CRUEL WORKS OF NATURE

11 ILLUSTRATED HORROR NOVELLAS

GEMMA AMOR

This is a work of fiction. Names, characters, businesses, places, events and incidents are either the products of the author's imagination or used in a fictitious manner. Any resemblance to actual persons, living or dead, or actual events is purely coincidental.

Cruel Works of Nature
First Edition November 2018
Cover Illustration By: Mark Pelham
Interior Illustrations by: Gemma Amor

Read More from Gemma Amor:
gemmamorauthor.com

Copyright © 2019

All rights reserved. This book or any portion thereof may not be reproduced or used in any manner whatsoever without the express written permission of the publisher except for the use of brief quotations in a book review.

CONTENTS

Title Page	1
Copyright	2
FOLIAGE	7
JACK IN THE BOX	58
BLACK SAND	83
BACK ALLEY SUE	121
GIRL ON FIRE	146
SCUTTLEBUG	174
THE PATH THROUGH LOWER FELL	213
HIS LIFE'S WORK	233
SPECIAL DELIVERY	272
IT SEES YOU WHEN YOU'RE SLEEPING	297
SKETCHBOOK	352
AUTHOR'S NOTE	389
ABOUT THE AUTHOR	390
OTHER BOOKS BY GEMMA AMOR	391

Gemma Amor

To Mr. M, because you are a good man.

And to all of the bad men, because, without you, there are no horror stories.

Cruel Works of Nature

FOLIAGE

I WROTE MY FIRST letter to Louise a few months after she died.

It started as an experiment. I was stone cold out of my mind with grief, and anger. I sat in my bedroom, once our bedroom, with a half-finished bottle of bourbon in one hand and a pen and a notepad in the other. Bleary-eyed, I began to scratch words forcefully onto the paper.

Dear Louise...

Before I knew it, I'd written her a letter.

The experiment became a habit, and now I write to her almost every day. Because I miss her. The letters help me, a little. I can't talk to her anymore, but I can write.

That's something at least.

I know, I know. Writing letters to a dead woman. A pointless, futile endeavour. It's not like there is a forwarding address to send them to. I have a pile of these brown envelopes amassing in a cardboard box on a shelf in the cupboard where her dresses used to hang, before I went crazy one night and threw them all out. I regretted that so much, the next day. Grief makes idiots of us all.

But, futility aside, it helps. The ritual. Smoothing the first sheet down. Making the first mark. All these gradual little steps towards something brighter.

Today, though, the pen won't move across the paper. For some reason, even though I have actual news to share, for once, I just can't bring myself to say anything. Writer's block, I guess. Usually, I'd get over it by wallowing in a bottle of single malt, but today, I've got an appointment to keep.

Today, I start a new job.

✻ ✻ ✻

MY NEW JOB is very different to my previous employment. I realised, after Louise died, that I couldn't take it any longer, sitting in an office, pushing my fingers around a keyboard, imprisoned behind a glaring computer screen.

I quit, about six months after her funeral.

I went back to basics.

I'm what they affectionately call an 'odd-job man' now. I work outdoors, all day long, come rain or shine. It doesn't piss me off half as much as my old job, mostly because I don't see or speak to many people throughout the course of my day. The pay is fine, it keeps the rent man at bay. And the work is hard, physical labour. I fix things, lift things, move things around. I do gardening, and maintenance. By the end of the day I'm exhausted, which is good, because it means all that's left for me then is a cold beer, leftover pizza, and deep, dreamless sleep.

I used to dream about Louise. I used to dream about her body next to mine in bed, her skin, the smell of her hair. Now I just sleep, heavy and solid. And then, I wake up.

And she isn't there.

Ah, fuck. There I go again.

Anyway, this new job. Well, not the work itself, but the location.

It's at Norfolk Manor.

I am the fucking odd job man for Norfolk Manor.

✸ ✸ ✸

WHEN LOUISE and I were kids, we were enchanted by Norfolk Manor. We used to play around the edges of the estate where the woods met the boundary wall. We had a den down there, made of crates and tree branches and an old tarp we'd found in my Dad's garage. We'd sit and read comics, eat candy, stare at the rooftops of the manor house as they poked out from above the treetops. We smoked our first cigarette in that den. It's a wonder we didn't burn the whole fucking thing down around our ears, and the forest too, for that matter. Those were good times, the best of times. I miss being young. I miss having all the good shit ahead of me, instead of behind me, like now. I miss my wife.

Anyway, I found out about the job in the local paper.

The ad said:

Odd Job Man Wanted
Norfolk Manor
Good rate of pay
Required immediately
Enquiries to Fay Lockwood, 202-555-0176

I sat up straight in my chair when I saw the name Lockwood. A thrill of excitement went through me, and it's been a long while since that happened, believe me.

Fay Lockwood is the granddaughter of Anne and Vincent Lockwood, who used to own the manor and the estate when I was a kid. The same Lockwoods who then went missing, all those years ago. It was the biggest scandal of the day, back then. One minute they were there, rolling around in that huge house with all that money, and the next, poof! Gone. Vanished without a trace. Only Fay was left behind, a child, an orphan, an orphan with an estate.

Officially, the Lockwoods were listed as 'missing,' but everyone round here knew Anne and Vince were dead. Most people thought Fay Lockwood had something to do with it, despite her age. Maybe she'd murdered them so she could inherit the estate. My town is like that. People desperate for something to wag their tongues at each other about. I remember feeling kind of sorry for Fay at the time, with her grandparents missing and everyone blaming her for it. But I think I was the only one. It's no wonder she moved away, in the end. Townsfolk would give her the stink-eye for just walking down the street, back then. Poor kid. She was only about eleven when it happened. Too young to be left alone like that.

In time, the gossip died down, and the house remained empty until the inquest was done and dusted, the legalities tidied up. This seemed to take years, and in all that time the house stayed boarded up, fenced off from the world.

Fay Lockwood finally inherited the house and its grounds a month ago. Well, what's left of it, anyway. The place is in a pretty bad state of repair.

I re-read the job advertisement a few times, thinking about it. Then, I called the number printed there.

Fay Lockwood answered right away, in a pleasant, if timid voice. We exchanged pleasantries, then she said she wanted someone who could come and tidy up before she moved in, and could I start right away, that morning?

I said yeah, sure. As long as I got paid, I didn't care when I started. She laughed down the phone at me, and so here I am, ten minutes later, jeep loaded up with tools, ready to drive on over.

I make one, last effort to write to Louise before I go, tell her my news.

Dear Louise…

I start, but again, the pen stalls on the paper.

I sigh, screw it up, throw it into the corner of the hallway, and leave.

❊ ❊ ❊

NORFOLK MANOR IS every bit as eerie now as it was when we were kids. It is more decrepit, if anything, absolutely covered in ivy and these huge, strangling creepers, all the windows choked up with the stuff, the gutters, the drains. Roof tiles missing all over the place. Anything that was once painted is now peeling, or rusted. The driveway is more like a forest, almost too overgrown to get a car down. It's going to be a shit-ton of work.

As a kid I would stare at this house for hours, face pressed through the bars of the wrought-iron gates out front. It used to creep the hell out of me, but I just couldn't help myself. You know when, as a kid, and you'd scrape your knee on something, and then you'd get a scab over the wound which you would then pick at, and worry at, and then yank off, despite the pain? Norfolk Manor was like that for me when I was a boy. I hated it, it scared me, but I couldn't stay away from the damn place, couldn't stop picking at the edges of it, trying to find a way in. Louise told me once, when we were eleven, that it was haunted, and at night, you could hear the ghosts screaming in the house.

That made it even more hypnotic, somehow. To a small boy, at any rate.

As an adult, I pressed my head against those same iron bars now, and looked at the grey, crumbling stones of the Manor. This time, I felt sadness, not fear. I could see the decay, even from a distance. I get mad when places are left to rot like this. Back in its day, the Manor was the talk of the town. I'd done some research. Things had happened here: important guests were wined and dined, local business deals brokered, political notaries entertained. Later on, the house was the backdrop to my childhood, a fundamental part of the scenery behind the show that was me, and my future wife.

Dan and Louise, together always, since we were five.

Now, Norfolk Manor was nothing more than a ruin, and Louise was no longer part of the show.

The gates were held together by a rusty padlock hanging from a large, thick iron chain.

I rattled them gently, wondering how to get in. The padlock fell to the ground with a thud. I looked at it, lying there by my feet. It had rusted through completely. I shook my head, unwrapped the chains, and pushed.

The sound the gates made as they opened was indescribable, like the whole place was in pain, and shouting at me. Kind of like the sound my heart made when I got the news about my wife's accident. I made a note to come back with some oil and grease the hinges.

Once the gates were open, I drove my car carefully up the weed-strewn drive and parked opposite the house. I stood there for a moment, marvelling at the size of the place. The house was massive, and, up this close, the extent of the neglect was more evident. Windows smashed. Gutters overgrown with weeds and those thick, choking vines. Birds flying in and out of holes in the roof. A weather vane, crooked and half-dangling off of a turret. Green mildew coating the grey stone.

The front door opened, and a woman came

out. She was thin and pale, with short dark hair. She looked anxiously at me until she spotted my tools in the back of the Jeep.

'Dan?' She said, with uncertainty. 'Dan Burrows?'

'Yeah,' I said, holding out my hand, which she shook, timidly.

'How did you get in?' She asked, looking behind me at the wrought-iron gates.

I shrugged. 'Padlock's bust. Fell clean off the chain. I'll bring a new one tomorrow.'

'Oh,' she said.

I looked at her, so slender and fragile-looking, and then back up at the huge dark mass of the manor house. I tried to figure out if she was the sort of person who could have killed her own grandparents. It didn't fit. She was so...delicate. I sensed that she was out of her depth, here. Inheriting an ancient pile of decaying stone and vines at her tender age didn't seem like it was all it was cracked up to be.

I said: 'Where do I start?'

She looked at me with a strange, unreadable expression on her face. Like she was...scared of something.

'Don't worry,' I said, after an awkward silence. 'I'll take care of it.'

She nodded and disappeared back inside.

I looked about me and rubbed my hands.

I like having a project to focus on.

❉ ❉ ❉

I CAN'T STOP THINKING about what Louise looks like, now.

I mean, I know it won't be pretty. She's been in the ground a while, and I hate the idea. She should have been cremated, but we decided on a traditional burial instead. Big mistake. Now I lie awake in the mornings, before the day starts, and wonder what that soft skin of hers feels like, wonder if the worms have gotten to it.

It's not a healthy thought process.

❉ ❉ ❉

I DECIDED TO start on the weed-choked driveway before I did anything else, so that getting my jeep in and out was a little easier. I picked up a strimmer, and then realised there was too much growth to tackle that way, so switched to a Weed Wand blowtorch. God, those things are so much fun. You blast the weeds with butane gas, and within two days, everything just fucking curls up and dies. I felt like Kurt Russell in *The Thing* as I swaggered along, nuking everything in my path. Every man likes to destroy shit, there's a truth.

When I stopped to rest, I could feel a set of eyes on me. You know, there's a prickling sort of feeling you get when you become aware of it. The hairs on the back of my neck rose up, to use a cliché.

I looked up at the Manor house, and sure enough, Fay stood in one of the first floor windows, staring down at me. She vanished pretty quick after I spotted her, as if embarrassed that I'd caught her out. I didn't think much of it, just went back to destroying the weeds on the drive.

After that, it was lunch. I usually eat mine in the Jeep, scrolling through mindless shit on my phone, but for some reason there is no signal out at Norfolk Manor. Besides, it was too hot to sit in my car, so I took my wrapped BLT and went to explore the grounds to the rear of the manor.

If I thought the front of the house was a mess, then I was in for a real, certified treat. The gardens around back were a *lot* worse. I mean, almost impenetrable.

Large curtains of ivy formed barriers every which way you turned, and what wasn't obscured by that was hidden or choked by some sort of strangler vine, a type I've never seen before. The stems of the foliage were about the same thickness as a man's wrist, and they had a choke hold on absolutely everything: trees, old statues, walls, doors, everything. It looked like a mass of snakes, like medusa's hair, writhing and smothering the life out of the estate. I felt short of breath just looking at it, claustrophobic almost, but I could also feel myself rising to the challenge. Clearing all this was going to take weeks, but I couldn't wait to see what lay underneath.

The vine growth was so thick, I couldn't get further than the end of an uneven, rotting terrace that spread out from the rear doors of the Manor. From there I could just make out the top of a metal structure at the bottom of what was once a formal lawn, one which sloped downhill away from the house. I caught a glimpse of glass, and iron amongst the vines. Probably a greenhouse, or orangery, I thought. Intriguing.

I made a list in my mind of the tools I was going to need. Chainsaw, axe, pruner, shears, knife. This was a much bigger job than I'd thought. I was going to need to draft in some extra labour to help.

A voice from behind me on the terrace interrupted my thought process, and made me jump.

'It's sad to see the place like this.' Fay had crept up behind me, somehow. I turned and was struck by how melancholy she looked. In fact, she looked how I'd been feeling since Louise died. Lost, sad. Tired.

'Yeah,' I said, surveying the tangle of growth in front of us. 'It's a real shame. I've never seen anything like it, if I'm honest. These vines. But I'll clear it. I like a challenge.'

'I admire your confidence,' she said, looking dubious. 'Are you sure you can handle this by yourself?'

'I have a guy called Ted. I call him to help me with big jobs. But don't worry. I'm sure it looks worse than it is.'

'I was sorry to hear about your wife,' said Fay, changing the subject abruptly.

I looked at her, taken aback by the curveball, and unsure of how to reply. *Small town gossip still going strong,* I thought. Only these days, people don't talk about how Anne and Vince Lockwood disappeared and were likely murdered by their own granddaughter. No, these days people talk about my wife, Louise Burrows, and how she died. And they talk about me, and how sad it all is.

I fucking hate small town gossip.

'Yeah,' I said, scratching my head and avoiding eye contact. 'Yeah, me too.'

'Oh, God, I didn't mean to pry,' she said, realising she'd made a faux pas.

'It's okay. Don't worry about it.'

There was an awkward silence, and then she said:

'Know what I hate the most about people?'

I shook my head.

'They can never mind their own fucking business.'

I smiled. 'True. But...I appreciate the sympathy.'

'It was meant kindly.'

'I know. Seriously, don't sweat it. I've lived here long enough to know that news spreads.

People feel...involved in your life, even when they aren't.'

She smiled back, hesitantly. 'Isn't that the truth. I guess if anyone understands, it's me. My Grandparents were the most important people in my life. Losing them both so suddenly...it changes a person. I was orphaned, in the blink of an eye. And that's aside from the fact that the whole town thinks eleven-year-old me killed them so I could inherit...this.' She waved a hand at the crumbling, tangled estate and laughed, softly. 'Poor me. Wanna come to my pity party?'

I sighed. What the hell. If she wanted to share, I'd share.

'That's what all the surrounding people don't get, isn't it?' I said, looking at the wedding ring which still sits on my ring finger.

'What?' she said, not understanding. I tried my best to explain.

'People don't get that you change fundamentally when someone you love dies. But you change in a way other people aren't comfortable with. Like, I could sit in a bar with my buddy Ted and talk about football. But I couldn't tell him I wear my dead wife's dressing gown on really shitty days, so that I can smell her perfume one more time.'

There was silence after that. I'm pretty good at killing conversations dead.

'Sorry,' I mumbled. 'I don't speak to people much, these days.'

'Don't worry,' she said, and I felt grateful. She put a hand out tentatively and patted me on the shoulder. I thought I would mind, and realised I didn't. The human touch felt good, actually, after such a long time.

'What's down there?' I asked, changing the subject and pointing at the metal structure at the bottom of the lawn.

Fay looked and sighed. 'That's Grandpa's old potting shed. He fancied himself as something of a botanist. He used to spend hours in there, splicing different plants together and trying to create new species and doing God knows what else. Roses were his thing. He was obsessed with the idea of black roses.'

I chuckled. 'Men need their hobbies,' I said, my interest piqued. 'Did he ever succeed?'

She laughed too, and it was a nice noise. 'Look around,' she said. 'See any black roses?'

'Nope.'

'Well, there you go.'

She's nice, in an unassuming, low-key kind of way. I thought she'd be stuck up, rich girls are like that, sometimes. Too good for anyone else.

But Fay isn't. She's...nice.

We stayed like that in silence for a bit longer. Then she said:

'Well, I've got a huge old house to somehow clean up.'

'Sure,' I said. 'Good luck.'

'Thanks,' she said, smiling again. 'I'm going to

need it. So are you!' She nodded at the overgrown garden, and left.

When she returned to the house, I went to get a better look at the vines covering the terrace and lawn. I held one between my finger and thumb, noticing how thick each stem was, how supple and strong. I followed the line of it until I reached a leaf, ran my fingers over the rich, shiny green foliage with its blood-red veins. My fingers kept going, searching, until I eventually noticed something hanging down. It was green, and looked, on closer inspection, like a seedpod. It was long, almost the length of my forearm, and looked like a vegetable, like a zucchini, or cucumber.

I took out my pocket knife and cut it free from its vine. It came away reluctantly, with a squelching noise, leaking a thick, pungent slime as it separated. I turned it over in my hand, frowning. It wasn't a seed pod. It was a flower bud, the petals tightly locked together like the flower was somehow hibernating, getting ready to burst forth.

I put the tip of my knife under the edge of one petal and worked it loose from the bud. It came free with a wet, tearing sound that somehow made me feel a little nauseous. I kept going, peeling back petal after petal, hoping to get to the stamens in the middle so I could see what kind of flower it was.

I was nearing the centre of the bud when my

knife tip hit something and made a noise.

Ting!

It was a solid noise, and not organic. It sounded like... metal. Felt like it too as I wiggled the blade around.

'What the fuck?' I murmured, and ripped out the remaining few petals.

When I saw what lay in the centre of the bud on a pillow of pink, fleshy matter, I repeated myself.

'What the *fuck?*'

I hooked it with the tip of my knife and held it up. It glinted in the sun.

It was a diamond ring.

❉ ❉ ❉

THE NEXT DAY was a bad day. I knew as soon as I woke up that it was a bad day.

I dreamed of Louise in the night. When I awoke, for just a second, just a wonderful, bright, hopeful second, I forgot that she died. I rolled over, and put my arm out, and felt the empty bed, and bang! There went that hope.

The world feels cruel now that my wife isn't in it.

I called Fay and told her I was sick, food poisoning, I couldn't make it in. I know she could tell I was lying. But she seemed cool with it. Sympathetic. You know people will always be sympathetic. That's the great thing about losing your wife. Makes getting a day off easy.

Fuck their sympathy.

I gave into the huge emptiness inside me, and got drunk.

I sank a whole bottle of Jack, lay in bed and fiddled with the diamond ring I'd found in the middle of that fucked-up flower pod. I turned it over and over and tried to figure out how it had gotten in there. The more I drank, the less sense it all made.

When I finished my bottle, I dragged my ass out of bed, went to the store in my pyjamas, and bought another. The lady at the checkout stared at me with sympathy. I glared defiantly back at her, aware I was being an angry asshole, but unable to do anything about it.

Fuck you, checkout lady. I don't need your sympathy, can't you understand?

I just need my wife back.

I went back to bed with the second bottle of Jack clenched between my knees and tried to write to my wife again.

Dear Louise, I managed, and the page blurred as tears welled up in my eyes.

God, I miss you.

Why the fuck did you have to leave me alone like this?

I stopped writing.

✽ ✽ ✽

Cruel Works of Nature

MY DAY-LONG BOURBON marathon turned into a two-day pity party, to borrow the phrase from Fay Lockwood.

I woke on the third day with a crushing hangover, a raging thirst for more booze, and the diamond ring still clenched in my sweaty fist.

I decided that I needed two things: hair of the dog, and information about the Lockwoods. And I knew a guy, and I knew where he would be.

I pulled on a halfway-clean shirt and walked into town, too steamed to drive. It was eleven-thirty by the time I got to the Slide Bar.

Slide is like a million other small-town bars across America: dark, run-down, in dire need of a paint job, and a second home to many of the town's locals, especially those that have retired.

Retired like Sherriff Tidey, who sat hunched over the bar nursing a Bloody Mary when I walked in. He looked almost as bad as I did.

'Rough night, Sherriff?' I asked, pulling out a bar stool and flopping down onto it. I was still half-drunk from the day before, but like a lot of functioning alcoholics, I dealt with it well. So did Sheriff, who grunted at me in amusement.

'Ain't every night a rough night these days?'

I chuckled. 'True, true. Sherriff...can I trouble you for a moment?'

'You know I ain't Sheriff any more, right son?'

'Yeah I know, but old habits die hard, I guess.'

It isn't just me. The whole town still calls him Sheriff, even though he gave up the title five years ago. He's that kind of man: he demands respect, and as far as I'm concerned, he has mine. He's had it ever since the night that Louise died. I remember how he cradled her head in his lap as she lay there on the cold asphalt, struggling to breathe. I remember the look he gave me as I ran over, having gotten the call to get out there, and get out there fast. I remember how he held her hand, and then held mine, in a firm, rough grip.

I remember being thankful that he was there when my wife breathed her last.

Ah, fuck, it's hard to stay on track with these memories.

'You alright, son?' Sheriff asked, with kind eyes.

I shook myself.

'Yeah. I need some information, Sheriff. If you don't mind, that is.'

'Shoot.'

'How much do you remember about the Lockwood case?'

Sheriff looked at me for a few moments, then finished his Bloody Mary with an indulgent slurp, gesturing for another one.

'Anne and Vince Lockwood. If I had a dollar for every time someone asked me about that case I'd be a rich man, Danny boy.'

'So...the case... is it still marked as unsolved?'

Sheriff took a hold of his fresh Bloody Mary, and stirred it with the stick of celery that stuck out the top, before crunching into it with a satisfied noise.

'Yup, still unsolved. No-one has seen hide nor hair of either of the Lockwoods since they vanished into thin air all those years ago.'

I chose my next words carefully. 'And...what about the Granddaughter? Fay Lockwood?'

Sheriff looked at me again, wondering where this was going.

'Word is, she smothered ol' Granny and Gramps in their sleep, then fed em' into a chipper. And all so's to inherit a big fat crumbling pile of rot and ruin otherwise known as Norfolk Manor. Bit like me, huh! Fat and falling apart.' The retired Sheriff spat into the corner.

I raised an eyebrow at him.

'And what do you think?' I asked, trying to keep my tone neutral.

He wiped his mouth and snorted in amusement.

'Skinny little thing like her? Aged all of eleven years old? Naw.'

'So what did happen to them? I mean, in your opinion. Off the record, like.'

Sheriff sighed, as if he'd given this a lot of thought over the years.

'My guess is that they retired quietly to some remote island together. Probably fed up with all the gossip and small-town shit.'

'You mean, faked their own deaths? And left Fay all on her own, with no legal guardian?'

He shrugged. 'Why not? I mean, she stood to

inherit their full fortune, they knew she'd be well looked after. And she was enrolled into one of them fancy boarding schools, which would take her 'til she was eighteen. After that, she was an adult. Maybe they thought it would be better for her than living here, waiting for them to die before she could come into her own.'

'I don't know, Sheriff.' I shook my head. 'I mean, it kind of makes sense, but I also know that they were close to Fay. I don't think they would have left her like that, so suddenly, with no idea of what happened to them. Not when she was so young. I mean, she was a kid. No-one would just abandon a kid like that, not if they loved them, not even for the best of reasons.'

Sheriff shrugged again.

'Whatever, Dan. We found no evidence of any foul play. Damn, we found no evidence whatsoever. When they first disappeared, we did a thorough sweep of that house, and I mean, fine-tooth comb. I could probably draw you a goddamn floor plan of that place, I walked it up and down so many times. All of their gold and valuables were still there. The antiques, the paintings. All of it was untouched, so there was no burglary gone wrong or nothin' like that. There was no trace of anything like blood, no signs of a struggle, no nothin'. We dusted for fingerprints and found nothing out of place. The Lockwoods just up and vanished. And from experience, that usually only happens when someone wants it to.'

I remained unconvinced, but didn't want to argue with him. I was silent for a few moments and then brought the diamond ring out of my pocket. It glinted in the overhead lights.

Sheriff smiled in amusement as I offered him the ring.

'I'm flattered, son, but I'm already married.'

'Very funny. Look at it. Look at the initials on the inside.'

He fumbled in his pocket for his reading glasses and squinted at the ring. He spotted the ornate, scrolled letters engraved into the gold band:

A.L.

He peered at me over the rims of his glasses.

'Fay Lockwood hired me to do some work on the grounds of Norfolk Manor.' I said, by way of explanation.

'That right? Well, someone sure needs to pay it some attention. A real eyesore now, it is. Such a shame.'

'I agree, but that's not the point. I was...clearing back some vines in the garden. I found this, kind of... embedded in one of the plants. Like it had been there a long time, and sort of been... *assimilated* by the plant somehow. You know how tree roots grow around fence posts and things that are in their way? Like that, only inside the goddamn plant.'

Sheriff remained silent, turning the ring over in his hands.

'Point is,' I continued, 'That I think it belonged to Anne Lockwood.'

He was silent for a moment, thinking. Then he said:

'A diamond ring like this was listed in the itinerary of valuables the Lockwoods owned, if I remember rightly from the inquest. I remember 'cos the diamond was a two-carat one. Or was it three? Anyway. Big fucker, like this.'

'Did you ever find it? You said nothing was stolen or missing from the manor.'

He shrugged again, but I could see the wheels turning, reluctantly. 'I just assumed she was wearing it when she disappeared. Piece like that, looks sentimental. You'd think she'd take good care of it.'

I rubbed my face. 'I don't know. Maybe she dropped it in the garden right before she left. But...what if she didn't? What if she was wearing it on the day she vanished, but she never left Norfolk Manor? Did you...did you check the grounds carefully?'

Sheriff levelled me with a disapproving glare. There was a hint of something else in those eyes too, something that looked a lot like...

Well, shit.

It looked like defensiveness.

'Do I look like I leave loose ends untied, son?' He said, and I couldn't help but not believe him.

He continued, eyes shifting about all over the place.

'Of course we searched the grounds. Like I said, no evidence of any foul play. We missed the ring, but these things happen. And there's a big difference between a ring and a human body, son. We would have found the Lockwoods if they were in those grounds somewhere, trust me.'

I sighed, and wondered what it was about the Lockwood family that made people behave in such odd ways.

'Perhaps I'm over-thinking this,' I said, giving it one last try. In vain, as it turned out. If Tidey had a secret, he wasn't telling me what it was any time soon.

'Something about that house, though, Sheriff. It feels...unresolved, somehow.'

Sheriff patted me on the shoulder. 'I get it, son, I do. Cold cases are like that. They build their own folklore and mystery, become stuck in people's minds. You think you're the only one to tell me their theories about what happened to the Lockwoods?'

I smiled sheepishly. 'I'm sorry, Sheriff. I'm just...I'm just fixing for a distraction, I guess.'

He nodded kindly.

'I don't mind, son. I'd help you if I thought I could. And I agree, the ring is interesting. But my advice, is give it back to the lady of the house, focus on bein' a handyman, and not a cop.'

He winked at me, to show no hard feelings.

I smiled politely into my beer, my appetite for booze suddenly gone.

I went home, took a shower, got my pen and pad of paper out, started writing.

This time, the words came easily, and as I wrote, the clouds slowly lifted, just a little. Enough to let in a sliver of light.

Sometimes that sliver is enough to keep us going, in the darkest of times.

And Sheriff is lying, I just know it.

There is something about that house, that garden, those vines...something that just isn't right. And I don't care what anyone else says, Sheriff or not, diamond rings don't just end up in the middle of flower buds like that, sitting in the middle like it fucking grew there somehow.

And it's like he said, the ring looks... like it was special. Like an engagement ring. Something sentimental. Something you wouldn't part with easily.

I keep thinking back to what Fay said about her Grandpa fancying himself a botanist. Trying to create new species, splicing things together, messing with the natural order of things.

And then I think about how they vanished, Anne and Vince Lockwood, vanished without a trace, and I can't get the image of that damned flower bud in my mind, huge, and alien, and fleshy somehow.

❋ ❋ ❋

Cruel Works of Nature

I RANG FAY to apologise for my absence. She was surprisingly relaxed about it, which I appreciated. I thought for sure I'd lose the job at Norfolk Manor, and was strangely relieved when I didn't.

To make up for it I forced myself out of bed extra early the next day, despite my overwhelming exhaustion. I called my buddy Ted, and arranged to meet him at Norfolk Manor. I had an ice-cold shower, a bucket of aspirin, and did half an hour of sit-ups to sweat the booze out.

Feeling better, I got in my Jeep and went over to the estate, parked up, and waited for Ted. There was no sign of Fay anywhere, which I was oddly grateful for. I felt ashamed at how I'd cut out on her, and didn't want to deal with the complicated feelings that arose in her company at that particular moment.

Also, there was the diamond ring. I needed to give it back to her, but I still had a bad feeling about it. And I was done with bad feelings for a little while.

Ted met me at the gates, pulling up on an old dirt bike that coughed noxious black fumes from its exhaust. I met Ted in the Slide Bar a while back. He's younger than me, and skinny as a bean pole, but strong, and a good labourer. We work together on bigger jobs and split the pay. He's a good natured kid, and diligent. Kind of kid you have no choice but to like.

I took him round the back of the house, noticing with pleasure that the weeds were beginning to shrivel up and die off on the front drive. I'd clear up the dead stalks later. For now, I wanted to get rid of those vines on the terrace. Actually, if I was being honest with myself, what I really wanted was to get to that ornate old potting shed poking out of the undergrowth at the bottom of the lawn, and explore it. I felt like it was important, somehow, particularly when it came to the Lockwoods. Maybe I'd find a skeleton or two inside, or maybe even some black roses, who knew? I kind of liked that idea. I would take a cutting, and plant one on Louise's grave. Black roses are just the sort of thing she would have loved.

Or, maybe, instead, I'd find more of those horrible pods, with God knows what growing inside. I shuddered.

Ted blew out his cheeks as he surveyed the jungle on the terrace.

'Well,' he said, cheerfully. 'That is going to take a lot of chopping.'

'Yep,' I said, chucking him a thick pair of pruning shears. He looked at the vines, thicker than the width of my forearm, and frowned. 'I'm not sure these are going to be enough,' he said, scratching at his head. 'I mean, these things are huge.'

'Do your best with the smaller ones,' I said, unshouldering my cordless chainsaw. 'I'll deal with the big fuckers.'

'You got it, boss.'

'Oh, and a word of warning,' I said, remembering the diamond ring burning a hole in my pocket. 'If you come across any of these...ah, flower pod things, look like seed pods, about the size of your arm, cut 'em off and keep them, would you? Make a separate pile of 'em over there.'

He shrugged, puzzled. 'Sure,' he said, and I fired up the chainsaw. Flipping down my safety visor, I moved forward, and started cutting.

A few hours later, and we'd cleared at least half of the terrace. It was hard, slow work, and...well, it was unsettling, for both of us

Cutting through the vines was a messy, slippery undertaking. They were spongy, and fleshy, resisting our tools and only coming apart under the chainsaw or pruning shears after several attempts. They leaked a thick, pink sap that spread all over everything, and to which everything else stuck, like it was glue.

And while we were trying to clear through it all, there were the flower pods, prolific, as if we'd caught the plant in season. Ted found seven of them, and I found another twelve. We laid them out on a piece of tarp, where they sat, stinking in the hot sun.

Ted and I eventually stopped for a break, and looked at each other, wiping sweat from our faces with the bottoms of our shirts.

'I feel like I've been working a goddamned morgue,' Ted said, and I knew what he meant.

It didn't feel like cutting through foliage, it felt like cutting through human skin, and bone. It was a distinctly disturbing feeling, and didn't sit well with the remnants of my hangover, which clung to me stubbornly.

A voice came from behind us. 'Can I interest you in any lemonade?'

It was Fay. We turned and saw her standing on the newly opened up terrace, a tray clutched in both hands. She looked nervous, but hid it behind a tentative smile.

Ted whipped off his baseball cap as if royalty had just entered the garden.

'Thanks, ma'am,' he said, a goofy grin on his face, and I realised that Fay was wearing a short, white, cotton dress that clung to her hips and emphasised her smooth skin.

'Hi,' I said gruffly, dropping my gaze, which only made me aware of her legs- long, pale, and shapely.

Fay set the lemonade tray down on a crumbling balustrade along one edge of the terrace. Then she reached up to gather her hair into a ponytail, speaking around the hair-tie gripped in her teeth as she worked.

'Can I help you guys? It feels wrong to sit in the house watching you both do all the work.'

Ted looked at me, and I shook my head.

'Seriously, I wouldn't. This stuff... this stuff is unpleasant.' I gestured at the mutilated vines lying tangled in a pile nearby, and then plucked at my shirt, which was coated with a thick wet secretion from the foliage.

Fay looked over at the tarp upon which were stacked the flower pods. She wrinkled her nose.

'What are those? They stink!'

'Some sort of flower, or seed pod. I haven't quite figured it out yet.'

'Gross. Anyway, you have to let me help somehow. I insist. A bit of mess doesn't bother me,' she said, and I laughed.

'Fine,' I said, relenting. 'But do me a favour and change out of that pretty dress first.'

She raised an eyebrow at me, acknowledging the compliment. 'Obviously,' she said, shy and sassy in equal measures. She disappeared into the bowels of the house to get changed.

Ted whistled as she went inside. 'That's Fay Lockwood? *The* Fay Lockwood who murdered her Grandparents? Wow.'

'Have a care with that kind of talk, Ted,' I said, gruffly. 'Gossip is painful for some folks. She was just a kid when that happened.'

Ted shrugged. 'Ah, I'm sorry, Dan, but you know this town. I grew up with that story. It's kind of peculiar to meet her in the flesh. She seems...nice. Not...not like a murderer at all.' He laughed awkwardly.

I nodded, and reached for some lemonade. 'She is nice. But more importantly, she's paying our wages, so let's not piss her off with any more of that talk, okay?'

'Loud and clear, boss,' said Ted, in his good-natured way.

We finished the lemonade and Fay returned. She wore sensible boots, long trousers, long sleeves and a dark green cap. Her short hair was tucked up underneath the cap, the peak of which cast shadows across her eyes. The shadows made me think of the dark, empty windows of Norfolk Manor, hollow holes that continuously watched our progress.

'What can I do?' She asked, pulling a pair of thick gloves out of a pocket.

'You any good at lighting fires?' I said, pointing at the pile of undergrowth we'd cleared. 'Best thing to do with that lot is burn it,' I added.

She smiled. 'I happen to be good at lighting fires,' she said. 'Lot of time spent at camp.'

She set to clearing a patch of earth in which to build a shallow fire pit, wide enough to toss the vines into for burning. Ted and I picked up our tools and went back to our assault on the garden. The chainsaw roared, and before long, I saw sparks and ash fly into the sky as Fay got a fire burning.

After a while, I noticed my chainsaw slowing down, churning and grinding on the thick sap. I stopped, examined the edges.

'You alright, boss?' Ted called out to me, across the terrace.

'Goddamn chainsaw teeth are getting clogged up with all this gooey shit. Can't make any headway for love 'nor money.'

'I gotta backup saw at my place, boss.'

I was about to answer when something hit me. I wrinkled my nose. 'What's that smell?' I said, looking around me and spotting the fire that Fay had lit.

Ted gagged into his sleeve. 'Smells like a fucking barbeque. What the fuck?'

Fay stood staring down at the crackling fire which sizzled and popped reluctantly around the wet vines.

'Dan,' she said, her eyes wide over a handkerchief which she had clamped over her mouth and nose. 'Dan, what does this look like to you?' Her voice was unsteady, and I got a sinking feeling.

We came over to have a look, and I instantly wished I hadn't.

Lying in the fire at Fay's feet was one of the flower pods. It must have got tossed into the burn pile by mistake. She stared at it with a mix of horror and disbelief. My eyes followed hers. My stomach turned.

The heat of the fire had done something to the pod, triggered a flowering response. The petals had burst wide open, revealing the centre of the flower.

Only instead of stamens and pollen, there inside the flower lay something long, and pale, and far too familiar. Ted breathed out, incredulous.

'Is that a...is that..?'

'It can't be,' I murmured, and yet I knew it was.

'It's a finger,' Fay said, turning to me for confirmation. 'It's a finger, isn't it?'

I didn't want to touch it, get a closer look.

'I...what the fuck *is* this stuff, anyway?' Ted continued, repulsed, and I shook my head.

'You said your Grandpa liked to...experiment with plants?' I asked, turning to Fay and finally bringing the diamond ring out of my pocket.

She stared at it as if it were a poisonous snake lying in the palm of my hand.

'Where did you...where did you get that?' She asked, her voice choked.

I nodded at the monstrous flower in the fire. 'Inside one of those things.'

Fay's face was a frozen mask. 'That ring...it's my Granny's engagement ring. I think she...I think she was wearing it when she went missing.'

She took it from me, and slipped it tenderly onto her left ring finger with shaking hands.

We stood in silence, and then, in unison, turned and stared at the roof of the potting shed.

* * *

I CALLED SHERIFF. Told him to come on down to Norfolk Manor, speak to Fay.

'Dan,' he said, sounding tired over the phone, 'I'm retired, remember?'

'Don't you want to know for sure what happened to them, Sheriff? What if you were wrong? All these years? You could...I don't know. Clear Fay's name.'

He sounded irate. 'A court of law did that, years back, Daniel.'

I persisted. 'Yeah, but I mean... in the eyes of the town. Look, Sheriff, something is wrong in that place. We found...I can't describe what we found, but I think you should come. I wouldn't ask unless I was pretty desperate.'

He said he'd think about it, but I could tell he was lying. He clearly thought I was insane.

✻ ✻ ✻

AN HOUR PASSED.

When Sheriff showed no sign of being interested in our discovery, I collected up the pods and put them in a large canvas holdall. I told Fay to get some rest, and sent Ted home.

'What are you going to do?' Fay asked me, ignoring my advice about resting and eyeing the canvas bag nervously.

'Take these to someone to analyse,' I said, grimly.

'Who?'

I shrugged. 'Anyone who will listen,' I said.

She sighed, and twirled the diamond ring on her finger. It looked good there, like it belonged.

'I want to come with you,' she asked, politely

but firmly. I couldn't argue with her. Besides, I kind of liked her company. I liked having a female presence in my life again, one who was alive, and who wasn't my Mother.

The light was fading when we got in my Jeep. Embarrassed, I cleaned the front seat of all the clutter and shit that goes with my job, and tried to hide the beer bottles rolling around in the footwell before Fay could catch sight of them.

We threw the flower-pod bag in the back, climbed in and drove away, Norfolk Manor filling my rear-view mirrors with its gloomy, brooding silhouette.

I went straight over to Sheriff's house, and banged on the front door screen.

He opened it, face set in a bad mood which only darkened further when he saw us standing there, a great, smelly, leaking bag slung between us.

'I swear to God, Dan, you're a nice boy but I'm about done with this shit,' he said, scowling at us.

I bent down and unzipped the bag. The stench that rolled forth was overwhelming.

'Jesus!' Sheriff said, and hurriedly shut his front door behind him to keep the smell out.

'I'm not wasting your time, Sheriff, I know it.'

Before he could say anything else, I picked up one of the disgusting flower buds, and dug my penknife into it, peeling it like it was a revolting piece of fruit, held out at arm's length, my eyes

Cruel Works of Nature

watering.

As the petals began to fall away and I got closer to the centre, I could feel Fay and Sheriff tense beside me, reluctantly absorbed by what I was doing. An expectant silence fell upon us, and I felt my heart thudding in my chest with anticipation.

When I got to the centre, my knife stuck into something with a squelch, and I swore, dropping the blade and the bud to the ground.

'Oh, God,' Fay groaned as she saw what lay on the floor surrounded by discarded petals, a knife blade sticking upright out of the centre of it. All I could think of in that moment was a dartboard, or a target.

Bullseye, my brain said, over again. *Bullseye*.

'Are you kids playing a goddamn joke on me, is that it?' Sheriff said furiously, stepping back from the thing before us.

I pressed a hand to my mouth in disgust and shook my head. Fay moaned and put her head in her hands.

It wasn't a finger, this time.

It was an eyeball.

A fucking *eyeball*. Staring at us, real as the sun in the sky.

✽ ✽ ✽

THINGS HAPPENED FAST after that. Once Sheriff had

examined the pod for himself, and reconciled himself to the very real nature of it, he disappeared into his house. I heard him on the telephone, working himself into a temper as he tried to get hold of the new Sheriff.

Fay and I sat on Sheriff's porch, staring into the distance. The bag full of pods lay where I'd dropped it. A thick, black cloud of flies had amassed over the top of them.

Fay was lost, deep in thought and probably shock. I patted her on the hand to rouse her as Sheriff continued to bellow down the phone indoors.

'You okay?' I asked, softly.

'No,' she sighed. 'Are you?'

I shook my head. 'Nope.'

We were silent for a while longer. Inside, I heard Sheriff shout:

'I don't care if it's not procedure, you get his skinny, lazy ass out of his house and down to Norfolk Manor before I come get him myself! You hear me? I wasn't Sheriff of this town for forty years to be fobbed off by a jumped-up desk clerk! I'll come back out of retirement if I have to, and fire your ass in a *heartbeat!*'

I smiled, despite everything. Sheriff had never stopped being Sheriff, not even in his own mind. People who are good at what they do never retire, not really.

❋ ❋ ❋

WE WENT BACK to the house. The damned place is a magnet, I just can't keep away. Can't keep from picking at that scab. Worrying at the wound. Digging around inside something I shouldn't. But I felt, somehow, like this was what I needed. To solve something. To understand something. After all this time, when nothing made sense in any context. I just wanted to get to the potting shed, see what was inside. A simple thing.

What's inside the shed.

As if it held the answers to my own mysteries.

We found Ted waiting in the drive, unable to keep away, an unsteady look about him.

'Cops are here,' he said as we pulled up in my Jeep. He jerked a thumb at the rear of the manor.

'They better be,' Sheriff said gruffly, and we moved through the dying weeds and around the back to the terrace and lawn.

We found the town's finest crowded on the terrace, standing around in a disorganised fashion, staring in confusion at the mess of vines that smothered the land. Some of them were suited up in white overalls, and I could only assume they were a forensics team. Others, in regular police uniform, were taping a perimeter around the edges of the terrace.

There was an air of confusion, of being bewildered. *Better get used to that*, I thought, grimly.

Sheriff strode over to one of them and barked a question.

'Where's Sheriff Hoxton?'

The officer shrugged in apology. 'He's at a dinner dance this evening, sir. Gave us strict instructions not to bother him anymore.'

'Is that right?' Sheriff said, face reddening in suffused rage. 'In that case,' he continued, growling, lid barely kept on his mounting anger, 'You can all take orders from me. We need to cut a path through all this shit and get down to that structure you can see poking out over there. We need to keep a close eye out for...for human remains.'

The team didn't question him, just waited for more orders. He turned, gestured at me.

'This is Dan Burrows. He's got experience with the foliage you can see covering everything. He's going to lead, with me up front. He knows what to look for. We need you to follow behind. Photograph and collect any evidence we discover, anything at all that doesn't fit within the context of this garden, got that? Clothing, jewellery, personal effects... and, like I said. Human remains.'

One of the uniformed cops raised a hand, slowly. Sheriff waved him off, dismissive.

'And yes, this is about the Lockwood case, before anyone asks.'

The cop lowered his hand.

They gave us white hazmat suits. I looked at Fay while getting into mine. 'You sure you want to do this?' I asked, softly.

She nodded, unable to answer, sliding her thin

limbs into the white suit carefully, is if feeling unsteady on her feet. I put out a steadying arm, and she leaned on me. I smiled gently, reassuringly, but she didn't acknowledge it. She looked sick to her stomach.

We picked up our tools, looked to Sheriff for confirmation.

'Let's get on with this,' he said, grimly.

We cut a slow, arduous, sticky swathe through the vines, noticing that the flower pods were more prevalent the closer to the potting shed we got. As we moved forward, our brand new police issue chainsaws roaring in unison like a terrible engine of destruction, I noticed that some buds were actually flowering. I stopped to breathe for a moment, covered in sweat and sticky sap, and found myself staring into the heart of a huge, black flower, petals unfurled fully, each one easily the size of a tennis bat.

My breath caught in my throat, and I almost choked in shock, spluttering and closing my eyes in denial.

In the centre of this flower lay another eye, a rheumy, milky, sore-looking eye.

I steadied myself, and then carefully pushed my face right up into the heart of the thing, trying to make sense of it, my own heart in my mouth. As I gazed in fear at it, aghast at this cruel, horrible perversion of nature, the unthinkable happened.

It blinked.

I yelled, and fell backwards into Fay, who stumbled and crashed to the ground. I landed heavily on top of her, barely registering her cry of pain.

Slowly, a withered eyelid lowered over the eye, thin, worn eyelashes brushing against the black petals. Then, it opened again, as if from sleep.

It looked at me, fixing me with a milky pupil, and the flower...shuddered.

As if it had seen me, and didn't like what it saw.

I screamed. I couldn't help it. It rang out into the thick, scented air like a strange bird call, bitter and ragged. A few of the white-suited guys behind us let out their own scared noises, one of them turning as if to leave.

Sheriff rounded on them savagely.

'Don't even think about it!' He snarled. 'If we can stick it out, you can too. We got a duty here, you understand?'

They stared back, not answering, but not running either.

A white suited man came forward, took pictures, then, trembling, removed the shuddering flower from the vine with a surgical scalpel, and bagged it. The eye rolled back in its socket as the fine blade cut through the stem.

I got back to my feet, sweating. I helped Fay to her own feet. Her skin was grey as if she was going to puke.

'That eye,' she said, struggling. 'It looked...it

looked...'

'Don't think about it,' I said, squeezing her hand, and trying not to throw up myself.

* * *

IT TOOK ANOTHER hour for us to reach the potting shed. The closer we got, the tighter and more impenetrable the vine growth became. A high, rich stink permeated the surrounding air, and the heat and humidity became overwhelming.

We began to make out a noise as we moved. It was a creaking, groaning noise, audible in the silence between chainsaw bursts. It was the vines tightening, closing like a fist in response to our assault, squeezing together into a writhing, slithering mass, like a nest of snakes, like Medusa's hair. The message was clear: you shall not pass. Whatever was in that potting shed was the centre of all of this, I was sure now.

The plants were guarding whatever was in that shed.

Sheriff grunted and puffed with exertion as he fought his way through the foliage.

'I don't have a Goddamn-fuckety clue what's happening right now, but I'm damned if I'm turning back,' he said, his jaw set grimly. I caught a movement out of the corner of my eye and called out a warning.

'Look out!' I said, my voice hoarse.

A tendril snaked suddenly across Sheriff's path to block him. He stabbed it, lightning quick, with a scalpel. The vine recoiled as if in pain. Sheriff grunted in satisfaction. I kept him in my sight at all times. He was a rock.

And then, at last, we came to it.

The potting shed.

We found the top of a door. A mesh of vines as thick as my leg wove a defensive shield across it. I put down my chainsaw, chest heaving, sweat pouring off me. I turned to the team behind me. 'Any of you bring a flamethrower?' I asked. I was filled with a sudden urgency to burn the whole fucking place down, and then run, run as if my life depended on it.

I was half-joking, but one of the forensic team nodded at me, silently. I raised an eyebrow, wondering if it was a standard issue police flamethrower, like the chainsaws, or if they borrowed it from someone.

The flamethrower was passed down the line of white suited men. I slipped the fuel tank straps over my arms, freed up the fuel line, took a deep breath, and let the rage fill me up as I took hold of the gun.

Fire shot forth from my hands. It felt *good*.

One jet of flame was all it took. The plant reacted as a human would to the fire: it flinched, and...

Shrieked.

Fay clamped her hands over her ears, and I had

a moment to worry about her sanity. She was not going to like what she found inside the potting shed, instinct told me. The vines fell away, dropping to the ground like a hand dropping a hot coal, then scuttling backwards and retreating away.

In their absence, we saw an old, wooden door with cracked panes of glass set within, each pane engraved with ornate etchings of flora and ferns and other household plants.

Sheriff put his shoulder to the door. It gave way easily, with a definitive crash. He drew his gun, looked back at me, Fay and Ted, gestured to the team behind us to get them to stay put, then ventured inside.

I swallowed and took Fay's hand in mine. It was cold, and pale, like my wife's hand was when she died.

We went inside and found Anne and Vince Lockwood.

✤ ✤ ✤

FIRST, WE FOUND more black flowers. Not roses, but still, black as midnight, petals shaped like that of a sunflower, only longer. They grew in abundance from a huge mass of vegetation, in the centre of which we found the Lockwoods.

The plant had assimilated into their bodies so completely that at first, it was hard to spot them, but they were there. They were barely recognisable as human. They had become a thin, stretched, membrane-like mass of skin, veins, tissue, hair and plant matter. The vines burst out of this membrane like intestines, and I could see that over the course of many years, they had taken bits and pieces of the Lockwoods and distributed them across their rapidly expanding network of growth.

An age-spotted hand, fused with a glossy green leaf the size of a dinner plate, trembled to the left of us, fingers opening and closing uselessly.

Over to the right, an ear grew in the centre of a flower, and inside another flower, I saw a tongue flapping around listlessly in the fetid, humid air of the potting shed. The noise it made was obscene, a sound I'll never forget.

Human teeth, long and yellow, lined the stem of a tendril by my right elbow.

On the floor not two yards from where I stood, a distorted, gnarled old foot disappeared into the ground, as if kicking its way down, and out of this hell.

Sheriff shook his head, mesmerised and horrified by what lay before us. Ted wiped a hand across his mouth, making quiet retching noises into his fingers.

Fay just stood there, her cold, clammy hand gripping mine so tight I thought idly that she would break all my fingers, but I didn't feel it. I couldn't feel anything at that moment.

Cruel Works of Nature

The Lockwoods had been missing for nearly twenty years. Twenty years is a long time in the life of a plant.

It's a long time over which to systematically deconstruct two human beings and rearrange them organically.

I understood now what Mr. Lockwood had been doing in his shed. He had been trying to create a new species, only not a species of plant. He had spliced human matter with organic matter. He had given himself, and his wife too, to the foliage.

It was a form of suicide, I guess.

Only...

Oh, God.

Only, the Lockwoods weren't dead, you see.

We heard a low moaning coming from the centre of the tissue mass. It was a vaguely feminine, throaty, rasping moan. Faint at first, and then louder, and louder.

We froze and scanned the shed to locate the source of it.

And found what was left of Anne Lockwood's skull, upon which the lower half of her face was still visible, just about. Her mouth was still connected to a tongue, and that tongue, somehow, was still connected to a set of functioning vocal cords.

After that, I lost track of what was human and what wasn't.

All I knew was that Anne Lockwood, or what

remained of her, was moaning: a long, drawn-out, pained moan.

Fay burst into panicked, wretched tears, and grabbed the gun from Sheriff's hand. Without hesitation, she fired it at what she could find of her grandmother's skull, over and over again, round after round. It shattered in a splattering mess of sap and brain matter. The moans stopped, and Fay said something incoherent, then fainted.

* * *

I SCOOPED HER into my arms and carried her out of that place. I pushed through the circle of shocked, whitesuited men and took her back across the newly cleared lawn, laying her down on the terrace.

Then, I lay down on the ground next to her, taking huge breaths of air into my lungs, and I thought about Louise.

I thought about her dying, and her last words to me.

It doesn't hurt, she'd said, blowing bubbles of blood through her lips as she spoke.

Don't worry, darling. It doesn't hurt.

She lied to me, with her last breath, because that's what you do when you love someone.

* * *

Cruel Works of Nature

TODAY I WROTE my last letter to my dead wife.

It's funny, but I didn't think I would have a reason to be grateful for much after she died. But seeing what became of the Lockwoods made me...grateful, somehow.

My wife didn't die an easy death. I was there, I saw. She died in pain, but she died...how can I say this? It felt... natural, somehow. People die in car accidents all the time. It's brutal, but it's a truth we can cope with, eventually. A fact of life. A shitty one, but a fact nonetheless.

But the Lockwoods?

Nothing about that was natural. Nothing about that was a recognised fact of life. It was a twisted, artificial design, a type of life and death that had no business on this earth.

So, yes. In a strange way I feel somehow...better about Louise's death since that day in Norfolk Manor.

When Fay woke up, I took her away from that place as fast as I could. I took her back to mine, wrapped her in a clean blanket, and put her to bed. She slept for hours, and when she woke up, we talked. For hours. Hours turned into days, and we kept on talking. Like we were both making up for all the time we'd spent alone, talking to no-one.

The days turned into weeks, and she didn't leave. And I was okay with that. She's with me now, curled up catlike on my couch, staring off into the middle-distance, thinking about the foliage.

And what of the house? The gardens? The Lockwoods?

Fay had the whole place bulldozed, in the end. The manor house, everything. She sold the land to developers, and they poured concrete over everything within days of arriving on site.

As for me, I'm moving. I need a new start.

I told Louise about it, in my last letter. I told her about Fay, too. I think she would have liked her. I think she'd be happy that I found someone.

And so now, before I go, I have this box of letters I wrote, sitting here, and waiting for something. I'm going to bury the whole thing out on the edge of the Norfolk Manor estate, away from the bulldozers, in the woods, near where our den used to be.

Fay is going to join me. Anne Lockwood's diamond ring will go into the box with the letters, and the whole lot will go into an unmarked grave, ready for us to dig up in the future if we ever feel strong enough to do so.

Then, we're going to climb into my Jeep and head off, where I don't know, but it will be new, and free of memories.

For both of us.

Cruel Works of Nature

JACK IN THE BOX

'WHAT THE FUCK IS THAT?!'

This was not the response I was expecting.

My wife stared at her birthday present as if it was a steaming, freshly curled dog turd on a plate. She wore a potent expression of horror and repulsion on her otherwise handsome face.

It slowly dawned on me that perhaps, just perhaps, I'd misjudged the gift by quite some distance.

She turned her face to me, her voice reaching a tone of high-pitched disbelief.

'No, really. What the hell is that thing?!'

Cruel Works of Nature

I stared at my wife some more, baffled. I began to suspect, with a sinking feeling, that there was not much I could say at this point to make things better.

'Well...' I hesitated, looking at the gift in her lap.

'Well?' My wife echoed me, her voice grown shrill, and demanding.

I shrugged, defensively.

'It's a Jack-in-the-box!'

We looked at the offending object in silence for a few moments more.

The Jack-in-the-box rested on the bed between us, partially shrouded with hastily discarded wrapping paper. Its head wobbled around on the end of its spring as we shifted on the bed. It had burst out of its box while my wife was unwrapping it. She'd screamed, and dropped it as if it were a burning hot coal. And so it lay, untouched, unwanted.

Apparently not the best birthday present I've ever chosen.

It was, I suppose, a little...unusual. Perhaps not quite to everyone's taste. But really, I couldn't see what all the fuss was about.

My wife turned her head, looked at me once again.

'Why would you buy me this?' She stared at me, her eyes wide with what now looked like reproach, and sadness. I groaned inwardly. There was nothing worse than that face. It meant I'd be spending the rest of the week grovelling for forgiveness. It meant a week of stony silence, the cold shoulder.

It meant that poor old Barry was in the doghouse, once again.

Why didn't I just buy her perfume, like I usually did?

Well, for precisely that reason, actually. Because I always bought her the same thing, year in, year out. This year I'd wanted to be spontaneous, because she was always complaining: I was predictable. Our marriage was dull, she'd say, boring. Hum-drum. *Why can't you ever surprise me?*

So when the Jack-in-the-box had caught my eye at a local yard sale as I was walking past, I'd stopped.

To begin with, I hadn't known what it was. I'd seen the colour, first, a flash of bright vermillion, a brilliant red flickering in my peripheral. Turning my head, I'd seen a box sitting on a table in my neighbour's front yard.

I sauntered over. The box seemed to grow more intensely crimson in colour the closer I got. I picked it up, and saw that it was about as big as a man's head. I turned it over a few times in my hands. It clanked and clunked, the unmistakable sound of something mechanical rattling around inside.

The exterior surface of the box was inlaid with beautiful silver geometric patterns, thin,

Cruel Works of Nature

polished lines that traced impossibly complicated interlocking patterns across all sides of the cube. I thought maybe it was some sort of Chinese puzzle box, until I saw the handle, and suddenly understood what it was.

There was an old-fashioned crank handle inserted into one side of the box. Underneath the handle, painted in an ornate cursive, were the words 'Crank me'.

So I did.

I cranked the handle until it would turn no more, and waited, anticipation tickling the edges of my nerves.

Music began to play, softly at first, then increasing in volume. It was gentle, tinkly music, like the music you heard when a jewellery box was opened. It was classical, and soothing. I think it was Beethoven's Moonlight Sonata, although I was never the musical one in our family. It overlaid the noise of something whirring mechanically inside, like the sound that an old clock makes when you wind it up.

The music and the whirring continued, and the suspense grew as I waited for the inevitable to happen, until I could hardly bear it.

Then, with a sudden BANG! Jack, in all his glory, jumped out of his box.

He was a large Jack, about a foot long, and dressed in the traditional jester clothes I'd expected, complete with a large, ruffled collar. He wore a three-peaked hat with bells sewn on. The bells jangled as he moved around. His clothes were beautifully made, with patterns stitched into the fabric that matched the silver tracery on the exterior of the box. He bounced around on his large, tightly coiled spring, his arms waving around in merriment. As his momentum calmed, I got a better look at his face, and I gaped.

The head appeared to be fashioned from a small, delicately painted skull. I touched it, and felt a thrill as I did so. It was a real skull, not a plastic one. It was tiny, and perfectly formed. I assumed that it was the skull of a small monkey, or a marsupial of some sort. I guessed that this Jack-in-the-box was a handcrafted, probably Victorianera curio, meant to look human without actually being so. *A collectible*, I told myself.

Painted onto the skull were red, swirling lines which again, matched the patterns on the box and on the exquisitely embroidered clothes. The lines made the face look as if it were covered in tribal tattoos. There were no eyes inside the eye-sockets. Those had been left empty, and blank. Long, black eyelashes had been painted around each socket, and gave Jack a childlike, owlish quality I found appealing.

The skull's tiny jaw bones sagged open then, and I saw that they were expertly wired together, not unlike the way a ventriloquist's doll is wired, so that the mouth opens and closes to mimic human speech. Jack's skull still had all of its tiny teeth intact, from the molars to the slightly pointed canines. The twin rows of teeth clacked together in an approximation of mirth: *Clack, clack, clack!*

Then, the mouth opened again, and *Clack! Clack!*

Clack!

The skull chattered away in glee.

A high-pitched giggle bubbled forth from deep inside the belly of the box, a giggle that in no way sounded mechanical, but was somehow engineered to sound... human. Like a small child chuckling at a good joke. I laughed out loud myself, shock and delight making my heart bump along fiercely in my chest.

I was enchanted. It was quaint, and kitsch, and quirky, all at once. Everything we had in our house was so staid, so safe. This was fun, and colourful, and terrifying all at the same time. I had to buy it for my wife. I just had to. There was no way she wasn't going to love it.

'How much?' I'd said eagerly to the lady behind the table, fumbling in my pocket for some spare cash.

'Take it," she'd said, sourly, staring at the Jack, which was now dangling loosely from the box, its teeth still clacking together at irregular intervals as the mechanism wound down.

I raised both eyebrows. 'Are you serious?'

'I've been tryina' get rid of the damn thing for years,'

she said, giving me a funny look. 'You'd be doing me a favour.'

'Sweet!' Not one to look a gift horse in the mouth, I'd thanked her, and walked away with my trophy clutched tightly to my chest.

It would make the perfect present for my wife's birthday, I'd thought, as I sauntered home like a cat who'd had all the cream.

She was going to love it. Of course she was!

My wife didn't waste any time destroying my naïve hopes.

'You do understand what that is, don't you?'

She stared at me in disbelief, her voice strained.

'I mean, you can't be that dumb, can you? You at least know what this is?'

And now, the more I looked at the Jack, the more I realised that my wife was right, that there was, in fact, something horribly familiar, and yet somehow amiss with the thing. And then, as it eventually dawned on me, as the pieces clicked together, I furiously tried to backpedal.

'Look, honey, please, I didn't--'

She shouted at me, her eyes bulging in their sockets.

'You've bought me a toy made out of a human skull, Barry.'

'Well, hang on a minute, honey, I...'

'It's a fucking HUMAN SKULL BARRY!'

'Please, honey, sweetheart, come on, I...'

'A HUMAN CHILD'S SKULL.'

I swallowed, nodded sheepishly. Not a monkey skull. I could see that now.

'Babycakes, look, I didn't realise. Honest! I thought...'

'WHAT DID YOU THINK??' She screamed at me, her face turning a frightening shade of red.

I swallowed meekly.

'I thought it was a monkey!'

She began to laugh then, incredulously at first, and then in a more and more crazed manner.

'Even if it was a fucking monkey, Barry, why on earth would you assume I'd like that any better? Who buys their wife a fucking *monkey skull* on a spring for their birthday, Barry? Who does that? Who makes a gift of a dead baby's skull in a box, Barry? Who else do you know that would actually do that to another human being?'

I spread my hands out, pleadingly, the magnitude of what I'd done only now beginning to sink in.

'What the hell is wrong with some fucking perfume, Barry?' My wife raged, in full flow now. 'Why choose now to deviate from your comfort zone? You've bought me perfume every year since we first got married! I hate it, but it's better than...that...goddamned monstrosity!'

The Jack-in-the-box twitched, and clacked its teeth together.

Clack-clack-clack!

My wife cried out in disgust, and pushed the toy further away from her.

I blew out my cheeks, a feeling of total helplessness washing over me.

'I don't know,' I said, staring at my hands, which were still outstretched. 'I just thought it was...kind of cute...Peculiar. Different.' I trailed off, wordless again.

Tears welled up in my wife's eyes.

'Barry, it's a child's skull. Jesus! What were you thinking?' A little sob escaped from between her clenched lips.

'Yeah, I...yeah.' I sighed, and gave up, defeated. There didn't seem to be anything more to say.

Except...well, it was me. And I never knew when to keep my mouth shut. So...

'Happy Birthday, babe!' I said, suddenly, in a forced, celebratory tone, and then I attempted to hug her, clumsily, to try to make up for my faux pas.

'Oh my GOD!'

She erupted up out of the bed in an explosion of sheets, pillows and fury. 'You are literally unbelievable!'

She threw the Jack-in-the-box against the bedroom wall, and locked herself into our en-suite bathroom, where she stayed for the next hour or so, sobbing.

The strange toy clattered onto the floor, and I felt a sudden anxiety, not wanting the thing to break. I went over and scooped it up, cradling it protectively in my arms, inspecting it for any signs of damage. The human skull stared back at

Cruel Works of Nature

me with its empty eye sockets. I must have inadvertently triggered the laughing mechanism, because that childish, impish giggling came out of the chattering mouth once again. The teeth knocked against each other with the noise that was fast becoming familiar.

Clack clack clack!

I gazed at the Jack-in-the-box with admiration.

I mean, come on. The ingenuity of the thing!

Now, you might be wondering why my wife had such an extreme reaction to my well-intentioned, if macabre gift. I mean, sure, the thing was weird, and yeah, I get it: no-one really wants a toy made out of an actual child's skull sitting there on their mantelpiece, but she didn't have to be such a bitch about it, right? It was, after all, an honest mistake.

Well, here's the thing. This would probably be the case in another household, with another woman, a woman who hadn't had to bury her only child in the cemetery right across the road from our house only three years ago.

Wait a minute! I can hear you think.

Yep. I know, I just dropped that one right in there, didn't I?

But there's not much point in beating around the bush with these sorts of things. It is what it is. We had a baby, a beautiful, bouncing baby girl, and she died. It wasn't anyone's fault. We didn't do anything wrong, as parents. It just happened, quietly, one night when she was asleep. Not even the doctors could explain why. The autopsy was inconclusive.

So, with hearts full of disbelief, shock, grief and unanswered questions, we buried our angel on a sunny day in spring. The daffodils ran riotously through the cemetery. Birds sang joyously in the budding trees overhead. It felt like nature was mocking us as we lowered the tiny white box into the ground. My wife shook with sobs from head to toe, crying so hard I thought she might fly to pieces before my eyes. My own eyes were curiously dry, itchy and sore. I remember that I ached all over, the kind of ache you get before you come down with the flu. A priest droned on and on in prayer as our little girl was fed into the waiting, gaping mouth in the soil by our feet. I put a hand on my wife's shoulder, but she didn't pay any attention to it. This was to become an enduring theme in our marriage over the coming years.

Now, you're probably thinking what most people do when they hear this story. It seems odd, doesn't it, living within yards of our daughter's grave. Our house overlooks the cemetery where our own daughter is buried. But, for some reason, maybe because it felt that one degree too final, we couldn't bear the thought of a cremation. And there is only one cemetery in town. All of our other family members are buried there, and in a small place like this, tradition...well, it

Cruel Works of Nature

has a strong chokehold on a family. We never even contemplated burying our baby anywhere else.

'Don't you think it's a bit...morbid?' My mother said to me in hushed tones, during the wake. Her timing was impeccable, as usual. 'I mean, can't you sell the house? You'll just be stirring up your grief every time you look out the window.'

She had a point, no matter how unwelcome it was at the time. If you were to look out of the north facing windows of our house, you can see the tiny headstone, lying on a bed of soft grass underneath a willow tree. The white marble stone reads 'Charlotte,' and once you'd gotten your head around the dates, you'd realise that she was only nine months old when she passed. That was, indeed, a difficult thing to be reminded of every time you opened the curtains in the morning and looked out the window.

But my wife refused to move. She found it oddly comforting, being able to see our baby whenever she made herself a cup of coffee, or sat down on our front porch. Morbid it may have been, but I was happy to do anything which meant she would stop crying, so in the house we stayed, although at times it felt more like the cemetery, and Charlotte, was watching over us as we slept, instead of the other way around.

Okay, okay, I know. Now that you understand the context, my wife going bat shit crazy about that Jack-in-the-box makes a lot more sense.

Yeah.

I mean any normal, *sane* human being would have thought twice before bringing what was essentially the head of a dead child into our home a mere three years after we'd lost our own child so tragically, and suddenly. And I'll be the first to admit that I'd made a colossal mistake, a huge error of judgement.

But then, as my wife would be the first to tell you, what's new?

In her eyes, I think I've always been something of an idiot, navigating the complicated twists and turns of the corn maze of marriage with a combination of ignorance, blind hope and in a generalised state of perpetual confusion. I mean, I never knew what the right thing to do was. Buy her perfume every year, and I'm Mr. Boring. Buy her something else for a change and look what happens. Tears, tantrums and getting locked out of my own bathroom for hours on end.

So, I did what any self-respecting man with a failing marriage hanging around his neck would have done in my situation. I tucked the Jack-in-the-box under my sweater, went to the front porch, cracked open a beer, and sat staring at the cemetery until darkness fell.

My wife eventually unlocked the bathroom door and went to bed, exhausted. I heard her soft movements as she readied herself for sleep, removing her tear-streaked makeup, putting clothes away, shutting drawers and switching off lights. After half an hour, her gentle snores floated out of the window and down to the porch where

I sat.

Across the road, the cemetery lay bathed in weak moonlight. My little girl's headstone glowed faintly under the stars. I closed my eyes, rocking myself back and forth as I sipped beer. For a moment, I drifted off, and imagined I was cradling my baby to my chest, humming to myself tunelessly to get her to fall asleep. Her warmth and her smell were mesmerising, a smell you never, ever forget. Her little chest rose and fell. Her eyelashes fluttered against her cheek.

Clack, clack, clack!

I jolted awake, and realised I was cradling the Jack-inthe-box, and not my daughter. The darn thing was chuckling at me again, clacking its pearly whites, now no longer pearly, or white.

I went to bed in my usual place on the couch downstairs. I pushed the Jack back inside the box, closed the lid, gently, and set it on a windowsill where I could see it when I woke up in the morning.

As I drifted off to sleep, I heard it chuckle once more, faintly.

✤ ✤ ✤

I WOKE to find my wife standing at the foot of the couch, a suitcase in one hand, and her jacket in the other.

'I'm going to stay with my sister for a day or two,' she said, a sad frown on her face.

I looked at her, and once again, I found myself bereft of anything useful to say.

'Okay,' I managed, propping myself up on one elbow.

'Okay? Okay?'

Surprise surprise, that was not the answer she'd been looking for.

'You could at least try to look a little heart broken, Barry. You know. Make a pretence if only to save my feelings.'

'Well...' I tried to unstick my furry tongue from the roof of my mouth. I'd just woken up, for Chrissakes. I hadn't even taken a piss before being dragged straight back into marital warfare. Even soldiers get time to piss on tour.

I tried to think of something to say that would amount to damage control, although, honestly, the idea of a few days of peace and quiet, with no arguments or animosity... well, it was kind of an attractive proposition.

'I mean, I'd rather you didn't go, obviously.' I hated how my voice sounded: weak, wheedling, insincere. I was like a lap dog, whining and scratching against the back door, dying to be let out. It was not a terrible analogy for my situation, on thinking about it.

'Obviously.' Her sadness had morphed into open hostility, punctuated with lip-curling sarcasm.

'You'll forget about me five minutes after I walk out of that door. I'll bet you can't wait to see the back of me.'

A little, malicious, child-like voice popped up inside my head.

Too fucking right, it whispered, and then giggled.

My eyes went unbidden to the Jack-in-the-box, sitting on the windowsill where I'd left it. I shook my head and attempted to inject some reason into the conversation.

'Honey, come on. It's early, I've just woken up…'

'It's eleven-thirty in the fucking morning, Barry!' My wife yelled, swiping a vase from atop the mantelpiece, and hurling it at me.

'Jesus!' I yelped, and she stormed past me, making her way to the front door, heels stomping into the wooden floor with real, livid force.

She turned when she reached the door, eyes flashing hate, and snarled at me.

'And I swear to God, Barry, if you call me 'Honey' one more time, I'm going to rip your balls off with my teeth!'

With that, and a slam of the door, she left. I heard the engine of our car start up, and then the squeal of tyres on gravel as she put her foot down and sped away.

'Bye,' I said, waving at the back of our car as it disappeared down the lane. 'Don't hurry back!'

Clack. Clack. Clack.

Jack was out of his box again, bouncing around and chattering his teeth together.

I sighed and waved good morning.

* * *

MY WIFE DIDN'T COME HOME for three weeks.

During that time, Jack and I got to know each other pretty well. We sat and talked, or rather, I talked, and Jack listened, clicking his teeth together and chuckling whenever I told a good joke or recited one of my better anecdotes. To be honest, life had been so quiet since Charlotte died, that there wasn't that much to talk about, but Jack listened nonetheless.

I got into a daily routine that agreed with me, in the absence of my wife bossing me about all over the place. I stopped going to work and unplugged the phone. I slept a lot, and took long walks in the cemetery every morning, to visit Charlotte. Then, as the sun went down, I'd settle into my comfy chair on the front porch. I'd put Jack on a coffee table beside me. I liked to pour myself a vodka, chase it down with some clozapine, and wind the crank handle. When Jack popped up, I would ask him how he was. His little bony face would set into an enquiring expression, as if to ask me how my day had been, in return. We'd greet each other like old friends. It was the most meaningful interaction I'd had with another being for years.

Then, one evening, as I stared at Charlotte's grave glowing ethereally in the deep night in front of me, a small, clear voice interrupted the deep reverie I'd fallen into.

'Barrrryyyy,' it said softly, in babyish tones.

My head whipped round.

Jack was upright on his spring, his empty eye sockets trained on me, and he looked...somehow alert. His jaw moved slowly as if testing itself out.

'Barrrrryyyyy...' He said again, wistfully this time.

I frowned. 'You're not supposed to talk for real,' I admonished, waving my almost empty vodka glass at him. 'You're just a...I dunno, an imaginary friend that I can talk to. You know, so I don't go fucking crazy sat here by myself in this big old empty house.' I tipped my head back and finished off the vodka, then poured another. Should I take more clozapine? Would it take the edge off, stop the voices?

'Barrryyyyy...' Jack was not giving up easily, it seemed.

'Oh my God, what?' I snapped. 'You sound like my wife, moaning away. Barrrrryyyy, why you always gotta buy me perfume? Barrrrrryyyy, why you gotta be such a shit husband? Baaa-aarrrrrryyyy, why you gotta let our daughter die like that? Yeesh.'

Jack chattered dutifully, and a mournful chuckle rippled out across the porch.

'So what do you want?' I said, somewhat regretting my harshness. Poor little guy was only trying to get my attention, was all.

'I'm lonely, Barry.'

Was it my imagination, or were there faint lights glowing in his eye sockets? Little red pinprick lights?

I blinked, and this time reached straight for the vodka bottle, bypassing the glass tumbler.

'Me too, buddy,' I said, slurring a little. You're not supposed to mix booze and medication, but then, you're not supposed to bury your child at nine months old. You're not supposed to see your wife walk out on you three years later. You're definitely not supposed to sit making light conversation with a tiny human skull skewered on a spring in a box.

'I'm so lonely, Barrrryyyy,' Jack's curiously infantile voice continued.

I blew out my cheeks, made a whickering sound like a horse.

'So what do you want me to do about it, pal?' I said, gazing at my daughter's headstone. A tear trickled unbidden down my face. I turned to face the Jack, needing to see anything other than that tiny, pathetic, awful little block of stone which sat, rigid with accusation across the road from me.

A pulsating red glow was building up within

Cruel Works of Nature

Jack's skull. I registered it, and then found it hard to look away.

The glow grew brighter and more intense. My own eyes grew wide, so wide I thought they might pop out.

The Jack-in-the-box began to whisper instructions to me. I saw the red tattoo lines on his bony face move, writhe about like live worms. The red light grew brighter and brighter until my eyes watered and my ears began to ring with a loud buzzing noise, but still, I couldn't look away. Jack's teeth clattered together, *clack! Clack! Clack!* I sat hypnotized, ramrod straight in my chair, pinned into the cushions behind me by the force of Jack's gaze as firmly as if I were being pressed into them by a giant, invisible hand.

After that, things got a bit...patchy.

I remember looking down and seeing a shovel in my hands.

Then, later, I remember standing, panting, covered in sweat and mud, next to a great, deep hole in the ground. Gravestones poked out of the turf like wonky teeth all around me. Something small, white, polished and oblong glimmered at the bottom of the hole.

Something that was roughly the same size as a nine month old baby.

I reached down for it.

Then I was in my garage, at my work bench, tinkering around with some springs, screws, a welding iron, a glue gun and a patch of what looked like human hair, dark and matted.

After that, I remember vaguely heaving myself upstairs, exhausted, and crawling to bed, filthy, covered in mud and twigs and bits of wood and metal and grease, my hands sore and blistered. I was asleep within seconds. The faint *clack! Clack! Clack!* of Jack's teeth sent me to dreamland, but what was that, before I descended into oblivion complete?

It sounded like an echo, like a *second* set of teeth chattering.

Clack! Clack! Clack!

❋ ❋ ❋

I AWOKE TO the sound of the front door closing behind someone.

'Hello? Barry?' It was my wife's voice. It echoed around our house like an unwelcome smell, lingering in the air. I dragged open my eyelids.

My wife stood in the doorway, hesitant, almost apologetic.

'I'm sorry,' she said, taking a breath as if to continue. Then she registered my clothes, spattered with dried mud, the fact that I was in bed fully dressed, dishevelled, bruised, cut, and that my hands were covered in grubby sticking plasters from hundreds of tiny cuts I'd inflicted upon myself, somehow.

Then, I saw her eyes move from me to the windowsill where I usually placed the Jack-in-the-box, in a position where he could watch me as I slept.

Her mouth dropped open, and all the colour drained from her face. She fell to her knees, and began to wail, an animal, howling noise that sounded like a dog in pain.

'What have you done?' Was all she could say, over and over again.

And then: 'My baby. Not my poor baby. Not my poor, poor baby!'

I closed my eyes, and let her carry on, too exhausted to do anything else.

'What have you done to my baby?!' She screamed, and the sounds of her grief closed in around me as I drifted into unconsciousness.

* * *

A POLICEMAN WOKE me this time. He shook me awake, rather gently, considering.

'Come on, buddy,' he said, and his face was ashen, his breath sour, as if he'd been sick recently. 'We gotta take you in, buddy. Okay? I'm going to put these handcuffs on you now.'

In the background I saw a paramedic give my hysterical wife a shot of something. She slumped to the floor once again, her wails of distress fading into mumbles, and then silence.

I was aware, as the handcuffs were placed on

me, that the policeman was reading me my Miranda warning.

'Barry Lincoln, I'm arresting you on suspicion of corpse robbery and defiling a grave.' The Policeman fumbled with the handcuffs, cursing under his breath mid-speech. Once they clicked together, he continued.

'You have the right to remain silent,' he said, swallowing as if the words were difficult to pronounce. 'Anything you say can, and will, be used against you in a court of law...'

I zoned out, struggling to crane my head around and find my Jack-in-the-box. I wanted one last look at him before I got taken away.

There he was, his delicate skull bouncing around on his spring, his teeth gnashing together as usual.

Clack! Clack! Clack! They went.

And then, as with the night before, I heard a second set of noises, almost identical to the first.

Clack! Clack! Clack!

My eyes moved along the windowsill to the source of the noise.

Next to him, a second box, crudely made, had burst open.

It was another Jack-in-the-box, this one made... by me.

On the end of an old, discarded bed spring, which was the only thing I'd been able to find at the time, a tiny, perfect nine-month-old baby skull rested.

Small, grey patches of skin remained attached to the skull. Dark, matted hair stuck out at odd angles from the crown. I'd tried to paint a smile on the tiny, wizened face, tried to replicate the smile my baby girl had given me when she'd been alive.

Charlotte hadn't had many teeth when she'd died. But the teeth she'd had now clacked together in unison with Jack's.

Clack! Clack! Clack!

I began to chuckle as the Policeman struggled to finish the Miranda rights.

Jack wouldn't be lonely anymore, I thought.

Then, came the tears.

Gemma Amor

BLACK SAND

It was on the second morning of my vacation that I came across the drowned body of a young man, washed up on the beach outside my hotel.

He sprawled face-down across the sand as if asleep, waist-deep in the lapping waves. The sea gently and insistently tugged at him, like a small child tugging at the hem of its mother's skirt.

I had been out for my morning run along the shoreline, and spotted him in the distance. From afar, he looked like a low, grey rock.

Up close was another matter.

I slowed from a jog to a cautious shuffle, and approached warily. My heart sank as I gradually realised what I was looking at. I stopped at a safe distance from the body, and crouched down, covering my mouth with my hands.

'Oh, Jesus,' I said from behind my fingers, as the waves continued to move up and down the tideline at my feet.

His skin was greyish-green, and his body was bloated from being in the water a while. I could smell decay and rot, rot scented with salt and the smell of the sea. I was grateful he was face down, because I didn't want to see what the ocean had done to the softer parts of him, his eyes, his lips, his nose. I could see the remnants of stubble peppering one cheek. A tiny crab crawled out of his right ear, and wandered drunkenly down his neck, disappearing under the collar of his shirt. His hair was dark, and matted, and caked with something black, something that was either mud, or sand, I couldn't tell which.

I had seen dead bodies before, but never this early in the morning.

I kneeled sheepishly beside the corpse in the water, my mind a blank.

'Oh, Jesus,' I said again, for want of anything better to say.

I knew I needed to get him out of the water, in case the tide took him while I was fetching help. I scanned the surrounding beach, in the vague hope that someone else was around, perhaps also out for their morning walk or run, but it was far too early. I glanced up at the Hotel Bianco, which overlooked the beach, and saw no-one there either.

There was nothing else for it. I'd have to drag the body higher up the beach by myself.

It was a good job I hadn't eaten breakfast yet.

Taking a deep breath, and holding it, I steeled myself, and slowly took hold of the back of the man's ragged tshirt, taking care not to brush my knuckles against the wet, clammy skin of the corpse inside the shirt. The waterlogged fabric felt slimy to the touch, and I flinched, then tightened my grip.

I pulled. Nothing happened.

'Come on, you stubborn bastard,' I said, through gritted teeth.

I pulled harder, grunting with the effort, hoping against hope that the fabric wasn't about to tear, or worse, any of the flesh underneath. I had a sudden mental image of the man's head rolling free from his neck, tumbling across the beach like a football, and almost gagged.

Still no movement. He was heavy, and waterlogged. I pulled.

Then, the man's torso shot up out of the water and onto the sand in a sudden rush. I toppled over backwards, landing hard on my ass.

The torso came free.

The rest of the man did not.

He was missing from the waist down.

I yelled in disgust, and scrambled up to my feet. It was as if the man had been guillotined in two, from the waist down. I'd seen worse injuries, but I'd never seen one so clean, so decisive.

I ran for help as fast as my legs could carry me.

It was not a great way to start my holiday.

❋ ❋ ❋

THE ITALIAN POLICE arrived, surrounded the remains quickly with a fluttering tape cordon held up by iron poles poked into the sand. A small crowd of spectators gathered on the beach- other hotel guests, locals, children, joggers. They stood about gossiping, sharing snacks, smoking, catching up. For such a small island, there were a lot of nosy folk. They lent an almost festive air to the sombre proceedings.

I sat higher up, on the hotel terrace overlooking the beach, wrapped in a blanket I didn't need, nursing a cup of coffee I didn't want. A policeman was taking my statement via the hotel receptionist, who spoke English and translated for me. There wasn't much to tell: first I was running, thinking of what to order from the room service menu for my lunch, and then I was wrestling with a rotting corpse in the tide-line. As you do.

I was calm, and gave my statement with no hesitation, or theatrics. This made me appear cold, dispassionate. I hoped it would be mistaken for shock.

It wasn't shock.

Not much shocked me anymore.

The policeman asked me how long I was staying. I hesitated. I'd originally planned to be here for some time, at least a week or two, but now I wasn't so sure. My room had a sea-view. Did I really want the memory of the dead man's body sliding out of the surf and practically into my lap every time I looked out the window?

But, still.

I didn't have the money to relocate to another hotel, or the energy. Perhaps I could ask for another room, one without a sea view.

I chewed my lip, then told them I would be around for at least a fortnight. The hotel receptionist looked relieved, and offered me a discount on meals, to make up for the distress caused by my 'discovery'.

I took the deal, and kept my room.

The ocean view really was fantastic, drowned man or no drowned man.

❋ ❋ ❋

TWO DAYS LATER, another body washed up on the shoreline outside the hotel.

This one was a woman, in her fifties. She was later identified as a tourist, American, like me, and, unlike the other corpse, she'd managed to hang on to her legs. She was, however, missing her right arm, and the right side of her face. I didn't find her this time, thank God. A member of the hotel staff had that honour, a cleaning lady I think. I heard her screaming incoherently all the way from my hotel room. I went out onto my balcony, looked down to the beach, and saw what was happening. I sighed, picked up my in-room phone, dialled reception.

'Signorina?'

'You need to call the Police again,' I said. 'There's another body on the beach.'

The Receptionist swore under her breath in Italian.

'Cazzo!'

I hung up.

I didn't go down to the beach this time. Fifteen minutes later the island police were back, and another cordon of fluttering, flickering hazard tape was put up. More spectators gathered. More gossip shared. The party started all over again.

I sat on my balcony and drank cold white wine from a local vineyard.

I mean, I was on holiday, after all.

✼ ✼ ✼

A WEEK LATER, and the furore had died down at last. The sea had brought no more rotting bounties for us to find. The hotel grew quiet again, and it was fantastic. You cannot place a price on

Cruel Works of Nature

peace, on solitude. We are so rarely alone, anymore. There are too many people in the world, or certainly, there are too many people in my world. I crave solitude. I finally had it.

I sat on my balcony, a book open on my lap, abandoned mid-paragraph. I stared at the sea and let my tired body relax slowly into the chair beneath me.

What price solitude? I thought, dreamily, my mind wandering across different thoughts and feelings in a lazy, sleepy manner. No price. Priceless.

I stared straight down onto the small, curved beach littered with piles of dried seaweed, dredged from the bottom of the ocean. I wondered about the dead bodies, and wondered if there would be anymore. How had they died? Had a boat gone down somewhere? Why were so many parts of them missing? Were there sharks in the water? Surely not, not in the Mediterranean. And it wasn't a shark, I knew that. The separation of legs from body on the corpse I'd found had been too clean, too surgical for an animal or shark attack.

How much did I really care, though?

I mean, from one point of view, it was interesting. Two bodies in a week, both exhibiting signs of great violence. Sure, I could see why the locals were getting all excited about it.

But I'd been around death a lot, and it had lost its ability to impress me beyond than the initial dismay of discovery. My encounter with the torso on the sand had only served to make me feel tired, tired and useless and futile, as was death's way.

The sea beyond the beach was grey that day, grey and churning, frothy white waves lurching at the shoreline and smashing into it over and over again. A restless sea, an angry sea. Spray erupted over rocks and plumed high into the air. A cool wind tore through the fronds of the palm trees that lined the beach. Leaves ripped free from their stems and landed in the murky swimming pools around the hotel. It was off-season, so the pools, the beach-bars, the terraces- it was all closed, waiting for better weather, for sunshine and blue skies, for planes full of people. The Hotel Bianco was therefore nearly empty. I preferred it that way. I felt like a Queen alone in a grand palace by the sea. Sometimes I left my room, and wandered corridors and gardens, solitary, content. Occasionally I would see another resident, but only very occasionally. When I did, we would smile politely, but offer no conversation.

For now, it was enough to be sitting on this balcony, wrapped in a warm jumper, a blanket around my knees, the pages of my book lifting up hopefully in the gusts of wind that chased across my lap. I ignored them, and stared at the beach, and the water. It was soupy with debris and weed, murky and yet hypnotic. There would be time for reading later. At this moment in time, I just wanted to revel in the ocean, and the wind, and the quiet patter of rain against my sea-facing windows. My clothes grew damp, and a faint chill crept along my skin, but still I remained, staring out to sea. Just a little while longer. Just a few moments more.

After a time I spotted a small, dark figure scrambling across the rocks to the left of the bay. As it grew closer, I could see that it was a man dressed in jogging gear. I could see the neon brightness of his shoelaces flashing against the grey stone. The tide was higher now than it had been an hour ago, and still coming in. If he did not get across the rocks quickly, he'd find himself cut off, stranded on a tiny outcrop until the sea receded once more.

The approaching tide didn't seem to bother him much. Clearly a fit and healthy man, he hopped from rock to rock with ease, using his hands to brace himself, scrambling along like a goat. He made it to the edge of the outcrop and jumped, landing on the beach nimbly. He then jogged along the shoreline towards the hotel.

Minutes later he was on the terrace below me. I watched him with a mild curiosity. He glanced up, saw me looking. He grinned, and waved. I didn't respond. He shrugged, in a good-natured sort of way, and disappeared into the bowels of the hotel.

My eyes drifted back to the sea. Just a little

longer.

Just... a few moments more.

※ ※ ※

EVENING FOUND me in my favourite spot in the bar, martini in hand, neglected novel in the other. The rain was still beating against the hotel windows, and the sea and the sky had merged into a vast, midnight-blue expanse, with occasional lights flickering in the distance as ocean liners made their ponderous way along the coastline. It had been a good day, peaceful, restful, and my heart was feeling fuller than it had for a long time.

I took a sip, grimacing in pleasure at the strength of the martini. Quiet bar music played in the background, a saxophone compilation of hit songs from the nineties, the kind of music you never listened to outside of hotels. I turned a page of my novel, and the barman, who was called Jisepu, placed a bowl of snacks in front of me, wordlessly. We smiled at each other.

'Grazie,' I murmured, and he nodded.

'Prego,' he said, and left me alone. *Marry me*, I thought. All I'd ever wanted was a man who could pour a stiff drink and learn to leave me the hell alone when I needed solace.

A shadow crossed my vision. I became aware of someone sitting next to me. I frowned,

Cruel Works of Nature

marked my place on the page with my index finger, and looked up, annoyed.

It was the running man from earlier, the man who had been scrambling across the rocks. I looked at him blankly. He stuck out a hand, smiling the sort of smile you wore when you were about to try to sell something to someone who didn't want or need it.

'Hi,' he said, and his voice was thick with a southern drawl. 'Am I interrupting?'

I blinked at him, ignoring the hand. The answer was so obviously 'Yes' that I didn't need to say it. He showed no signs of moving, so I sighed, and put the book down.

'Can I help you?' I said, pointedly, sipping my martini and glaring coldly at the man over the rim of the glass.

'Ah, fellow American, I see,' he said, unperturbed by my rudeness. He smoothly withdrew his hand and gestured at Jisepu instead. He ordered a beer in Italian, and smiled winningly. Jisepu shot me an amused look, and turned away to grab a beer bottle from the fridge. He popped the lid off with practiced ease, and poured half of the contents into a tall glass, letting the foam settle, and asking the man for a signature so he could charge the drink to his room.

'I'll get this one too,' the man said, gesturing at my martini. 'And the next one.'

I sighed, exasperated. 'Really, there's no need,' I said, impatiently, looking around me for an escape route. I spotted one- a blonde, slim German woman who was about my age. She'd been in the hotel longer than even I had, and seemed to be a fixture in the bar in much the same way. We'd never so much as even said 'hello' to each other. We both seemed okay with that arrangement.

'Look,' I said, gesturing at the woman. 'She looks lonely, why don't you try to buy her a drink? I don't mean to be rude, but I've just started this chapter and I'm not feeling that sociable, if you catch my meaning.'

The man chuckled, and sipped his beer, making no effort to move. 'I love it when women say things like "I don't mean to be rude". You just know that by saying that, they are about to be really, really rude.'

I groaned, and took another gulp of my drink, desperate to make a hasty retreat but loathe to leave the cocktail unfinished.

'I'm Thomas, thanks for asking,' the man continued, waiting for me to venture my own name.

'That's nice for you,' I said, refusing to play ball.

His smile never wavered. 'I saw you looking at me earlier,' he continued, lifting an eyebrow as if to try to insinuate something.

'Don't flatter yourself, I was looking at the sea,' I said, crossly, drawn into the conversation despite myself.

'Sure, I believe you,' said Thomas, smirking. I let out an exasperated noise, and made to get up

Cruel Works of Nature

from my seat.

'Have you been this obnoxious your whole life?' I asked, as I drained the dregs of my martini too quickly, and got down from my bar stool. Jisepu looked at me sympathetically as he polished wine glasses with a crisp white cloth.

'Pretty much,' said Thomas, undeterred. 'But my Momma thinks I'm cute.' His eyes twinkled.

'Your Momma must be a very patient woman,' I said, gentling my tone a little. 'Anyway, if I *was* watching you, it was because I thought you were going to get stranded on those rocks. The tide comes in quickly around here. You were cutting it fine.'

'Is that right? Well thank you, I shall bear that in mind for tomorrow.'

'Why, what's happening tomorrow?' The words were out of my mouth before I could stop them. I cursed inwardly.

'I'm heading around the bay to the 'Spiaggia di sabbia nera'. Want to join me?'

I stared at the man, flummoxed and exasperated.

'First off, I literally just met you. So I'm flattered, but no. I'm not going anywhere with you. Second, my Italian is not so hot.'

'Spiaggia di sabbia nera,' Thomas repeated, patiently, as if I were a slow child. 'It means "the beach of the black sand". It's a local geological phenomenon. The sand is completely black, made of volcanic material, a real sight to behold, they say.'

'Wow,' I said, sarcastically. 'Black sand.'

Jisepu interjected, politely. 'Excuse me, sir, but that beach...it is closed to the public. Conservation reasons, you see. There is a rare species of bird that likes to nest near the beach. The authorities close it this time of year to...to encourage them to breed.'

Thomas shrugged. 'The trail leading to the beach is still worth exploring, no? The coastline is so beautiful around here. Can we still walk the trail?'

Jisepu nodded in assent. 'Si, si, the trail is still open, but it is not advised to go to the beach.' There was something in his tone which spoke of a hidden subtext to Jisepu's words, a subtext the brash American man in front of me was not hearing. I kept quiet, listening to the exchange.

Thomas waved a hand dismissively. 'Yeah, yeah, I get it. Don't go near the beach. Still, a hike will be better than staying here. Fancy it?' He renewed his invitation to me, and I scoffed at him in disbelief.

'No!' I said. 'How many times do you need to hear that word before you get the message?'

Thomas shrugged. 'Suit yourself,' he said. 'I tried.

Enjoy sharing the hotel with three hundred guests tomorrow.'

I froze.

'What?' I looked to Jisepu, confused. He nodded, apologetic.

'They didn't tell you, signorina?'

'Tell me what?'

'Ah, excuse me, but tomorrow, we have the three hundred guests arriving for a wine and cheese tasting event. They will stay for two days.' Jisepu nodded, as if trying to reassure himself that it would be alright. 'It is a national holiday this weekend, you see. And the locals, they can get a bit...how you say...excited on holidays. Maybe they will get quite...loud.' He trailed off, and picked up another glass, intent on polishing away his sudden embarrassment.

I stared at him in horror.

'Three *hundred*?' I imagined them all, sprawling across the couches in *my* lobby, taking up all the bar stools in *my* bar, thrashing around in *my* indoor swimming pool, tramping all over *my* beach.

I shuddered at the thought of it.

Thomas looked at me. 'The offer is still open,' he said, trying to appear nonchalant.

I shook my head in disbelief. 'While I admire your persistence, there is no way on this earth that I'm going anywhere with you, I'm afraid. I know enough about you already to know you'd drive me insane within ten minutes. I'll just have to hole myself up in my room for two days, until everyone has gone.'

'Suit yourself,' he said again, and I rolled my eyes, shook my head, and marched irritably out of the bar.

Behind me, I heard Thomas call out.

'The offer is still open! Meet me by the beach bar at ten-thirty! You know you want to!'

'I'd rather stab rusty forks into my own eyes!' I called backwards to him, over my shoulder. I heard Jisepu chuckle, discreetly.

That night, I slept a restless, churning sleep, dreaming of a hotel full of bloated, dancing corpses, black sand filling the sockets of their eyes and their nasal cavities, pouring out of their open mouths. Jisepu worked tirelessly around them, serving black martinis, bowing apologetically every few moments as the jerking, frenzied bodies performed a parody of movement about him. Clichéd jazz music played incessantly in the background, drowning out the sounds of the sea, and I watched, helpless, as the corpses danced until their legs fell off, then continued to writhe around on the floor, still trying to dance, mouths agape in a ghoulish revelry that was unlike anything I'd ever imagined.

I woke in a cold sweat, and went out onto my balcony, slowly emptying the remains of a bottle of white wine. I stared at the night, listening to the raging sea, caught in the fist of a worsening storm. Thunder crashed overhead. I leapt from my chair, and dove under the table I was sitting at, shivering. Thunder pealed again, and I cried, trying to forget the bodies I'd seen, both real and imagined, throughout the course of my reasonably short life.

I spent the rest of the night under that table, shaking, curled up into a ball, while the rain came down all around me.

※ ※ ※

THE NEXT DAY dawned clear and placid, the sea a glassy, flat lake instead of the churning grey mass it had been only a few hours earlier. Gardeners and groundsmen righted furniture that had blown over during the night, when the storm was at its worst. Meek, delicate waves lapped at the beach quietly, as if the ocean were offering little apologetic kisses for its behaviour the day before. A strong, hot sun shone down from the blue sky overhead, promising to dry out the bedraggled umbrellas that hung limply from their anchors all around the terrace. The storm was over. The sky was sapphire. Heaven was restored.

I watched the sunrise, my eyes gritty and sore through sleeplessness. I showered, warming my shuddering, cold limbs under steaming hot water. I picked up my book, and made my way down to breakfast.

It was obvious, even at this hour that the hotel was gearing up for a whole new level of activity. The breakfast tables, usually dotted at reasonable distances from each other in the bright and airy restaurant, were now shoved together to form long banqueting tables. Staff hurried around, their usual, relaxed morning routines now infused with a panicky urgency, as if they felt unprepared for the arrival of the three hundred guests. I had to wait twenty minutes before anyone would take my order of coffee and poached eggs. A man riding a floor-sweeper drove in manic circles round and around on the terrace in a frantic quest to erase all traces of debris from the storm the night before.

I grew increasingly frustrated.

Wrong, this was all *wrong*.

Thomas strode past my table with a knowing look on his face as I chewed at my eggs, listlessly. He winked as he passed.

'The offer still stands,' he said, and I nearly threw my coffee cup at him.

The hordes arrived at ten in the morning.

Within the space of an hour, every part of the hotel that had once offered me any solace, apart from my room, was overrun with chattering women, laughing men, shouting teenagers, and crying, over-excited children. They filled every available chair and lounger and stool, swarmed the spa area and swimming pool like a plague of insects, and choked the beach and terrace with ball games and card games and circles of jolly, cigarillo-smoking ragazzi.

I retreated hastily to my room, as promised, and hung the 'do not disturb' sign from my door handle.

I'd not been there longer than ten minutes before there was a knock at the door. I opened it, feeling decidedly unfriendly. The hotel receptionist stood before me, wringing her hands with that expression I now knew so well, the expression that was the bearer of bad news.

'I am so sorry, signorina,' she said, and I knew I was about to be turfed out of my room, into the chaos that was a local holiday down below.

'I am afraid we need to do some essential maintenance in your room, signorina. The man has to test the smoke alarm and rewire the faulty socket by your bed, signorina.'

I sighed, and admitted defeat. 'Give me five minutes to pack a bag, and then I'll be gone,' I said, heavily. The receptionist smiled gratefully at me, and thanked me for my understanding.

I packed a rucksack with sunscreen, water, a hat and a muesli bar from the mini-fridge. I looked at my watch.

The time read ten-thirty.

Of course it was.

Fate, it seemed, had plans for me today.

❈ ❈ ❈

I WALKED through the throngs of locals running around in the hotel lobby, and passed a harassed and red-faced Jisepu, trying to navigate his way around a tangled pile of squealing children who wrestled with each other on the floor by the bar. He looked up as I passed, and we smiled at each other ruefully.

'Even black sand is better than this,' I said, gesturing at the chaos all around.

He extricated himself and came over to me, his face suddenly very serious. Curious, I waited for him to speak.

'What is it?' I asked, barely able to hear myself speak over the babble of Italian in the background.

He put a hand on my wrist, a gesture that was strictly out of the bounds of normal hotel staff behaviour. It made me nervous, because I could see that whatever he was trying to say was important.

'If you go to that beach, I must tell you one thing.'

'And that is?'

'The beach...it is very, very dangerous. The authorities have not closed it because of the birds. I can't say more, but please. Don't leave the boardwalk. Don't touch the sand. Better not to go at all. Just...trust me. Please, signorina.'

I thought about this for a moment. I remembered the corpse I'd found only days earlier. I remembered a sticky sort of black substance in the dead man's hair, a substance part way between mud and sand. I remembered how the corpse had slid free of the water with a wet, sucking sound, toppling me off of my feet.

'The bodies on the beach...?' I said, leaving the question open-ended.

He nodded. 'Just don't touch the sand,' he said, and squeezed my wrist again.

And this is where the contrary vagaries of the human character made themselves known, because, instead of being frightened, or perturbed by his warning, I immediately became intrigued, and this, coupled with my frustration at the unwelcome new guests running riot everywhere, and the godawful night I'd spent hiding from the thunder during the storm, made for a heady combination of emotions in my mind that I didn't understand, or have the mental capacity to untangle.

Jisepu called after me as I left the hotel, thanking him and wishing him a good day.

'Don't leave the boardwalk!' He said, and then repeated it in Italian.

Thomas was waiting for me by the beach bar, as he'd promised, arms folded, self-assured smile planted firmly on his features. He wore mirrored sunglasses and a Florida print shirt, which looked ridiculous

Wordlessly, sullenly, I gestured for him to lead the way, and we set off, away from the hotel, in search of the beach of black sand.

✽ ✽ ✽

WE WALKED in silence for an hour, picking our way along a path that wound over rock shelves and through pools of crystal blue seawater. The temperature began to rise as we walked, and a thin layer of sweat beaded up on my arms and across my top lip. We walked, and I listened to the waves moving in and out, in and out, in and out. Thomas seemed content with the lack of conversation, which surprised me. I should have been more grateful about this, at the time, because when he did eventually speak, it was to ask a question I was not expecting.

'So,' he said, brightly, stopping to rest on a rock for a moment, and mopping sweat from his forehead with his hands. 'Are you fucking the bartender?'

I almost choked on the mouthful of water I was drinking.

'Really?' I managed, regaining my composure. 'An hour of silence and that's your opening line?'

He shrugged, grinning. 'There's just a...you know, a vibe between you two.'

I glared at him. 'He talks a lot less than you do.'

'I bet he's not as rich as I am.'

'God, you really are an idiot,' I said, half to myself, and moved along the trail without waiting for him.

'Seriously though, are you fucking the bartender?' Thomas jogged to catch up with me, and there was a slight uncertainty to his voice.

'Why do you care so much?' I asked, not slowing down. A rise in the coastline had appeared in the distance, and I assumed it was the trail heading up to the top of a cliff, underneath which would be a bay, the bay of black sand. I guessed at another hour of walking, at the most, less if I kept this pace up.

'Well, it's just... well. You're pretty.'

I stopped, and turned to see Thomas sheepishly rubbing the back of his head, a lopsided smile on his face. Was he for real? It had been so long since I'd thought, or cared about my appearance, that his compliment caught me off guard.

Pretty? What did that even mean, anyway?

I stared at him, perplexed, and then turned wordlessly, and carried on along the trail.

Thomas gave up on his flirtation pretty quickly after that. I kept my relief to myself. There was no room in my world for those kinds of conversations, not anymore. Not after the things I'd seen.

Soon, we found our steps angled upwards, and we began to climb slowly up to the top of a rocky ridge, as I'd guessed. Vegetation screened us from what lay beyond, and the trail very nearly disappeared into the undergrowth. I trampled it purposefully underfoot, ignoring the stings and scratches of thorns and weeds.

I broke through, and stopped abruptly.

He wasn't kidding, I thought, and I was momentarily awestruck.

Black sand lay before me.

* * *

THE BEACH WASN'T JUST black. It was *black*. Not the colour. An absence of light. A void in the fabric of the earth. I had never seen anything like it in my life before.

My eyes ached looking at it, drinking in the perfect, curved arc of midnight-coloured sand, cutting a dark scythe through the blueness of the sky and the sea up above and off to my left. It was so dark it absorbed the sunlight from all around.

I stood, and felt my eyes burn as I looked.

'It's quite something, isn't it?' Thomas said from behind me, unnecessarily. For once, I agreed with him.

'I'm at a loss for words,' I breathed, and I was.

He beamed, proud, as if this was his own, personal discovery.

Jisepu's warning played suddenly in the back of my mind. *Don't touch the sand*, he'd said. But it was so beautiful. I longed to run my fingers through it, feel the silky, cool grains pour from my palm.

'So...why is it black?' I said, unashamedly hypnotised by the spectacle before me.

'It's something to do with basalt,' Thomas said, sounding unsure. 'This island is volcanic. So the beach is a large deposit of basalt fragments.' 'Wow,' I said, and breathed out. 'Wow.'

And here I was, thinking I had seen it all.

The path descended steeply down the other side of the ridge and into the bay below. I moved dreamily along it, until I stood almost on the edge of the beach.

'Wait for me!' Thomas was itching to get there first. He made to push past me, but I held up one arm to block the path. He pouted, but also frowned as he looked at the hand gesture I'd made without thinking about it. He assessed me with new eyes, then, but I was too preoccupied to notice.

I couldn't deny that the sand had a certain... *pull* to it, and that I longed to run barefoot on the beach, but old habits die hard, and so first, I did what I always do these days when entering new territory. I stood still, and scanned the dunes around the edges of the beach, looking for potential danger.

I spotted it quickly: not more than ten feet before me, I could just make out the faint gleam of shiny, newly strung barbed wire. It made a thorny garland around the dunes, cordoning off the beach. I could see that the trail we were on, which headed down that way, passed under the wire, and then seemed to connect with a bleached white boardwalk that cut through the middle of the black beach beyond. Signs were peppered along the walk, painted in both Italian and broken English. 'Do not leave path', they said, over and over again. I thought once more of Jisepu's warning.

My senses alive, I walked up to the barbed wire, feeling...strange.

'Jisepu said not to go onto the beach,' I said quietly, as Thomas tested the wire to see if he could find a way over it. I let him. I was not overly fond of barbed wire. It brought back too many memories.

'I won't tell if you won't tell,' he said, and when he looked at me, he had such a hungry gleam in his eyes that I felt something unwanted inside of me lurch in an excited response.

'There were bodies on the beach, last week,' I continued, trying to talk over my own suddenly tumultuous feelings. 'Jisepu seemed to think they were linked to the sand, somehow. I found the first body, you know. There was black sand in his hair.'

Thomas looked at me, surprised. 'That was you?' he said, incredulous. Then he narrowed his eyes.

'You don't seem too disturbed by it.'

I shrugged. 'I've seen a few dead bodies in my time.'

Thomas stopped fiddling with the fence, and folded his arms, giving me his full attention.

'I've been wondering what it is about you that has been bothering me, aside from your general rudeness. It's your mannerisms, the way you act, and sit, and talk to people. It's the hand signals you make when you don't realise you're doing it. Not to mention your... physique.' He gestured to my figure, clad in sensible walking gear. My arms were still corded with tight muscles, and my legs were still lean, strong, conditioned. I trained every day, out of habit, in the gym, out running, swimming, walking, keeping the bag of bones that was my body in top form for no other reason than the sheer habit of it all.

'You're ex-military, aren't you?' He said, and I nodded, reluctantly.

'Combat medic,' I said, not wishing to elaborate.

'Okay,' he replied, and then:

'See much action?'

'I was in Iraq for three years.' I avoided eye contact. People had mixed feelings about war. I had mixed feelings about it myself. I was young when I signed up.

'Discharged?' he asked, not letting it drop.

I lifted up my vest, reluctantly.

His eyes widened as he saw the scars that wound their way around my abdomen, and the chunk of skin missing from the right side of my chest. The knotted scar tissue disappeared under my underwear and snaked down to my right thigh, which ached whenever I grew seriously tired, which I was suddenly, now.

'I.E.D.,' I said, and then finally met his gaze. An echo of the explosion went off in the back of my brain, and I twitched, as I always did when I remembered my own scars.

'Is that why you don't like people much?' He asked, quietly, and for him, it was a surprisingly insightful question.

I nodded. I didn't much like anything, anymore, except for the sea, and the sky, and silence.

I lowered my vest, and walked over to the wire barrier. I stood on the top strand of barbed wire that blocked our path, squashing it down to the ground with my body weight, holding it for Thomas so that he could climb over.

'You sure?' He said, suddenly hesitant.

'What else is there to do around here?' I asked, a rhetorical question.

The wire snapped back into place behind us as we walked towards the beach. Against my better judgement, against all my instincts, I lifted one foot, and placed it on the boardwalk.

❋ ❋ ❋

WE TESTED our footing on the old, weathered planks. The black sand lay beneath us and all around us, forbidding and yet somehow very tempting. I fought the urge again to strip my shoes off, dip my toes in the sand, feel the grains against my skin. I restrained myself, just, thinking of Jisepu's warning. But the further we walked, the more I wondered if perhaps the warnings were just a lie, perhaps this was noth-

Cruel Works of Nature

ing more than what it was: an anomaly of nature, a beautiful black stretch of sand, sand made of basalt, sand that was not dangerous at all.

I had grown so accustomed to danger. What would it be like to relax, to walk about as other people do, without the weight of my experiences hanging from my shoulders like a dark velvet cloak, heavy, and stifling?

I trod carefully, fighting with something complicated happening in my heart, and all around me was the colour black, as if night had fallen, but in contrasting mockery, above us, the sun beat down in the bright blue sky.

Soon, we stood in the middle of the bay, boardwalk underfoot, smooth banks of dark matter to either side. I closed my eyes and breathed in. A curious smell tugged at my senses- something a little sulphuric, something a little acidic. I listened for the sound of the ocean, and found that here, the familiar noise of waves crashing ashore seemed dampened, reduced. I looked up at the sky above me and saw no birds. I scanned the rocks that surrounded the bay for vegetation and found none. No shrubs, none of the ubiquitous pine trees that covered the rest of the island, no vines, or creepers. I examined the sand, looking for debris, seaweed, shells, crab carcasses. The sand was pristine, flotsam free. It was as if the beach had been swept free of all clutter except for the sand.

I thought back suddenly to the storm the

night before, to the hotel swimming pools full of debris, to the overturned tables and chairs, the small, pebbled beach heaped high with mounds of ragged seaweed. And yet, only a mile along the coast, we had this, clear sand, crystal blue sea. It was as if the storm had never visited this bay at all.

Thomas winked at me, trying to steal my attention away from the surrounding sights. He swung a leg over the rope handrail that lined the boardwalk.

'Shall I do it?' He asked, his face naughty, and I had a sudden insight into what he'd looked like when he'd been a child. His foot hovered a few inches above the black sand. He was wearing his running shoes, neon orange and blue. They clashed with the colours of his shirt and stood out harshly against the darkness of the beach. Looking at his foot so close to the sand gave me that old familiar, foreboding sense of something being very out of order. I shook my head, feeling uneasy.

'I wouldn't,' I said. 'Jisepu said not to leave the path.'

Thomas was full of bravado and a blatant desire to make an impression upon me. He grinned, in a devil-maycare sort of way, and before I could stop him, he hopped over the rope, both of his feet landing squarely on the beach with a quiet thump.

Something clicked into place in my mind.

The legless torso I'd dragged inland last week.

The legs, shorn off at the waist.

Thomas, jumping feet first into the sand.

My uneasy feeling grew stronger and more urgent.

'Thomas, get out of there,' I said, in a low and commanding voice.

He shrugged, looking at me and grinning with a lopsided smile. 'Nothing ventured, nothing gained,' he replied, and started skipping about in the sand, kicking at it, whooping and cartwheeling like that small boy I'd glimpsed moments before.

I stood and stared at him, half-afraid, half-jealous. He frolicked about. Sand sprayed into the air around his head, and he laughed. He wasn't in the slightest bit selfconscious. I had to admire that, begrudgingly.

Relax, I told myself, ignoring the warnings firing off in my brain. *Relax, it's fine. It's all fine.*

It wasn't.

Thomas stopped suddenly in his tracks and looked at me with an expression of consternation.

'What's the matter?' I said, and felt that old, well-used surge of adrenaline flood my body, and my fight responses kick in. I tensed, attuned my senses to the surrounding environment.

And that's when I heard it.

A faint hissing noise, the sound of something moving quickly through smooth sand.

A ripple appeared in the blackness behind Thomas, a long, sinuous ripple that moved with a hypnotic, lazy sort of grace towards him. I was reminded of a snake sliding through long grass.

'Thomas!' I called, ordering him to obey. 'Get off the beach!'

His eyes widened, and he grimaced with panic.

He looked down at his feet. A sizzling noise filled the air. The ripple snaked ever closer.

'It burns,' he whispered, in disbelief, and then he said it again, only this time, he shouted it, and I saw steam rising from his feet.

'It BURNS!'

And then the sand rose up, like a great, black hand, with a rush, and a hiss, and it grabbed Thomas by the ankles, swallowing his feet hungrily. He was yanked downwards, into the burning sand. I could smell scorched flesh, and once again, the body of the man with no legs flashed into memory.

I have to get Thomas out of the sand.

The message flashed in my brain once, and then again.

I have to get Thomas out of the sand.

I went into combat mode. I let my instincts take over.

I peeled off my backpack and threw it into the sand. I ripped off my vest and threw that down too. The items lay there, not smoking, and I guessed that it was only live, organic material that reacted to the sand.

Cruel Works of Nature

I looked around me, found a wooden warning sign on the boardwalk to my left. I ran to it, and charged it with my shoulder, again and again, until the wooden pole holding it up cracked, and eventually crashed over. I wrenched it up off the boards and ran back, hurling the sign into the sand next to the bag and my vest.

Then, I took a deep breath and jumped over the rope.

I landed on my bag, and wobbled furiously, windmilling my arms in an effort to stay upright. Ahead of me, beyond the makeshift stepping-stones I'd thrown down, Thomas screamed in agony. I leapt from the bag to the vest, from the vest to the wooden sign.

I grabbed hold of Thomas' hands.

'Help me!' He screamed, steam rising all around, and the black sand roiled and shifted like a hissing, contorted worm.

'Come on!' I yelled, clenching my jaw and pulling. Whatever was in the sand pulled back, and Thomas became the shrieking rope in a deadly game of tug-of war. I pulled, and felt my stepping stone begin to shudder beneath my feet, and the smell of burning wood rose in my nostrils, and I knew there was not long before my tiny platform was taken by the sand, and then it would be my feet smoking.

'Come on, Thomas! *Try!*' I shouted again, and my voice cracked. My arms shook with the effort, but the sand was stronger than I was, and it pulled at the man, yanking him further down into the black silt, and I realised it was up to his knees, and the screaming had stopped, because Thomas had fainted with pain as his legs dissolved beneath him.

The sand quivered and shifted, as if swallowing, and I realised the wood beneath my feet was now little more than charcoal. I'd been wrong about the sand only eating live flesh, the sand consumed everything, it just took longer with inanimate, dead objects. I could feel heat rising up under my toes. Thomas was a lost cause, I knew that now. If I didn't run back to the boardwalk, I would be next.

Cursing, I let go, and he sank down into the blackness. I turned and scrambled back to the boardwalk, falling over the rope and collapsing on my back onto the planks, which I realised now must not be made of any ordinary sort of wood, or else the sand would have taken them, too.

I heard sizzling and fizzing and turned my head long enough to see the last few inches of Thomas sink into the ground. I watched his eyes soften and melt, I watched his hair curl and disappear, and then there was nothing left, nothing but a gently shuddering expanse of deadly black sand. It belched, throwing a bubble of dark, sticky sand up into the air, before settling down into smooth, deceptive perfection once more.

Then, there was silence, except for the muted

sounds of the sea nearby.

I didn't vomit. Soldiers are trained not to do shit like that. I lay on my back, and remembered the last time I had felt like this, the last time I had lost someone to evil. I had been showered with the fragments of his body, made blind and deaf and dumb by the same blast that disassembled him from head to toe. Shrapnel had ripped through my skin, and I remembered nothing after that except for pain.

I screamed into the air, a futile, desperate scream, a scream from the depths of my long-internalised anguish.

Was I going mad?

Why survive, for this? Was this God's plan? Was this fate?

What was the fucking point of surviving if only to come to this? What was the fucking *point*?

I screamed again, as if my whole body was a bomb, a bomb that had been cleverly hidden for so long since that day, hidden behind medication and booze and aimless wanderings as I tried to rediscover life out of active service.

The ground shuddered beneath the boardwalk. I stopped my racket, and lay flat on my back, panting. There was movement in the sand once more. I sat up, trembling, and saw the shifting grains coalesce into a mockery of a giant, open human mouth.

The mouth screamed back at me.

Blood erupted from my nose and trickled down from my ears. I clamped my hands over them and squeezed my eyes shut.

The blackened beach screamed at me, a monstrous noise that obliterated all other sounds and sights and smells.

And then it was over.

I scrambled to my feet, lurching and stumbling, and ran back to the barbed wire fence.

✣ ✣ ✣

THEY FOUND ME, later that day, wide-eyed, shivering and curled into a little ball on the trail. Of Thomas, they found no trace, but this didn't seem to bother the police that much. There was a resigned feel about things as I was carried to safety. There was a feeling of repetition, as if this tragedy had played out many times before.

I shuddered in the arms of a policeman who carried me as if I weighed no more than a small child, and then I was on a stretcher, and then a bed. Doctors administered clear syringes of fluid that sent me into dreamless sleep. I would wake, and thrash around in rage, and cry out, and then sleep again.

Eventually, as had been the case years before, after the explosion, I was discharged, and pretty much left to my own devices once again.

I sold everything I owned back home.

And now, I rent a room at the Hotel Bianco. I have paid in advance, using my army pension and the money I made from selling my home. Every morning I wake, go to the window, and stare out at the sea. Every night Jisepu makes me a martini, just the way I like it. I have a collection of books that I still have not read, and my skin is brown, now, sun-kissed, not pale.

Every day I walk along the trail towards the beach of black sand.

Every day, I stand on the ridge overlooking the bay, staring at the deceptive, smooth tide-line, looking for answers.

One day, I'll set foot on the boardwalk again. I'll get the answers I need. I'll run my fingers through the sand and let it take me.

Until then, I'm going to sit here, and study the ocean.

What price solitude?

No price.

Gemma Amor

BACK ALLEY SUE

'**G**OT ANY CHANGE LOVE?'

The sound of high heels clacking along the pavement nearby grows louder. I lift my head up from my knees and look at the feet approaching. They are shiny red stilettos, the type of shoe I would have once bought for my wife as an anniversary gift, the type of shoe that was a preamble to a sexy weekend spent rolling around together in bed with a few bottles of red wine for company. Those days are long gone now, and my wife is long gone. I still have a thing for high heels, though. High heels, slender ankles, long, dark hair.

Those were the days.

The shoes stop before me, and I repeat my question.

'Got any spare change, love?'

The woman wearing the red heels rummages through a crimson handbag, draws out her purse, and finds a few coins. She hands them to me with a kind smile. They clink into my cold hand, which trembles a little.

'Here you go.'

I nod gratefully, and pocket the cash as swiftly as I can. My fingers don't work well these days, the joints are swollen and painful.

'Thank you.' I say, and try to smile.

'No problem.' She moves away, and I watch her go wistfully. The sound of her heels mingles into the general hustle and bustle of the high street. I catch crimson flashes, her feet moving smartly, one in front of the other. Then she is gone.

I lean back against my bundled belongings and watch the city as it gradually wakes up. It's a Monday morning, and that special time of day where people are kicking off their weekly routines, dropping children off at schools, opening up shops, marching to important office jobs in their smart suits and expensive shoes. I like this time of day. The noise swells like an approaching tide: engines revving, horns honking, traffic crossings beeping, people chatting, music playing, feet stamping on concrete. Seagulls squabble and squeal over a pile of discarded food cartons to the right of me. A postman unlocks a postbox to the left of me, and scrapes a mound of envelopes into his delivery bag. A dog barks in the distance.

The cafe across the street has its doors and windows thrown wide open, to let in some fresh morning air. Every summer they do this, and I can hear the music from their sound system playing across the square I'm sitting on. It's part of the reason I like this spot. The song currently booming out is 'Hotel California' by the Eagles, which in my mind is the greatest song ever written. You might have a different opinion, which you're welcome to, but you'll be wrong. Greatest song. Hands down. No argument.

I raise my voice and croak out my daily hopeful chant as a young mother with a small, wailing child in a buggy approaches. She looks harassed but I try my luck anyway.

'Got any spare change please, love?'

She ignores me and walks swiftly past, her face drawn tight into a strained frown, her toddler wriggling and screeching fit to burst in the buggy. I don't watch her go. I'm used to being ignored. I'm used to being invisible. When you live on the streets, you lose your face, lose your voice. You cease to exist in what people think of as the real world, those passers-by with their headphones, their pinched faces, their noses glued to their phone screens. I must speak, on average, to over a thousand people a day, saying the same sad little words over and over again: 'Got any change?' 'Got any change?' I'm like a scratched record, the worn needle returning to the same point in the song over and over again. Over a thousand people I'll reach out to, and I'll be lucky if even ten of those thousand will look in my direction.

I didn't always live on the streets. I had a life once, and a wife, a house, a car, a good job. I had friends and money. I went on holidays abroad, and ate nice food. People shook my hand when they met me, and held my gaze. Eye-contact is something I miss the most, you know. People don't like looking at me anymore. They look at the pavement to the left or the right of me, or above my head, or off into the distance. Anything but look straight *at* me. In the old days, my old days, people always used to comment on how blue my eyes were, how bright my smile.

But then my wife left, you see, and it all went a bit… wrong from there. Hero to zero, as the saying goes. Riches to rags. Funny how quickly your life can unravel if you let it. Once I stopped caring about anything, it was as if my world were nothing more than a stack of playing cards: flimsy, unstable, easy to knock over in one fell swoop. Down tumbled the cards, and down tumbled I, and here I remain. Sitting on the pavement on a Monday morning, begging for change. Not quite what my poor wife hand in mind for me, I bet.

Nowadays, if anyone ever asks me for my address, which rarely happens, I tell them 'No fixed abode'. I do have a home, of sorts: this stained, flattened cardboard box that I'm sitting on, and this filthy, coverless duvet that was once white and is now not. Hardly a palace, but there is one advantage. It's mobile. All I have to do is bundle the cardboard up inside the rolled-up duvet, tie the lot together with some rope, swing the bundle over my back, and I'm away.

'Hotel California' has finished playing in the café, and that is my cue to leave. I parcel up my tatty little house and move along, slowly. My hands aren't the only thing bothering me. My knees are also swollen, and stiff. My shoes don't fit so well, either. The heels have gone on both feet, so I shuffle along slowly, like an old man, even though I'm not yet fifty. I look much older. Sleeping rough through seven winters will age a person well beyond his years. The average life expectancy these days for a man sleeping rough is about forty-seven years of age, or so I've been told, which means I have about three years and seven months left to go. If I'm lucky.

I have a destination in mind as I make my slow and painful way across the square, moving in the same direction that the woman in red heels has gone.

In the middle of the city, there lies a huge, sunken concrete recess in the ground called the

Bearpit. It's an octagonal bunker with no roof, an open-air blister in the landscape, and it acts as a shortcut between the commercial centre and the start of the long, independent high street that snakes up the hill and out of the city entire. Inside this recess are some public toilets, a derelict double-decker bus that used to sell Mexican food, a few fruit stalls and pop-up cafes, some skateboard ramps and a large statue of a white bear standing on its hind legs. The bear is twelve feet tall, and called Ursa. The council want to get rid of her, clean the place up in a bid to tackle anti-social behaviour. There will be a campaign, no doubt, this is one of those cities where people campaign for things, and the council ignore them. Eventually, the bear will be pulled down, and the developers will move in, wipe the slate clean with fresh concrete and steel. They have a name for that, the protesters: gentrification.

The Bearpit is surrounded on all sides by a multiple lanes of traffic, and connected to the streets above by several concrete tunnels. These underpasses provide reliable shelter from the rain, and have a high footfall all year round, so make a decent spot for begging in. I spend a fair bit of time here each day, and so do other people like me: the down-and-out brigade. The homeless. The faceless.

The voiceless.

As I shamble on towards the Bearpit, my mind on the coins jangling in my pocket, I can hear

Cruel Works of Nature

the sound of seagulls crying again. I look up before I disappear into the underpass. A small flock of the birds are flying lazily overhead. A few of them seem to be squabbling over something fleshy- probably some leftover kebab meat, or a burger from the weekend. They tumble over themselves mid-air and the scrap of meat falls from the sky, landing with a wet splat at my feet. A half-eaten chicken drumstick. I kick it behind me, hearing the seagulls descend in my wake and continue their argument, playing tug of war with the drumstick and shrieking in that mournful way that seagulls have. My wife always hated seagulls. 'Evil things,' she would say, and refuse to make eye contact with them. She was funny like that, my wife.

I enter the underpass and emerge a few minutes later into the Bearpit, which hums with its usual array of sounds: commuters hurrying on through, skateboarders racing up and down the ramps, a graffiti artist tagging a wall with an anti-capitalist slogan. There is a muffled clink of glass from a small group of weary, dirty and rough-looking folk sitting on some steps. They pass a bottle around between them. It's vodka, supermarket own-brand, nothing more than re-packaged paint-stripper. A dog takes a piss against a wall not far from the group, its face a mask of relief as it goes about its business. A Born Again Christian sets up an enormous speaker on the far side of the pit, and starts ranting into a microphone, passages of the bible. His voice bounces off the concrete surfaces around me, hurting my ears. I definitely preferred the Eagles, thank you very much.

The group of vodka drinkers have spotted me. They wave cheerfully. 'Dave!' they shout, their husky voices difficult to hear over the evangelising of the preacher.

'Dave!'

I lift a hand in acknowledgement, and shuffle on over. I place my pack down on the steps where they sit, and lower myself gingerly onto the ground. Sitting on concrete doesn't get any easier, no matter how long you do it for. I'm too old to be this close to the ground, really, but I mustn't complain. For now, I'm warm, dry and in good company. It doesn't take me long to get stuck into the vodka, and when that bottle runs out, we club together, pool our meagre resources, and buy another. And the day passes as these days do: slowly, minute by minute, bottle by bottle, until I sink into a pleasant stupor and then eventually, pass out on the steps, my pack behind my head, the seagulls wheeling and crying in the sky above me.

❊ ❊ ❊

WHEN I WAKE UP, it's to a very different world. Night is beginning to fall. The skateboarders

Cruel Works of Nature

have gone home for the day, as have the commuters, the Born Again Christian, the fruit stall owners, my friends, and even the dog. Ursa the bear is still there, her back to me.

I rub a hand across my bleary eyes and try to guess the time, sitting up slowly. I'm still drunk, but not as blind drunk as I had been when I'd passed out. Now I'm a mild sort of drunk that makes everything a bit fuzzy around the edges, the sort of drunk that makes life that little bit more tolerable. Grunting, I look around me, unsteady. My eyes travel across the pit, and stop, dead.

A shape stands illuminated in the underpass opposite me. It's a tall shape, sinuous, feminine in a vague, suggestive way. I see long hair, slender arms and legs, a thin waist. Despite the darkness closing in I hear seagulls, suddenly. I realise a crowd of them are circling overhead. I shake my head, several times over, to rid myself of the vision. The tall woman remains there in the flickering strip lights of the underpass, motionless, waiting for something.

I'm still drunk, as I've said, and suddenly full of bravado.

'Bugger off!' I call out, waving an unsteady hand at the figure, attempting to shoo her away.

Then a wave of faintness washes over me. This happens sometimes, something to do with dehydration or drinking in the sun all day, probably. I feel dizzy, and close my eyes, wait for the ground to stop spinning and lurching underneath me.

When I open my eyes again a few moments later, the woman is standing right in front of me. She is bent over, and her face is a mere couple of inches away from mine.

'Hello, Dave,' she says in a deep, throaty voice that has a strange, wheezing, whistling quality to it. A seagull flies down and lands on her shoulder, squawking at me.

I don't get the chance to study her features properly. She lifts a thin, white hand to her face, grabs a hold of one papery, slack cheek, and pulls.

Her faces comes clean away from her skull with a tearing sound like a newspaper being ripped in two.

Underneath there lies nothing but a wet, dark veneer that is oddly smooth and featureless, except for a black liquid that drips down her neck like melting wax. Underneath the liquid I can hear laughter bubbling away, laughter that echoes the cries of the seagulls above. The gull on her shoulder throws its head right back, exposing its white neck, and screams in glee.

I issue my own scream to the gathering gloom.

And then the woman is gone. In the blink of an eye, just like that. Poof! Gone.

After I've stopped shuddering and shivering, I decide it's time to call it a night. Whatever was in that vodka is not doing me much good. It is time to find a spot to rest my head, and start tomorrow anew.

I move slowly and cautiously, cradling my sore head, packing up my belongings which have somehow become scattered about on the surrounding steps. I keep any eye out for anything else strange, but gradually, the fear wears off, and is replaced with a profound tiredness.

Time to visit the alleys, and get some rest. A single, lonely seagull lands on a step not far away, hoping to rummage through the trash we've left behind. I shake my fist at it, belligerently.

* * *

IF YOU WALK ABOUT two miles north of the Bearpit, you come to a heavily terraced residential area full of nice families, expensive cars and well-maintained, flowerfilled gardens. As is the way with most terraced streets, those gardens are all roughly the same length, and so all come to an end at about the same place. That place will usually have an alleyway running behind it, parallel with the streets. There are hundreds of these alleys in the city, a little network of green, overgrown, curiously deserted tunnels that spread out across the streets like the veins on the back of a hand.

The locals are fond of these alleyways, and

even have a legend, the story of Back Alley Sue. Back Alley Sue was an unfortunate woman who got lost in the network of passages and paths one day long ago, and never made her way out again. She haunts the back streets at night, they say, mournfully wringing her hands, doomed to wander and drift for all eternity. 'Don't go into the alleys by yourself,' the locals tell their children, keen to manipulate local lore to keep them from wandering off alone. Maybe they are worried their precious darlings will bump into an unsavoury type, skulking around, a type like me.

And rightly so. My new favourite place to sleep are these alleyways. There's enough vegetation to shelter me from any rain, enough privacy for me to take a piss without being judged, and enough peace for me to get a good night's sleep.

So I lurk in the deepening dark of the night, and eventually find a good spot behind a disused garage that backs onto a narrow alley at the end of a park. I spread out my cardboard, and wrap myself in my duvet, sliding quickly off into sleep. Another day, ticked off the calendar.

Another day, closer to death.

I dream of seagulls.

※ ※ ※

I WAKE EARLY, I always have done. A thin, weak

sunlight filters through morning mist. Yesterday has disappeared, today is a new day. I stand up and relieve myself against the garage door, watching as my urine spatters downwards in a brightly steaming arc.

I shake, put myself away, and turn around, muttering and mumbling to myself as I do, these days, in the absence of anyone else to talk to.

The tall woman from the Bearpit is standing in the alleyway, staring at me.

I jerk backwards, coming up sharp against the garage door.

She is tall, and thin, swaying on her feet like a reed in a pond. Mist curls delicately around her legs, playing with the strands of her floor-length, jet black hair.

A cloud of seagulls circle lazily, and somehow silently, over her head.

She crooks a double-jointed finger at me. 'Come with me, David,' she says, and her voice makes my ears throb.

She takes a strange, loose and limping step towards me. My brain clicks slowly into action.

I throw the only thing I have to hand at her, with all the force my tired, frail body can muster. It's the empty vodka bottle, which I somehow clung onto last night and fell asleep with, cradling it in my arms like a small and precious child. I snatch it up from where it lies on the ground and hurl it straight at the woman.

It flies through the air and hits her, square on

the forehead. I don't have time to admire my own accuracy. She screams at me, a noise of pure defiance, and sticky black spittle flies from her red lips. She doesn't have any teeth, and her gums are the colour of tar. Her voice is like nothing I could have possibly imagined, even in my darkest days. It feels as if someone has hammered nails into my eardrums. I clamp my hands over my ears in a futile attempt to protect my fragile sanity.

Then, her body collapses, suddenly, awfully, into a thousand writhing, wriggling pieces of flesh. They splatter onto the ground in a great big mound, and begin to flop about, like so many fish out of water, gasping for air.

I stare open-mouthed at what she has become: a squirming mass of skin and bone and hair and sinew, and then I realise that the pieces of Back Alley Sue are moving in unison, wriggling and pulling themselves along towards me, like a horde of pink leeches questing for my blood. I cry out in disgust and scoot backwards on my arse as quickly as I can, but the garage door is behind me, and there is nowhere to go. The flesh creeps steadily on, little rotting flaps and shreds of it all stretching out in my direction, a rippling wave of mottled, decaying meat, and I'm suddenly aware of just how much I want to live, of just how much I value my body, broken and beaten as it is.

In the split second it takes me to make this

Cruel Works of Nature

realisation, the pieces of Back Alley Sue are upon me, covering every part of me, cold, clammy, obscene.

I open my mouth to scream, and her flesh invades me, forcing my tongue to one side, sliding down my throat, choking me.

Then, I feel the earth beneath me soften, start to give way. My body begins to sink through the ground, and it's like I'm falling, slowly, as if in a dream, and the wormy parts of Back Alley Sue have started to fill my belly and my lungs, and she drags me downwards into the bowels of the earth, and I realise that no matter how much I've suddenly decided I want to live, that this, well... this is it for me. My heart has longed for death for so long, and it's finally happening.

But wait! I don't...not like this!
Not like this!
Catherine, I think as I sink towards oblivion. *I love you, Catherine. I'm sorry.*

❈ ❈ ❈

I AM AWAKE.

I am underground.

I start screaming, thrashing around, the memory of Back Alley Sue still raw and terrifying. My arms and legs shake with uncontrollable spasms, and I can't stop yelling, tears flowing down my cracked and weathered face, mouth stretched so wide I can feel my lips splitting in several places, a little trickle of blood coursing down my chin.

I carry on like this for some time, until my voice breaks, until my horror subsides enough for me to realise that I am still alive, and that my body is still in one piece. I cannot get the taste of her out of my mouth. I feel something move beneath my tongue. Gagging and spitting frantically, I see several white, fat maggots fall from my mouth and land on the floor in a little puddle of my own yellowish spit. I retch, but nothing else comes out.

I look around me, groggily.

I am in an enormous cave, a cavern as big as a cathedral. I know instinctively that I am beneath the city, that there are people walking about above me, free and happy in the sunshine, clueless as to what lies beneath their feet. I've heard the stories about the network of tunnels and caves that lie underneath the streets, but never taken much interest in them. I never imagined anything like this. It's like someone is holding a mirror up to the world, and I am now a reflection. Is this how I am going to live out the rest of my life, trapped in Underland?

Back Alley Sue.

My heart thunders along irregularly in my chest as I search for her and find nothing. Where is that bitch? Where is she?! I can't see her. Just a cave. Nothing else.

The ceiling of the cave stretches up high above my head, and I can see lights up high, swirling slowly around in the air, green, glowing lights that look like glow worms, or phosphorescence.

Then, something rustles, and my gaze travels down. I freeze midway through the act of standing up. Lining the walls of the cave are roughly hewn stone shelves. Sitting on those shelves are thousands upon thousands of seagulls, silent, still, all of them watching me with their yellow, unblinking eyes.

There is a rumbling noise, and the earthen floor of the cavern erupts in a shower of dirt and rocks and long, ragged tendrils that must be tree roots. They rocket up towards the roof of the cave, reform, sink, and settle into the shape of a massive throne.

Then there is a sound like that of rain, and a black, thick liquid oozes through the walls of the cave, seeping through the stone as it were porous sponge instead of granite, moving like mercury, molten, fluid, purposeful, and I know that there is only one thing on this earth that can move like this: Back Alley Sue.

The liquid flows towards the throne, swells, bubbles, grows, and reforms into the shape of a woman, a woman with long, black flowing hair, a woman with no teeth, a woman with no face, who sits, crosses one leg over the other, and smiles at me.

'Hello, David,' she says, and a ripple passes

through the gathered seagulls, a thousand pairs of wings shudder and ruffle, her audience, waiting, hanging on every word.

I realise she is waiting for me to say something.

'What are you going to do with me?' My voice sounds tiny, and weak in the vast cave. 'Why am I here?'

She smiles again, her rotten gums gleaming between her livid lips.

'You know the answer to that, David.'

'Is this hell?' I ask, wearily.

'Why would you be in hell, David?' 'Because…' I cannot bring myself to say it.

Back Alley Sue leans forward and chuckles.

'Because you killed your wife?' She purrs like a cat, and a blinding flash of realisation goes off like a beacon in my mind.

'She asked me to do it!' I shout, suddenly filled with rage. My words hang in the air.

There is only silence, as the woman enthroned judges me, a mocking smile on her lips.

'She did! She *asked* me to do it!'

The seagulls take flight. They circle around us, a tornado of wings and feathers and beaks. The sound of a thousand harsh cries fills the air. Back Alley Sue throws back her head on her long, soft neck and laughs, cackles, *shrieks*, her mirth mingling with that of the seagulls, swirling around me, a deadly vapour, a cloud of poison gas.

I am filled with anguish, and the face of my wife floats before my eyes, bloated, purple. My hands are around her neck.

'Don't hurt me, David,' she said, but I'd had no choice. She'd *wanted* me to kill her. There is no way to kill another human being quickly and peacefully. Death is pain, it would have hurt her whichever way I'd done it. Her eyes, her deep, dark, green eyes, had bulged as I'd applied pressure, and then I realised I'd gone too far to stop, so I had tightened my grip, squeezed and squeezed until I felt her body spasm beneath me.

'SHE ASKED ME TO DO IT!' I scream, and then I begin to cry with my mouth hanging open slackly, thin trails of drool falling to the floor, great, heaving, undignified sobs wrenching through me.

But, wait.

Wait just a minute.

I frown.

That's not how it happened.

My memories change direction, morph into another vision, and my wife is still there, but this time I have a pillow in my hand, and I am kneeling on the bed beside her, pushing down with all my might against the soft, feathery fabric of her death. Small muffled noises escape from underneath the pillow, and I am crying, shushing her, telling her it will be over soon. She jerks and fights, arches her back, then falls silent and still.

No, wait!

It wasn't that, either!

We are on a cliff. She looks at me with those sad, sad eyes. 'I don't want to hurt anymore,' she says, her voice echoing around the cave, drowning out the seagulls and the mad laughter, and if I don't do it now I will never find the courage, so I push. Her body flies backwards into the air, her thick, lustrous hair forming a dark halo around her head, and then she sinks, falls, everything happening in slow motion, until her body meets the rocks below and splits apart.

I smack my head with my hands, over and over, babbling nonsense words. The seagull cries rise in a horrible crescendo above me.

I have a gun in my hand. I press it to my wife's head, chest heaving with grief, and pull the trigger. Her brains exit her skull in a small fountain of crimson matter, spraying patterns onto the wall behind her.

No, it's a knife.

A big kitchen knife.

Or was it poison?

I can't remember how I killed my wife.

I just know that I took her life.

Because she asked me to.

Only because she asked me to.

I sink to my knees. Back Alley Sue raises herself up on legs that are long, black, rotting vines, and slides across the cave floor until she is standing above me.

'You're mine now,' she hisses, and her hands cup my face, tilting it up so that I have to look at

Cruel Works of Nature

her, at her yellowed eyes, her maniacal grin, her tangled, black, disgusting hair. I see worms moving around inside her nostrils, and a huge beetle clambers down her neck and disappears under one thin, long, sagging breast.

Chuckling, she leans forward to kiss me, a spotted, blue-black tongue snaking out from between her filthy gums, reaching for me, and I didn't think I had any screams left in me, but I do, and I fight, because I don't want the taste of her in my mouth anymore, but she holds me fast, and the seagulls fly faster and more frantically in circles around us, a blizzard of white noise, swirling, whirling... and her mouth is on mine, her lips are on my lips, and I scream, and scream, but she will not let me go.

'It wasn't my fault!' I struggle and shriek against her face as best I can. 'It wasn't my fault! IT WASN'T

MY FAULT!'

And then something happens.

The seagulls stop crying, stop their incessant wheeling.

They disperse and vanish, like evaporating mist.

A peaceful silence descends around us.

The kiss becomes a gentle kiss.

The lips become soft, and no longer taste of decay, but carry the faint taste of strawberries.

The hands on my face soften, grow smooth, still strong, but now they hold me tenderly. The hair becomes glossy and sleek to the touch.

She lets me go, and it's no longer Back Alley Sue.

It's the woman with the red shoes, the woman who dropped coins in to my hand yesterday morning, the woman who looks remarkably like my dead wife.

Her eyes are filled with tears.

'I know, David,' she says mournfully, and her voice is soothing, musical. My heart swells with longing and loss.

'Catherine,' I say, my voice full of wonder.

'It wasn't your fault, David,' she says, and she kisses me again. 'I love you,' she says, and the light starts to fade, and the blackness returns, and I can hear music faintly playing from somewhere. Is it the Eagles?

'There she stood in the doorway;
I heard the mission bell...'

My wife strokes my face, murmuring sweet reassurances. 'Not your fault,' she says, and the music grows louder.

'And I was thinking to myself
'This could be heaven or this could be Hell...'

She moves back, her face a beautiful mask of sadness. 'Goodbye, David,' she says. 'Don't carry me around with you anymore.'

The music is deafening now. Her red shoes are the last thing I see as I start to lose consciousness.

'Then she lit up a candle, and she showed me the

way...'

Then, there is nothing, nothing but the taste of strawberries.

❊ ❊ ❊

I'M IN THE BEARPIT.

I open my eyes, and the worried faces of a small crowd of people stare down at me. I cannot move, or speak. I can barely breathe. Tears stream from my eyes, and I cannot stop them.

Catherine. My Catherine. I love you, Catherine.

Men in fluorescent jackets arrive. They load me onto a stretcher, and an ambulance carries me away from the Bearpit, carries me off to a sterile, white haven.

Before the ambulance doors close, I see a row of seagulls sitting perched on a tree nearby. They stare at me with yellow, beady eyes.

❊ ❊ ❊

I GOT MYSELF INTO A SHELTER. I have a room, for now, a small but clean room and a bed with a pillow, a real pillow to lay my head on. I left my duvet and flattened cardboard box behind in the Bearpit. I never went back for them.

I've got a plan, to quit the drink, to clean up, to try to get back into society, whatever that means. There is a woman who works for the shelter helping me. She is soft and pretty, about the same age as my wife was when she left. She has dark hair and likes to wear red.

I tell her I killed my wife, and she tells me firmly that I'm talking nonsense. She tells me my wife left many years ago, but lives, hale and healthy. She tells me that my sense of loss at her departure turned into something dark and poisonous, and created memories that weren't really there. She says there are doctors who can help me with this, trained professionals I can talk to. Medication I can take. She doesn't believe in Back Alley Sue. She says I am sick, but that I can be treated.

Her words are kind, but I know the truth. Back Alley Sue still wanders the alleys of Bristol, a cloud of seagulls at her back.

Listen for them, and when you hear their cries, walk away as quickly as you can. Find a place, a crowded place, full of people and warmth and laughter. She preys on the weak and the lonely, the desolate and deprived.

She feeds on your secrets, your dirty, precious little secrets.

Be wary of Back Alley Sue, the locals say. You should listen to them, you know.

Cruel Works of Nature

GIRL ON FIRE

MY CAR IS OLD, AND SHIT. OLD, SHIT AND YET SO, so beautiful. It's a cherry red 1989 Pontiac Bonneville. It's the first car I've ever owned, and will probably be the only car I'll ever want to own. I saved every pay check from my first regular job to buy it. I got no help from the bank of Mom or Dad. This car is a symbol of my independence, my freedom. I love it more than anything, or anyone.

The engine throbs as I put my foot down on the accelerator. I have my window open, as the car is too old for functioning air con. My red hair whips around my head as I push down with my foot. Red hair, red car. The needle creeps to seventy-five. Seventy-five, and I feel *alive.* I feel happy. There is country music on the radio. Around me, the dry, arid plains of Nevada stretch out into the distance. The highway slices through the middle of it all like an arrow, pointing to my future. They call this 'the loneliest road in America'. Well, I don't know about that, but it sure is one of the prettiest. In the distance, mountains loom. Overhead, a blue sky stretches out into infinity. A hot sun burns in the blue.

I am free.

I throw my arms up in the air, letting go of the wheel for a moment, unable to restrain myself any longer. I crow, and yell out joyously. My voice is whipped away like a dry leaf on the breeze.

'Wooooooooo-hooooo!'

I try to push the needle further around the dial, and the engine starts to protest, unused to this kind of speed. I'm not going to win any races with this car, but this is faster than I've ever driven it before, and my baby isn't sure about it. It's more used to crawling around the city than my current pedal-to-the-metal style of driving.

'Come on baby, you can do it,' I croon, and then I scream again, unable to keep it inside me, this joy:

'Yeahhhhhh!'

The car races faster along the asphalt. I throw my arms up into the air once more, fists clenched tight, punching out, victorious, queen of the fucking world.

And then, it happens.

There is a *bang!*

And a jolt.

My car has hit a pothole in the road, a pothole I could not have seen, because I am driving too fast.

I am thrown sideways. My head whacks the window frame hard on my right-hand side. I am not holding the wheel, so I can't control the sudden swerving of the car as both tyres on my right-hand side burst. I feel the rims of each wheel scrape along the ground. They make a hideous noise. The car begins to veer wildly off the road.

Panicked, I finally manage to grab hold of the steering wheel and yank it over hard to the left to try to correct my trajectory, but this only sends me further off. The car speeds towards the verge of the road. The road is raised higher than the surrounding land, only by a small measurement, but enough to create a ledge between the asphalt and the scrubby green plants that poke up through the sand all around.

Me and my car hit the ledge, still doing about seventy.

I slam my foot on the brakes, but it's too late. The car squeals as if in agony, then shoots off the road and into the desert.

There is a moment, a split second when I think everything is going to be okay, that the car will stop, dragged to a halt by the sand and the scrub.

The car will stop.

It will all be okay.

Instead, my car, my baby, unable to cope with the drop in ground level, tilts dangerously onto its side, flips, and then rolls down the slight incline away from the highway.

My world is turned literally upside down, and then right way up, and then wrong way down again. I am strapped into my seat. I put my arms up, not in joy, now, but in fear, for protection, and brace myself against the roof of the car. I am dimly aware that I am screaming, that blood is dripping down my face from where my head hit the window frame.

The car rolls two, three times, and then comes to an uneasy rest, leaving me suspended upside down, and half unconscious.

Gradually, the dust settles around me.

The car creaks and moans in pain, as do I. I hang from my seatbelt, my head squashed uncomfortably against the roof, which is now the floor.

A stillness falls.

Blood begins to pound in my ears. I lack the energy to try to unstrap myself. I'm afraid I might hurt myself if

I try.

I call out, knowing it is futile. This is the loneliest road in America, after all.

'Help!' I whimper, to the empty world. Then, slightly louder:

'Please, someone, help me!'

It's a waste of my time, my energy. I stop,

feeling faint. I close my eyes and try to find the strength to undo my seatbelt. I can't. The full weight of my body is hanging downwards, pressing against the belt, locking the mechanism. It won't budge. I start to pant, and panic, and then I faint, black out momentarily.

Gradually, I am woken again, this time by a sound.

Well, two sounds, actually. The first is the unmistakably wet noise of something liquid trickling out of my car and into the sand.

Fuel.

The second is a hissing, juddering, fizzing sort of noise coming from underneath the hood of the Pontiac. I have a moment to wonder what this means. *The upper intake's gonna go*, I think fuzzily. Faulty fuel pressure regulator? Punctured...engine...wall? What the hell am I talking about? I don't know shit about cars. I have no idea. Daddy would know.

Wait, no, don't think about Daddy, not now. Focus. Focus!

Then, the car explodes.

❊ ❊ ❊

A WALL of fire and heat blasts against my face. A fireball envelops the car.

I am screaming.

I am burning.

I am burning!

First, my clothes.

Then, my hair, which disappears in a flash, curling crazily first and then simply melting away.

The stench of my own flesh roasting is unbearable.

Everything around me is red, orange, black. The roaring of the fire is so intense, so loud, so terrible, and I am in the middle of it all, I am the fire, I am the eye of the fucking storm.

I open my mouth to scream again, but this one is wordless, and the fire invades me, licking the back of my throat, filling me up from the inside out.

It is too much.
It is too much.
Pain.
Burning.
I close my eyes.
I die.

❋ ❋ ❋

OR, not.

Slowly, carefully, disbelievingly, I open each eye.

I am lying in a blackened heap of ash, and twisted metal, and scorched earth.

The charred skeleton of my car rises from the

desert like a sad, ancient shipwreck rises from the sea-bed: an echo of a life that once was. A blackened footprint in time.

A memory of the old me.

I see smoke, dark and noxious, curling up into the sky. Small, residual fires burn in a few places on the scrubland around the car wreckage. They glow a muted orange, little distress signals that no one can see except for me. I focus on my body, trying to assess how injured I am. I can't feel anything wrong. How is that possible?

I am curled up like a newborn, tucked into the foetal position, arms and hands clasped to my chest, knees drawn up to my chin.

There is no pain, none of the pain I expected at any rate. No burning, no bleeding, no broken bones.

A thin, keening cry sounds out overhead. I blearily look at the sky, and see the outlines of birds circling my body, vultures, or crows, I can't tell: my vision is still blurred, misty, my eyes raw from heat and smoke.

I unfurl like a reluctant flower, slowly, cautiously, still reeling from the shock and the impact of the crash.

A thought worms its way into the front of my mind.

How am I still alive?

How can anyone survive an explosion like that?

I shiver with the cold, and it dawns on me that

Cruel Works of Nature

I am naked, that my clothes have burned clean away. If I stay here, lying on the ground, I will freeze. Nights in the desert get real cold, real fast.

I stand, the remains of my car, my life, scattered around my feet. I can still feel the heat from the blaze. I hold my arms out in front of me, inspecting my flesh in the rapidly fading light.

No burns, no blisters, no scars.

I run a hand over myself, up each arm, over my belly, my legs, and finally up over my head. The hair on my head and my body has gone, leaving behind a fine, fuzzy stubble. Otherwise, I'm untouched.

Completely unscathed.

And alone.

Unsure of what else to do, I start to walk unsteadily along the road, back the way I had driven only a few hours earlier. I see the pothole I hit whilst driving too fast, whilst waving my arms in the air like an idiot instead of holding the steering wheel. It's small, but the edges are jagged. I stare at it, and then move on. It is in the past now. What has happened has happened. What matters is what comes next.

And clothes. God, I need some clothes.

I throw a last, longing look at the wreckage of my old car over my shoulder as I walk away, and feel my heart breaking a little in my chest. I have no idea what is happening to me, or how, or why, but I know there is no going back from this.

There is no going back to who I was before.

I am a Phoenix from the ashes, but what that means for my future, I have no idea.

I face forward, walking slowly along the highway, headed towards I don't know what.

❋ ❋ ❋

IT ISN'T long before I hear the sound of engines approaching. I know enough about motors to recognise the sound of multiple Harley-Davidson twin-cams roaring towards me. Bikers. Four of them, riding side-by-side, hogging the highway, as bikers do.

Moments later I am illuminated by the glare of headlights, and a cavalcade of Harleys surround me, engines chewing up the night air.

They slow, and then stop, putting down the kickstands, removing helmets, leaning on their handlebars, assessing me. There are three men and one woman. They are heavily tattooed, and look like they belong to a gang.

They stare at my naked, shivering body. I put a hand up to protect my eyes from the glare of the headlights.

The leader of the gang dismounts, and walks over to me, heavy boots jingling slightly as he moves. He pulls a cigar from his jacket pocket and lights it with a zippo covered in skulls. Skull rings gleam on his fingers. There are roses choked with thorns tattooed on his face. Entwined with the roses, a green snake, which winds down his neck and vanishes under his wife-beater.

He lights the cigar and continues to peer at me, a slow, predatory smile spreading across his face.

'Well,' he says, looking me up and down. 'What do we have here, then?'

I work my dry mouth, not sure how well my voice will work.

'Please,' I say, hoping against vain hope that this isn't all about to go horribly wrong. 'Please. I was in an accident. My car...it...came off the road.' I pointed back up the highway behind me.

'I need help. Clothes, water... anything. Please.' The biker laughs, and it isn't kind.

My heart sinks.

'Help? Well, I can see that. You need a lot of help, girl.'

The others laugh with him, and my neck prickles as a warning sign. I think the expression is "Out of the frying pan, and into the fire," except I've already been in the fire, and now I am here.

I turn my attention to the only woman in the group, trying to ignore how the men leer at my naked body, eyes lingering on my breasts and ass, hungry. I'm young, but I know that expression, I've seen it countless times before, and it doesn't bode well for me.

I need clothes, and I need to get away from

these people, quickly.

'Please,' I plead with the female biker who looks at me like I'm an alien. 'I don't want any trouble. I just want to cover myself up. Even just a blanket, a scarf. Anything. Please.'

I shouldn't have to grovel like this, but I am desperate, my body quivering. The words fall on her and slide off like rain down a windowpane. She narrows her eyes and sneers at me.

'Do I look like a fucking charity service, bitch?'

I am taken aback by the malevolence in her voice. I'm in trouble, can't they see that? What does a girl have to fucking do to get some help in this world?

Mom always told me to never rely on others, to only look out for yourself.

Easier said than done, I think, as I look around at the leather-clad crew surrounding me.

The leader speaks up, amused.

'Now, Violet, no need to be like that. We can help out this little lady, can't we? What do you say, boys? Shall we...help her out?'

I read the subtext in his voice. I know what is coming next.

I turn and try to run, but the leader catches me around the waist easily, throwing me to the ground.

'Oh, don't be like that, missy,' he says, kneeling in the sand next to my nude, prone body.

'See, the way I look at it, we can help you out just fine. But things in this life don't come for

Cruel Works of Nature

free, understand me?'

He starts fumbling with his fly, unzipping it with a degree of ceremony that speaks to his opinion of his own virility. He holds me pinned to the ground easily with his other arm, and as he continues to fumble with himself, the other two men in his gang join us on the dirt, taking my arms and my legs, holding me firm. I struggle and buck and squeal, but that only excites them more, and they start crowing, and guffawing, and grunting the more I try to escape.

The leader's eyes are hot with excitement.

'Nothing comes for free, like I said, missy. So, I can help you, sure. But you gotta help me first, alright?' And all I can think is:

No.

Not again. Oh Christ, not again.

No.

I said I would never let it happen again!

NEVER!

The man's face moves close to mine, and he drags his thick, wet tongue down my cheek.

NO!

And that's when I feel it.

It starts in my fingertips, which grow hot, so hot my skin begins to hum, to *vibrate*. The heat travels up my arms, down my chest and spreads to my legs. I have a moment to see something burning and red reflected in the man's eyes, which have widened in shock.

And then I explode, like a fucking volcano.

For the second time that day I am on fire, but this time… I do not burn.

Flames spurt out of every orifice, fire roaring up into what is now the night sky in great, twisting columns, a tornado of fire, a goddamn pyre, born of rage and pain and anger at where I find myself, held down by three disgusting horny fuck-pigs, men who would rather rape a woman in trouble than help her.

Through the sound of the fire I can hear all three of them screaming in agony, and it only makes me burn brighter.

I burn and burn until their faces melt clean off their skulls, until their bones lie around me like blackened sticks. The scent of charcoal and cooked meat is thick in the air. I savour it.

The flames die down, slowly, slowly, and I stand. The desert is quiet, peaceful almost. I feel lighter, although suddenly overwhelmed with tiredness.

I have just killed three men.

I clench my fists.

They fucking deserved it, though.

I look over to where the Harleys are parked. The female biker, Violet, is still sitting astride her bike, immobilised with fear, her face white, her mouth open. I walk towards her with heavy, measured paces.

She fumbles for something, brings up a gun, shoots at me before I have time to react.

'Stay away, you fucking freak!' she shouts, and

shoots again.

Both bullets hit me square in the chest. I should die, right now, and bleed out on the sand. But I know I won't. I am the fucking Phoenix. Nothing can kill me.

I watch with a detached curiosity as the bullets work their way out of my chest and fall to the ground, glowing white hot. *I must be made of fire now*, I think.

Does it fill my veins?
If you cut me, do I not burn?

I start to chuckle, and then throw my head back and laugh aloud, hurling my mirth into the night like an offering.

Violet stares at me, lowers the gun, and starts to cry.

'Shut up,' I say, sternly now, my laughter subsiding. 'Shut up and give me your clothes.'

She obeys. I dress in borrowed leather, order the pathetic creature off of her bike, and mount the Harley, from the left side, as is etiquette when it comes to bikes. My brother had a bike like this once, back when life was simpler. I know how to ride.

I start the engine. I feel the Harley throb underneath me. I feel the weight of the bike, the weight of my own actions. I warm up to the bike and it warms up to me.

The now naked biker shivers and sobs in the dirt at my feet, where she belongs.

I hold a hand out, and a small, campfire-sized

blaze springs up from the ground next to her. It will keep her warm until the morning. Then, the stupid, cruel cow is on her own.

'Don't leave me out here with them,' she croaks, throwing a sickened look at her former gang mates.

There's not much of them left to look at.

She should consider herself lucky, really.

I put up the kickstand, rev the engine, cannot resist a final word.

'Do I look like a fucking charity service, Violet?' I say, relishing each word, and then I drive away into the night.

Before all this madness, I'd been headed for the mountains.

Time to head for the mountains again.

Second time lucky.

* * *

I DRIVE until the Harley runs out of fuel, then I ditch it, and set it alight so no-one can track me. Then I steal another bike, or car, or whatever I can get hold of, and continue until that vehicle runs out of gas, and repeat the cycle. I figure it isn't a good idea to refuel. I don't have any money, and I'm paranoid about someone spotting my stolen ride, calling it in. I do not want to be found. I never want to be found, ever again.

Besides, I also figure that the new, flammable

Cruel Works of Nature

version of me and a gas station are perhaps not such a great combination.

I have a destination in mind. I have a plan, too. I am going to rebuild my life.

You see, back when I was in my Pontiac, driving through the bright afternoon sun, I was happy about it for a reason. I was leaving my home behind, and my family. I was escaping the prison that had held me captive for so many years. Most importantly, I was leaving Daddy behind, and I planned on never seeing him ever again. For the first time in my life, as I drove too fast along that desert highway, I was truly free.

I see no reason for the status quo to change now that I've died, and risen from the ashes. It's symbolic, really. Out with the old, and in with the new.

My destination is North, as far away from my birth town as it's possible to get without leaving the States. I plan on getting a job in a bar, or wherever will take me. I plan on setting up on my own. I plan on never having to rely on anyone else ever again.

Day turns to night, and night to day, and I am driving. Driving until Nevada merges into Idaho, getting through car after car after bike after truck.

I don't seem to need to eat anymore, or sleep.

I do however get thirsty. The irony of this is not lost on me. I seem to always be fighting off dehydration, and I get terrible headaches if I don't drink at least a litre of water every hour. There is only so much water a person can travel with, so I end up stopping more than I am comfortable with. Most roadside places I pass allow me a glass of tap water, which I drink quickly, head down, staring at the counter, avoiding all eye contact. I issue a brisk 'Thanks' and leave as quietly as I arrive.

I manage two weeks of this before the Police catch up with me.

Well, one Policeman.

❖ ❖ ❖

OFF HIGHWAY 26, there is a small town called Glenns Ferry. It's sparsely littered with cutesy wooden houses and an old livery barn. It's the kind of place where large, old guys in dungarees hang out on street corners all day, chewing the fat. There's a rail crossing right in the middle of it. Directly opposite the train tracks is the uninviting Oregon Trail Cafe & Bar.

It's in this bar that Officer Bright finds me.

I am sitting hunched over a table in a corner, my back to the room. I'm still in my borrowed leathers, which fit me surprisingly well. I like them, they feel like armour against the vagaries of the world.

Officer Bright sits down at my table, uninvited. I know his name is Bright because it's stitched to his lapel badge. He finds me in the middle of making a really terrible decision: to drink beer instead of water, in an attempt to find a little liquid satisfaction on such a hot day. Sometimes, water just doesn't cut it like cold suds do.

There is a collection of four empty bottles on the oiled red gingham tablecloth between us, and I'm just about to finish my fifth. I am beginning to realise that beer has a bad effect on my new body. It makes me feel mean. My fingertips are already starting to buzz when Officer Bright takes off his sunglasses and tries to establish eye contact with me.

'Ruby?' he says, softly. 'Ruby Miller?'

There's no point trying to deny it. He takes an old photograph out of his jacket pocket, slides it across the table to me. It's a school photo from a few years back. My thick red hair is the main feature of the picture, and I am hiding behind it as much as humanly possible. I was shy in school.

I don't feel shy anymore.

I beckon to the waitress, who shuffles over.

'Yeah?' she drawls, rudely. 'Can I getcha?'

I ask for more beer, ignoring the Policeman, and she obliges, grumbling under her breath, looking between me and Officer Bright with a verminous breed of curiosity. She pops the lid off a bottle and hands it to me.

'Shall I put it on your tab?' she asks, and then blows a bubble with the blob of gum she's been chewing since I got here. The bubble pops, and I grit my teeth. People.

God, people suck.

'Sure,' I reply, taking the beer.

Condensation beads the glass, and instantly sizzles as it hits the hot skin of my fingers.

The policeman notices this, and frowns. He then shakes his head slightly, dismisses it as a trick of the light, or a figment of his imagination.

I slowly meet his gaze, and let just a little, tiny ember glow in each of my eyes.

He blinks, and then opens his mouth, resolute.

'Are you Ruby Miller?' He asks, flatly.

'It's not a crime to leave home,' I say, not answering him directly. 'I'm nineteen years old. An adult. I can leave without it being a Police matter.'

He narrows his eyes. 'True. But I'm not interested in you running away, although your Mother is beside herself with worry. Nope.' He sighs, and fiddles with the label on an empty bottle of bud, gearing up.

'No,' he continues, heavily, 'I'm interested in the burned out wreckage of one abandoned Pontiac, a 1989 Bonneville, very distinctive, and registered to you. And, I'm interested in the three abandoned Harleys we found close by, back on a certain highway in Nevada.' There is silence as I listen and sip my beer.

'I'm also interested in the remains of the three men we found near those bikes, remains we had

Cruel Works of Nature

to ID with dental records, because those remains were no more than cinders and ash. Not to mention the naked woman we found neardead from exposure not half a mile away. She kept shouting about a... girl on fire. 'Girl on fire!' she screamed at us, over and over again. She's in the hospital now. But we showed her your picture, and she recognised you. Despite the...haircut.'

He gestures at my bald head. The hair that burned away has not regrown, but I am fine with this. It's a lot easier to manage. I am thinking about getting a tattoo across my scalp, of a Phoenix, but I don't know how my new skin will respond to this.

My fingers tingle again with heat, and my beer bottle cracks suddenly, the glass unable to cope with the rapid shift from cold to hot. The contents of the bottle dump themselves all over the table with a definitive splash.

Neither myself, nor Officer Bright move. The beer spreads across the table and then starts dripping onto the linoleum floor all around us. The gentle splashing reminds me of the noise my car made as it leaked fuel into the desert that fateful day when I burned for the first time.

We stare at each other over the mess, a showdown at high noon.

There is no point denying it. I have no wish to deny it.

I had every right to do what I did.

I fold my arms.

'They were going to rape me,' I say, keeping my

voice carefully neutral. 'I needed help, and they held me down, and tried to violate me instead. All of them.'

Officer Bright's eyes flicker with sympathy, and then harden with resolve. He shifts in his seat, carefully.

'Be that as it may,' he says gravely, 'I have no choice. You're wanted on suspicion of three counts of homicide, and one count of arson.' He slowly reaches to his belt, produces a pair of handcuffs. 'Not to mention your underage drinking.' He says it as if it's a joke, as if any of this is remotely funny. It is meant to defuse the tension between us. It doesn't. I glare at him, and he sighs.

'It would help me out greatly if you'd oblige me by coming outside.'

'No,' I say.

He stands up. 'Ruby Miller,' he says, moving towards me, and reaching out to take my arm.

'I'm arresting you on...'

I hold up my hand to stop him, and my fingers catch fire. He snatches his own backwards in shock.

I twist and turn my wrist and my fingers, playing with the flames lovingly.

'No,' I repeat.

His eyes grow wide, and his mouth drops open.

'How are you doing that?' he whispers, and I am dimly aware that the rest of the room has grown deathly silent.

Cruel Works of Nature

I shrug. 'I don't know. It happened after I crashed my car. But that's not important. What's important is that things can get real hot, real quick. And I don't want to hurt you. You're just doing your job. But I will burn this whole fucking town down if I have to.'

Hopefully he can see from the expression on my face that I am deadly serious.

'I made a promise to myself, you see. A man once kept me a prisoner, for years, in my own home. He called himself my Daddy, and thought that gave him free reign to do whatever he wanted to me, if you catch my drift. So I resolved to never let another man lay a hand on me again, unless I wish it so. And to never be holden to another person, or to other people's rules, for the rest of my life. So you see, I can't come with you. Those men tried to rape me. They got justice for that. I'm guilty, but I'm sure as fuck not going to jail for it. What would be the point? I'd just raze the whole place to the ground, anyway.'

The confusion on Officer Bright's face is palpable, and I feel almost sorry for him.

'I'll tell you what's going to happen now,' I say, and wish I hadn't drunk so much beer, because the anger is raging inside of me, and I want to just let rip, to incinerate everyone in this shit-hole town, just burn it all fucking down so that I can feel better.

'What's going to happen is that I'm going to leave, get in my stolen car, and drive away, and you are going to go back to whatever depot you're from and tell your superiors that I gave you the slip. Then, you'll never hear from me ever again.'

He swallows. 'What about the next time you decide to...dispense justice?'

He's brave, I'll give him that. And he has a point. But I have no response to this. He can't tell me what to do. Fuck him. Fuck them all.

'I'm going now,' I say, backing away, and that's when the waitress hits me from behind with something large and heavy and metal. It makes a loud 'thunk' as it connects with the back of my hairless skull. The blow should knock me out, but it doesn't. I could have told her that, saved her the trouble.

I turn, a playful smile on my lips. She is holding a fire extinguisher out towards me like a talisman as if I'm an evil spirit to be warded off. I can feel the fire spreading up my arms now.

'Now that wasn't very friendly, was it?' I purr, rolling my head around on my neck to work out the crick she'd just bashed into it with the extinguisher.

'Get out of my bar, you fucking freak,' she snarls, her fat jowls wobbling with emotion, and I wonder at all these women who seem hate me so, hate me for being just a bit different.

She pulls the pin and sprays foam at me, foam which hisses impotently and then evaporates the second it hits my body.

Cruel Works of Nature

I grow hotter still with fury, and a steady white glow begins to pulse around me.

How dare she?

Can't people just fucking let me be?

Officer Bright is trying to mediate the situation. He does this by pulling his service revolver out and pointing it at me.

'Get on the floor, miss!' he says, his voice shaking.

I look back at him over my shoulder.

'How many times do I have to say it? No.'

'Please,' he asks, more gently, and again, I could almost feel some degree of sympathy for him if he weren't pointing a revolver at me.

'Please, I can tell you're angry. I don't want to shoot you. There are good people in this town.'

'I'm leaving now,' I say, and in the distance I hear a train approaching, a freight train, probably. It rattles towards Glenns Ferry at one a hell of a speed.

'Ruby Miller! Stop!' Officer Bright shouts after me.

I grow hotter still, and the waitress drops the extinguisher, holding up her arms to protect her face. The approaching freight train sounds its horn: it has no intention of stopping in this shit-hole town. It's going to shoot straight on through, which is what I should have done.

The horn sounds again, closer, and I make to push open the cafe's door.

Officer Bright fires three rounds off in quick

succession. They hit me square in the back of the head. He's a crack shot.

Time slows.

The furnace inside of me boils over.

I throw back my head and howl.

Then, I let the fire come.

It washes through the crappy, greasy, go-nowhere bar in the crappy, dusty go-nowhere town like a tidal wave, destroying everything and everyone in its path. I don't stand around watching the wood burn, the tiles blacken, the linoleum blister, the light bulbs explode. I don't look back as the people burn and collapse to the floor in a heap of ash, small piles of teeth scattering about like macabre confetti. I wonder why teeth don't seem to burn like the rest of the body.

I walk within the fire, and I leave hell in my wake. Before me, the train approaches, roaring along its track like a great ravenous beast, eating up the miles, dragging containers and tanks behind it, maybe thirty, forty pieces of cargo. The level crossing barriers come down, signalling the approach of the train, and the alarm starts to ding.

An idea hits me, and I act upon it, walking right up to the barrier, turning it to cinders with a mere touch. I am on the level crossing now, a blighted, burning torch, a beacon of years of abuse and pain at the hands of my Daddy, my precious Daddy who said he would never hurt me, but he did, people lie, and they deceive, and they manipulate, and they take.

Well now, it is my turn.

I hear shouting behind me, and screaming, as the fire spreads from the cafe to the neighbouring timber buildings on the street. A fire engine blares out in the distance, but it's faint, it's no match for the sound of the blaze and the approaching engine on the tracks.

There is movement, and a rush of electricity along the tracks under my feet. I summon up the last of my grief and my anger and I push it all into the flames, which tower ten feet or so above me. I register dimly the noise of brakes squealing against the train tracks, but the driver has seen me too late, everything is always too little, too late.

As the train thunders towards me I see a warning logo painted onto one of the tankards behind the engine. It's the symbol for a toxic substance, a liquid chemical of some sort, and next to it, a simple, stylized flame, meaning one thing: flammable materials.

The train smacks into me at fifty miles per hour, and the engine up front cleaves clean in two, a great squealing of metal and broken things trumpeting its death.

The tankard follows. I embrace it.

The resulting explosion, or series of explosions, as the tanks behind the first one go off in succession, like a chain of dominos- well. It is the most glorious thing I have ever seen or heard. The very earth shakes. Huge waves of impact roll outwards from the epicentre of my once-again naked body. Buildings fall. Trees catch fire. Cars flip and tumble over and over down the streets.

People die by the hundreds.

They deserve it, each one of them.

I am the fucking apocalypse.

My name is Ruby Miller.

And I am a Phoenix from the ashes.

❧ ❧ ❧

I WANDER through the blackened scar I have left on the land, and hear the distant sound of helicopters and law enforcement approaching. I hit the outskirts of town, and find a single street where the fire did not get everything, for some reason. A small pocket of peace in the maelstrom. As I walk down it, I see why. I see providence. I see the Gods smiling down at me.

At the end of the half-ruined street, three cars are parked on the sidewalk, still undamaged. The third of these cars is a rare car. You don't find many of them, anymore.

It's a cherry red 1989 Pontiac Bonneville.

I smile.

Time to hit the road.

Cruel Works of Nature

SCUTTLEBUG

Y OU DON'T KNOW WHAT FEAR IS.
 You might think you
 do.
You, hiding in your concrete bunkers so far removed from what the world has become. You, whoever you are. You may have experienced some... version of fear. Before all of this. Before they came along and rewrote all the rules. Something happened to you once, some tenebrous encounter, something that stays in your memory even now, something from your childhood, maybe, or from just before the world went to hell in a handbasket.

Can you remember how it felt to be afraid back

Cruel Works of Nature

then? In the good old days? Remember when your heart, already clamouring against the rise and fall of your heaving ribcage, began to scramble painfully up into your throat? When your skin pimpled with a sweeping rash of gooseflesh, a rash that crawled up your arms and down the back of your neck like a thousand tiny ants? Remember feeling your breath become shallow and ragged, the blood beginning to pulse in your ears, your mouth grow parchment dry?

This is how we used to talk about fear. We'd read about it, too, in dog-eared paperbacks of the type only found in thrift stores when such a thing existed, the sort that had lurid cover designs and coffee-stains tattooed across the preface. The kind of novel I used to keep in my own house when I was younger, thick slices of noir lining my bedroom shelves: vampires and demons and rabid dogs and serial killers. They were faithful companions that sent me to sleep, where I would dream pleasantly of the shadows until the morning. I used to enjoy being frightened, you see. I had no idea what actual terror was back then.

No, no. No.

What you felt, my friend, is a redundant, bargain-basement version of fear, a type of fear that was easy enough to overcome: with rational thought, with a brisk walk, with a steaming mug of coffee, or a scalding hot shower. Breathe slowly, count to ten. Think nice thoughts. The type of fright that evaporated and retreated from memory the moment you opened your curtains and let the sun stream into your life.

Are you shaking your head at me right now?

Perhaps you think I'm being unfair. Maybe I am. Hell, the way the world has gone to shit in these last few months… it's hard to imagine you haven't seen enough to turn your brain into deep-fried calamari.

I'll speculate a little: by now, you've probably seen one of… *them* in the flesh, haven't you?

One of the bugs, I mean. Up close. Well, what else would I mean? What else is there, these days, to talk about?

How did it make you feel? When you saw it, in all its glory, for the very first time?

Honestly?

Did you shit your pants?

If this is the case, then maybe I'm not shouting into the wind.

But, also, in the nicest possible way: Fuck you.

And the horse you rode in on.

You still don't know fear.

Not like I do.

But that's why you sent me your little drone messenger, isn't it? Because you want to know what I know. I can hear it behind me right now, recharging its batteries on my front porch as I write this reply to your letter. From the corner of my eye, it looks like an enormous bug, basking in the sun. I twitch every time I see it. My instincts are tight, these days.

Well, anyway, if you want my help, and you want my story, then you're going to have to hear it on my terms. And not that it's important any more, in these nameless days, but my name is Frank. Frank Teller. Again, you knew that already, but like I said. This is my story.

And I'll tell you what you want to know.

But first, I'm going to tell you about fear.

※ ※ ※

I DIDN'T NOTICE the noise right away. It darted around the edges of my consciousness, giving me a nagging feeling that something in the natural order of my day was offkilter. It poked and prodded at the verge of my awareness, an irritant, one of many that day.

I didn't give the sensation any time to gather ground. I was head-down and balls-deep into an assignment, and with less than five hours to go until the submission deadline was up, I didn't have time to think about anything other than the task at hand: trying not to fail.

If you're interested, at the point at which this tale begins, trying not to fail had become my very own personal motif, something to be inscribed on my headstone, because everyone who knew me back then knew it was true. 'Hi there', I would say to whoever would listen,

'Hey, beautiful, my name is Frank. Me? I'm just here trying not to fuck anything else up, thanks for asking!' Cute, huh?

At the age of thirty-five, this personal crusade against the armies of failure led me to become something of a cliché. I did what a lot of guys my age do: overworked, underpaid, under-appreciated, misunderstood, overloaded, overlooked... I became a giant, pathetic collection of 'overs' and 'unders' and late nights and used condoms discarded messily on my en-suite floor. One thing led to another, and before you know it: BAM! I awoke one Sunday morning in a sticky, stinking pool of my own vomit, nose crusty and bloody, having been made redundant from my soul-crushing job in finance two days earlier, having lost my girlfriend (who I didn't like that much anyway), having had my latest credit card application rejected. I was an eyelash away from losing my house to the mortgage company, I was beginning to develop a taste for tranquilizers- Xanax in particular- and my hair had turned almost completely snow-white in the space of six months. I also had a gut from drinking too much, which in the grand scheme of things, doesn't seem that important, does it? Yet every time I looked in the mirror and saw it hanging there, poking out absurdly over the belt-line of my pants, I felt an inexplicable surge of rage.

So yeah, there I was, fucking cliché central: broke, fat, single, unemployed, teetering on the edge of drug addiction, and brushing up against middle age.

In case you haven't guessed, I was also heavily into self-pity in those days.

Objectively speaking, though, self-pity aside, I was the kind of guy you crossed the street to avoid walking past. I was useless, and mean. I didn't smell great. I parked my car inconsiderately, and pushed in front of people in coffee queues. I swore loudly, chewed with my mouth open, kicked cats whenever I saw one, although generally, I still think they deserved it, furry little fucks.

Screw everyone, I used to think as I navigated around my quaint little town in a listless fugue.

What the fuck has any of this got to do with me? I hear you think as you read this. Having painted such an attractive portrait of myself, why should you give a shit? Beyond the obvious fact that you need my help, that is. Because clearly I'm a level-seven asshole, a waste of oxygen.

Well, you aren't wrong. But I'm getting to it. Give me time. Basically, without ruining this story, your survival depends on my survival. Your story is also my story.

Simple as that.

But... I digress.

So there I am, face down on the floor of my shitty house, the sour scent of vomit coating what was left of the inside of my nose, my head pounding, my coffers empty, and with a good thirty or forty years more of my wretched life stretching out interminably ahead of me.

And it dawned on me, finally, as I attempted to pull myself up and rest upon my elbows: life had become an absolute cluster-fuck of 'no'. My slow fall from grace, my daily and seemingly unstoppable degradation, well, it was worse than torture. My very sense of self was dissolving away. Soon, I would be nothing more than a haunted bag of bones.

It was time for a change.

I didn't have an epiphany, if that's what you're wondering. There was no bolt from the blue, no sudden calling or vocational inspiration.

It simply came down to this: I could carry on living the way I was living, change nothing, and end up dead before I was forty, and good riddance too.

Or, I could change something.

After another ten minutes of self-reflection as I stared at the contents of my own stomach on the floor beneath me, I shrugged, and stood up.

Time to change, I guess.

So, I drank half a carton of orange juice. I gently rescued a spider that I found trapped in the bathtub, and showered in lukewarm water. I went down to my bank, and re-mortgaged the house I lived in, despite already having done so twice to pay my mounting debts. I'm amazed the bank even let me in the front door, but they did. It was like vultures circling my dying body in the

Cruel Works of Nature

desert: they knew they had me. Every miserable asset I owned was now theirs. Well, they could have it. Owning things was overrated, anyway.

I raised some money from my trip to the bank. I logged into a computer in my local library, pulled up a list of affordable undergrad degree courses, skimmed through the course outlines, and decided on a degree in Psychology.

Well, why not?

Shrinks were well paid, weren't they?

And perhaps...perhaps it would help with my empathy problem.

I can hear you laughing. I thought it was pretty fucking funny, myself, at the time.

I applied, and again, astonishingly, I was accepted, the university in question needing more mature students in that year's quota.

And so there it was, my fresh life: me, in my house, with my books and my laptop, learning something new each day, and hoping against hope that it would be enough to keep me alive.

* * *

HAVE you forgotten about the noise? My bad. I don't get to talk to many people, these days.

Yeah, so. There was a noise.

The very first time I heard it, as I said, I was working on my first assignment, five thousand words on standardised intelligence testing, not that any of that matters anymore.

I was typing away furiously, the shallow keys of my laptop clacking away like chattering teeth, the smell of my cold coffee on the desk beside me acrid and heavy in the air. I remember so many things about that day, so many tiny little details. I guess that's just the old me, clinging on to the vestiges of our old way of life.

The noise, as I said, wasn't immediately obvious, because I was so focussed. After a while, however, the persistence of it broke through my study-bubble. I lifted my head, all other senses slowly coming back online. I heard the noise, and frowned.

Scuttle, scuttle.

What the fuck was that?

The noise ceased, as if sensing my sudden attention.

I stopped typing, and listened. My eyes flicked around the room as I waited. Nothing seemed out of place. The sun shone weakly through the window opposite me. An old cast-iron radiator ticked and creaked as it heated up. A tiny movement caught my eye: a long-legged house spider hightailed it across the rug, and disappeared under my bedroom door. I tutted. That was the second spider today. Must be cold outside.

Otherwise, just another normal day in Frankville. I kept on listening.

After what felt like an eternity, I heard it again.

Scuttle. Scuttle, scuttle, scuttle.

That's the only way I can describe it. It was a ... scuttling sound. It was coming from my bathroom, little irregular bursts of noise that carried across my house with surprising clarity. Have you ever been under a tin roof when a bird has run over the top of it? It was like that, only more purposeful, somehow. It sounded like tiny fingernails scraping against the insides of my bathroom walls. It was insistent, and determined, and a little creepy. Creepy because it was an unexpected and unfamiliar noise. It didn't belong in the landscape of my house.

Fucking rats, I thought immediately, listening intently to see whether the noise would come back. It did, with renewed vigour.

I sighed, and saved the progress I'd made on my assignment. I wandered into my bathroom, head cocked to the side in anticipation. Was there a rat or a mouse in there, chewing through my floors or, worse, the electric cables?

I pinpointed the sound. It was coming from the wall behind my toilet. I knew it was a cavity wall, and as it was an old house, I reasoned that there was a lot of room for something to make a home in there. Whatever it was, it was big, and very busy. Probably driven in by the winter weather like the spiders had been- it was colder than a witch's tit outside, I didn't really blame the critter for finding a warmer space, but still. If it was stuck in there, it would die eventually, and then it would rot and stink the house out, and I did not want a maggot infestation.

As the scuttling and scrabbling continued, I rose up on my tiptoes and peeked out of my bathroom window, which faced onto my neighbour's property. I was in luck. I could see Ted pottering around his front yard.

I slung on my coat, shoved my keys in my pocket, and headed over to next door. Ted would know what to do.

It was the last time I would ever see my house again.

❊ ❊ ❊

NOW, I had a lot of time for my neighbour. Ted was everything I wasn't: he was a good guy. He was kind, and wise, but with the good sense to keep his wisdom to himself unless asked to share it. He was moving along in years, and hovered around the seventy mark, although he was fit for his age, like so many manual labourers are. Ted had land around here, land he cultivated for soybeans. He also kept a few hogs out back, although I always got the impression that was more of a hobby than a farming decision. He loved those pigs like they were children. He called them things like 'Dolly', and 'Caroline', and 'Princess', and had photos of them pinned all over his kitchen wall.

Anyway. As I approached his yard he looked up and offered me a rare grin. The best thing about

Ted was that he didn't think I was an asshole. He was raking dead leaves off an already immaculate lawn. He looked happy to be distracted, and straightened up with a groan as I wandered over, leaning on the rake and greeting me amicably.

'Hey, Ted.'

'Hey, Frank. Nice to see ya. Want a cold one?'

The second best thing about Ted was the perpetually fully-stocked beer fridge that stood out on his porch, even in the dead of winter. The third best thing about Ted was how generous he was with it. He had an easy way about him that I liked, and for me that was something. I hated most people.

I hesitated, actually considering it for a moment, despite the fact that my breath made a halo of white around me as I spoke, then shook my head. 'Sorry Ted. Got an essay to turn in.'

'Oh, yeah, I forgot you was learning how to be a shrink these days. So do they teach you how to hypnotise people?'

I smiled. 'Not yet. I'll tell you when they do. We'll test it out on someone you don't like.'

He chuckled, and we stood there for a moment, while I glanced longingly at the beer fridge. Next to the fridge was a set of wicker chairs arranged around a table. We'd had more than a few nights sitting up there, sipping Bud or sweet tea and playing cards by the light of an old Hunter's lantern he kept hanging from the rafters of the porch. I remember the mosquitos used to flock around our ankles. Ted would light an incense coil to ward them off: I will never be able to smell that smell again without thinking back to those nights, to his kind, broad face and his gentle, easy wit.

Ah, Ted. There isn't a day that goes by that I don't think about him and wish his end had been a better one. He deserved better than what he got. But then, he'd had good innings, too. That's more than a lot of folks could say in the days that followed.

'So what can I do for ya?' Ted said, after a few moments of silence.

I sighed. 'Well, I'm not sure, really. I've got a deadline to meet with this essay, but there's this... noise in my walls. Pissing me off. Sort of a... scrabbling noise. It sounds pretty big. Been going on for a while now. I'm pretty sure I've got a rat trapped in the cavity somewhere.

I was wondering if you had any advice for getting rid of the little fucker. If it dies in there, it'll rot, and stink the whole place out.'

Ted nodded, and scratched his head for a moment, thinking. 'Well, I got a few traps in the back,' he said eventually, nodding in the direction of the huge, old-fashioned Dutch style barn that loomed behind his tiny house. Then, he winked. 'You can help me break up some old pallets for firewood while we're at it, if ya like.'

I sighed inwardly. I really did not have time, but if he was doing me a favour, the code of male friendship dictated that I should return the favour when asked. 'Sure,' I said, trying not to convey any of my impatience out loud, because Ted was pretty much my only friend.

I looked up at the flat, white sky as we ambled across to the barn, noting that the sun from earlier on had dwindled away, and wondering idly if it was about to snow.

As it turned out, it would, later.

* * *

THE INTERIOR of the barn was like something out of a different time zone. Old-fashioned, rustic tools hung from all four walls, swinging in the breeze of the opened doors like something out of a seventies horror flick. There were scythes, chains, shears, harnesses, saws, axes, sickles...you name it, Ted had it. If I didn't know him better, I would have thought there was something sinister about his carefully curated collection, but I did know Ted, and I was fairly confident he'd never hurt another human being in his life unless they really deserved it.

An ancient, hulking tractor sat abandoned at the back of the barn, hemmed in by hay bales, boxes, crates, cardboard and general landfill. Ted had been clearing out, and had stacked the detritus in here ready to be broken up and reused. Ted liked to recycle things, and hated waste.

He reached up and unhooked a long-handled axe, one of a selection hanging neatly up on the left-hand side of the barn, by the double doors. He handed it to me and gestured to the pile of crates at the far end. 'Knock yourself out,' he said, cheerfully. 'I'll try to find those traps.' Then he stopped, frowning and staring at the thresher floor. 'Looks like you ain't the only one with an infestation problem,' he said, slowly, and lifted his cap away from his scalp to scratch at his head.

I looked down, and yelped.

Streaming out across the barn floor in two, long, thick, sinewy lines, moving with a dreadful kind of choreographed urgency, were thousands upon thousands of tiny, tumbling spiders.

They boiled out of the barn like black water, moving almost as one, single, fluid organism. We must have disturbed them by opening the barn doors, the sudden burst of light and cold flushing them out from wherever they were hiding. The sound they made as they moved was unbelievable: it was like the rustle of silk, or the ceaseless whisper of a tiny waterfall. It dug under my skin, and I felt horror slide along my veins in a cold rush.

'Mother fucker!' I yelped, backing rapidly away from the writhing columns like the total pussy that I was.

Ted snorted in amusement. 'Well, blow me,' he said, and I could tell he was enjoying my reaction of disgust. 'Haven't seen a swarm like that in my life, I reckon. I know they like to come in out of the cold this time of year, but still. Damn.' He spoke as if he'd just heard a weather report on the radio, like this was all commonplace, like a million fucking arachnids carpeting his barn floor was an everyday occurrence.

'What are you going to do?' I said, watching the spiders with wide eyes, my heart in my mouth. I knew they were just insects, but *fuck*, there were just so many of them.

'Got some bug spray alongside the traps, somewhere in here.' He waved at the pallets. 'You can still have a go at breaking up them pallets while I look. They won't bother you none.' He waved at the spiders, and I gulped.

'You sure?'

'Not squeamish are you, Frank?'

'Yeah, actually I am.' I renewed my grip on the axe handle, and blew out my cheeks resolutely. This was turning out to be some shitty day. Why did I have to live somewhere so fucking rural?

'Ah, well,' said Ted, winking. 'Best get to it, anyway.'

And with that, he turned and trundled off to rummage around somewhere in the barn, whilst I warily eyed up the tiny spiders and hoped against hope that he was right.

❊ ❊ ❊

DO you know how spiders eat their prey?

I mean, have you ever really thought about it? We've all seen flies trapped in spider webs, their mummified corpses swaying in the breeze that rocks the web. But not every spider spins a web, and besides that, how do they actually eat their prey? Does a spider have teeth? Can it chew?

No. Their stomachs, it turns out, cannot digest solid food. Only liquids. Therefore, spiders inject their prey with their own stomach juices. Then they ingest the remains, by grinding them with these big fangs they have called pedipalps. I know that because I looked it up in an encyclopaedia I found in an abandoned gas station.

Actually, from an evolutionary perspective, spiders are really very beautiful creatures. They have evolved into perfect predators. Food too fast to catch? Trap it, catch it in a web, set a booby trap. Food too hard to eat, too solid to digest? Liquefy it first.

All these facts aside, at the time, I had no idea of, or interest in, the eating habits of spiders.

At the time, all I could do was watch.

❋ ❋ ❋

IT HAPPENED SO FAST I couldn't fully comprehend it to begin with.

I overcame my initial squeamishness about the spider infestation, and cautiously began to work on the crates piled up by the tractor that sat in the shadows way to the back of the barn. Don't get me wrong: I kept my eyes on the spiders as much as I could, shuddering at the seemingly endless stream that continued to flow out from somewhere behind me. After a few minutes, I found the rhythm and act of chopping wood strangely soothing, and the axe rose and fell with purpose.

'Found them!' I heard Ted shout, and I paused in my work, looking up. Ted ambled across the barn towards me, rattling a huge aerosol can as he walked, avoiding the spider streams with the lumbering grace of a big bear. Bug-killer spray. KILLS ON CONTACT, it said in bold, red capital letters along the side of the can. In his other hand swung two rat traps, as he'd promised.

'Christ, Ted,' I called out as he approached. 'I didn't know you could even buy bug spray in a can that size.'

He smiled, rattling the aerosol and moving purposely towards the back of the barn behind me. 'I reckon there's a nest back there behind them hay bales,' he said in that wonderful Dallas drawl he had still, even after all these years of living in North Carolina. I mean, we've got our own slow style, but his voice...it was something else.

'Might as well deal with this first, and then head over to yours. Gimme me a moment.'

'No problem,' I lied, looking down at the

bugs flowing around my feet. I hadn't realised how close they had gotten. I swallowed, and edged away slowly from the marching, swarming arachnids.

And then it happened.

A dark shadow streaked over my head, so fast I had no time to react, so quickly and so close I felt a breeze ruffle my hair.

It was huge, and moved with incredible speed, and it made a noise as it flew through the air: a grinding, squealing noise, like metal on metal, like someone screaming in pain. Like a fucking war cry.

The thing, whatever it was, landed on Ted.

I cried out, and watched in horror as Ted crumpled instantly to the ground under the weight of...what was it? What *was* that thing?! The can of bug spray and the rat traps hit the ground with a loud clatter.

My brain struggled to grasp what was happening. I rubbed my eyes, desperately blinking.

What the fuck?

What the actual, fucking fuck??

Small details began to filter in through my shock.

It was hairy, and sand-coloured.

It had eight legs. A thorax. An abdomen, and a head.

My mouth fell open.

It was a goddamned, mother-fucking, fuck-nuggety SPIDER!

Cruel Works of Nature

And not just any spider, no, that would be too fucking easy, wouldn't it?

I'm talking about a *giant* spider.

I'm talking about a spider of human proportions.

A spider as big as a man.

❋ ❋ ❋

NOWADAYS, I can barely remember the person I was when I think back to that first encounter. The food chain has altered irrevocably since those days, and I guess I have evolved like the spiders have evolved, I guess I have become a different beast.

For a while, though, I was prey. Then I adapted, I guess. I learned. Now, I hunt.

❋ ❋ ❋

THE SCUTTLEBUG, as I decided to call it, is a type of jumping spider.

It hunts like a wolf spider hunts. Turns out, they don't build webs. They dig tunnels. They get under things, and inside things. They hide, and watch, and wait. They crouch, prepare, make sure the moment is just right.

Then, they pounce. Like a goddamned lion, like something feline.

This fucking thing had been *watching* us from

the moment we entered the barn, waiting for us, waiting for Ted, waiting to spring an ambush.

Poor old Ted never stood a chance.

He didn't even have time to scream. He just went down like a ton of bricks. I screamed on his behalf. I screamed like a fucking girl as I watched what happened next. I screamed until I ran out of voice.

The spider lowered its face to Ted's prone form. A different sort of noise drifted across the air between myself and the nightmare that was unfolding before me. It was a wet noise, a fleshy noise… a squirting noise. It was the noise of a giant spider injecting something into a dead body. It sank its fangs into the mess that had been my buddy, and from between them shot something sticky, and viscous. The liquid squirted into the corpse and it jerked, and twitched, in a macabre display of animation.

Then, the Scuttlebug waited, stroking the body tentatively with its front legs, ignoring me completely, prodding it, and poking Ted as if to test whether or not he was ready to consume.

I should have run, at this point. I did not. I could not. I just stood there, clutching the axe, my new best friend, wondering what would happen now.

At first, nothing much.

Then, whatever venom the spider had injected began to do its thing, and Ted's body began to liquefy. Slowly, delicately, like an ice cream melting gradually in the sun, his shredded form began to collapse in on itself, and I thought, *there goes my sanity.* Bye bye, Frank. It's been nice knowing you. Don't let the barn door hit you in the ass on the way out.

Stupid, insane laughter bubbled up and out over my lips. I didn't even try to hold it in.

The Scuttlebug quivered and shuddered in what I can only suppose was anticipation. Then, it began to convulse, and I could see its stomach making a sort of sucking motion, and the spider lowered its head, and slurped at the sagging pile of pulp that was my neighbour, and drank him in like a fucking soda, until there was nothing left of him at all except my memories.

My memories. Oh, Ted. Ted, in the lantern light, dragging on a cigarette and passing me a beer. Ted, waving at me over the wire fence that separated his house from mine. Ted, taking off his John Deere cap and scratching at his head underneath while he puzzled over something.

Ted, being torn apart and dissolved by a giant fucking spider.

I looked at it. Its abdomen had expanded grossly, and seemed ready to almost explode. Sated, it sat there, motionless, mute, with two black, shining rows of eyes, all of which were fixed upon me.

It settled, rearranged its limbs, gave off the impression that it was getting comfortable.

And I saw something then, something that

changed me beyond recall, something that just could not exist in nature and yet somehow... did.

At the end of every leg was a brown, hairy appendage.

An appendage that looked and moved exactly like a human hand. With fingers.

Long, supple, wriggling fingers.

It had eight fucking hands at the end of each leg.

I turned tail and ran, scattering thousands of tiny spiders in my wake as I left the barn, yelling like a man who had lost his mind. The axe came with me, although I didn't realise this until later.

The bug did not follow. I knew it didn't need to, for it had eaten, and was content.

I ran anyway.

❊ ❊ ❊

TO BEGIN WITH, I began running back to my house, thinking to get inside, lock the door, call the police, call anyone, and then crawl under my bed and fucking stay there until, well, forever came and went again.

And then I stopped, dead in my tracks.

The walls. The scuttling sound in my walls.

What if there was one of those things in my house?

And I knew suddenly that it was true, that

there was another nest in the walls of my bathroom like the one in Ted's barn, although perhaps not so big.

I stopped running, my chest heaving, my blood thundering through my veins, my throat raw. The cold afternoon air closed in around me. I wasn't even wearing a proper coat, just a light jacket I'd thrown on for the purposes of visiting Ted.

Oh God, Ted.

I buried my face in my hands, about to sink to my knees with hopelessness, when I heard it.

A high, long, terrified scream, coming from further up the road. A dog barked frantically from the same location. It was happening to someone else.

I lifted my head, tried to still my wildly erratic heartbeat. I looked down, and realised I was still holding the axe. The screams continued, rising in pitch and intensity.

'Thanks Ted,' I whispered, and my indecision hardened into resolve. He'd given me this axe for a reason. If I'd been quicker, I might have saved him.

I jogged along the road, towards the screaming.

Maybe I could save someone else, instead.

❈ ❈ ❈

IT DIDN'T TAKE me long to find the source of the screams. The next house along the street belonged to the Armstrongs- an older couple and their twenty-something daughter. They had a Labrador called Peter. Peter was a nice dog when he wasn't trying to take a dump on my front driveway.

As I rounded the corner and their house came into view, I saw that I was too late to save everyone. A pair of the giant, sandy bugs loomed protectively above two corpses, and I knew from experience that there was no getting them out of that situation.

The Armstrong girl was another story. She'd managed to somehow avoid the death-pounce of the third arachnid, and was warding it off with a pair of garden shears, screaming and sobbing hysterically while Peter the dog barked and darted forward, snarling and nipping at the spider's legs. I realised that the three of them, the whole Armstrong family, had probably been tidying up the yard in preparation for the winter, just like Ted had- cutting back deadwood, clearing up leaves, burning rubbish.

This spider seemed aware of the threat it faced from the sharp shears. It was smaller than the other two bugs, who were too preoccupied with liquidising their prey to pay us any attention. Aware of its vulnerability, the smaller spider's defence strategy was to rear up on its hind legs and wave its front legs around menacingly in what I recognised an attempt to make its mass as large and threatening as possible.

I took a moment to assess the situation, drew in a deep breath, and ran towards the thing as fast as I knew how, my new best friend, Ted the axe, raised high above my head. Adrenaline gave me wings, and I was upon it before I knew what was happening.

It sensed me moving up behind it, and turned, lurching above me with outreached legs, those fucking terrible hairy brown fingers reaching and stretching for me. I yelled, and brought my own arms down as swiftly and surely as I knew how. The axe connected with the top row of forward-facing eyes, which erupted in a shower of green pus.

The spider shrieked, and then shrieked again as the Armstrong girl recovered her composure and stabbed the thing repeatedly in the back of the head and thorax with her shears.

I pulled the axe free from its ruined face and swung again, remembering how it felt to chop wood at Ted's place. There was a rhythm to this work, it was good, honest work, and I settled into it. Peter the dog, still barking non-stop, circled the Scuttlebug and savagely, and ritually, attacked each of its legs until the monster stumbled, and then crashed to the ground.

We finished it off within moments, and then stood staring at each other in shock, covered in gore.

A movement below me caught my eye, a familiar, rippling, silk-rustling movement, and I snapped my gaze back to the dead bug at my feet.

Another fun fact: female wolf spiders carry their young around on their backs.

So, it seemed, did this brand of spider. It was covered in a thick blanket of writhing, angry baby spiders. They erupted and seethed towards us like thick, brown lava, chittering and screaming in rage.

'RUN!' The Armstrong girl screamed, and I didn't wait around to be told twice.

The three of us ran back down the road, Peter the dog racing alongside us, and for a while, that was all there was. Running, running, running, and staying alive. We lost the spiders eventually, but that didn't stop us. We ran away from the ruined mess our old lives had suddenly become, and towards a future where everything had been turned on its head.

Nothing would ever be the same again.

But then, it was the end of the world. What did we expect?

* * *

ONCE WE RAN out of breath and adrenaline, we found ourselves on the edge of a farmer's field. As it was winter, there was no crop, only well-tilled soil from the harvest earlier in the year. It was a

Cruel Works of Nature

flat space, wide and open, and provided a clear line of sight in all directions.

I gently took the Armstrong girl's hand, and led her across the field, until we were in the very centre of it. From here I would be able to see any of those leggy fucks coming at me from a good enough distance, although what I would do then, I couldn't say. How many of these things were there? A few? A hundred? Thousands? It dawned on me that I was not thinking big enough. I thought about the millions of tiny spiders I'd seen running across Ted's barn floor. If they all grew up to be like their Momma, we were fucked. Forget the zombie apocalypse. Who wanted to live in a world run by hordes of those monstrous things? Not me.

Peter the dog whined, and I realised the girl had sunk to her knees, sobbing. I remembered that her Mom and Pop were now spider soup, and patted her awkwardly on the shoulder as she cried. Emotional shit was not my strong point, but the kid had had a tough day.

'What's your name?' I said as gently as I knew how, hoping to distract her with some banal conversation. 'Fuck off,' she sobbed, and Peter the dog looked at me reproachfully.

I blinked and did as I was told, turning my back on her and walking a few paces away to give her some space. I scanned the horizon constantly, in all directions, turning a three-sixty degree arc and clutching my axe tight. The events of the past hour or so began to sink in, very slowly at first, and then in a big rush.

Ted.

Spiders.

Fuck.

Fuck!

Fuck me sideways, upside down and round the fucking corner!

Fuck.

I had a flashback to the first spider leaping through the air, a textbook example of an apex predator, legs outstretched, emitting that hideous war-cry. Then my brain replayed the sickening crunching sound my axe had made as it sank into crispy, hard exoskeleton, and the shower of ichor that followed. I shuddered, waves of shakes rolling around my body like a palsy.

I thought about the scuttling sound in my bathroom walls, imagined one of those things hiding in there, nesting, getting comfy, waiting, watching me through cracks between the tiles.

I thought about throwing up, but somehow couldn't muster the energy. I looked around, helplessly, at the white sky over my head and the black soil under my feet, the trees on the skyline, the low-slung clouds.

It dawned on me suddenly that two things were about to happen.

The first, was that it was late afternoon. Which meant that soon, it would be early evening. And then, it would be night-time.

I did not want to be out here when night fell.

The second thing was more unexpected. As I continued to scan the horizon, and the clouds, my breath puffy like smoke in the air, I realised I could *really* smell the cold, that it had intensified. The afternoon had taken on an eerie, quiet, muffled feel that usually preceded one thing, and one thing alone.

'I think it's going to snow,' I murmured to myself. Curiously, I didn't feel cold.

'Don't be stupid. It never snows round this way.' The Armstrong girl had managed to get a hold of herself, it seemed. She rose to her feet, and came over to join me, looking like warmed-up, recycled shit: her eyes were red and swollen, her hair was plastered to her face, and her clothes were covered in thick, green spider goo. I looked down at myself and grimaced. So was I.

I stuck out my hand in a ridiculous, formal gesture of introduction. 'It does, actually. You're probably just too young to remember. I'm Frank.'

She shook my hand, trying and failing to raise a smile. Still, serious suited her. 'I'm Agatha,' she said, then shivered, wrapping her arms around herself. 'I'm cold.'

'We need shelter,' I said. 'It'll be night soon, and the temperature will just keep on going down. Plus those Scuttlers could be anywhere around us, and we don't know how many there are.'

'I hear you.' Agatha stamped her feet to get some feeling back in her toes. 'Where can we go?'

I looked about, lacking inspiration. Most of the land around this way that isn't covered in fields is covered in trees. I didn't think trees would be much protection. I mean, I knew what happened to folks who went into the woods in scary stories. I wasn't *that* stupid.

In the distance I could see a sort of rusty, corrugated iron lean-to standing at the edge of the field, up against the highway, right next to a blue 'Adopt a highway' sign that was peppered with bullet holes. 'There,' I said, knowing our options were limited.

Agatha looked sceptical. 'Are you sure?' she said, scratching the top of Peter's head. 'It looks like it's about to collapse. It won't give us much protection from... the spiders.' She shuddered, from both the cold, and her memories.

I looked her square in the eye, lifted up my hands in a shrugging motion.

'You got a better idea?'

She shook her head. 'Nope.'

The three of us made for the lean-to, our feet making peculiar squelching, crunching noises as they sank into thick, ploughed furrows of soil. We were close, almost there, when I heard the noise I dreaded above all noises once again. That sound will be with me now for the rest of my life, even if I dig my own brains out with an egg spoon. It's lodged into my psyche like a tick on a dog's ass.

Scuttle.

Scuttle, scuttle.

I froze, put my arms out to stop the other Agatha and the dog.

I crept forward, clutching my axe, listening.

Scuttle.

'RUN!' I yelled, but I was already too late.

There was a rasping, inhuman shriek, and a sandy coloured blur moved through the air at lightning speed towards me, and then I was on the ground, and the goddamned thing was on top of me, and I realised I had dropped my axe, and I realised also, that, despite my best efforts, this was it for me. I was fucked. *So long, Frank.* What a waste of time that all was.

I waited for the bug to vomit acid all over me, waited for the searing pain I knew must be the result of such a thing. I could hear Agatha screaming from somewhere nearby, and Peter the dog barking, frenzied. *Such a good dog*, I mused. *Such a nice girl, too.*

After a few moments, I then thought: *Why aren't I dead yet?*

I opened my eyes, which had been screwed shut in fear, and found the spider was looking at me. Eight colourless orbs, and every single one of those evil lenses was fixed firmly upon my face.

Thing like that will change a man, I tell you.

Why?

Because it was an appraising look, a focused, intense look that spoke of...intelligence.

I can't explain it any better than that, and I don't need to. The world will know about it soon enough.

Wait though. It gets better.

I didn't have long to wonder why I was still alive.

Seconds later, it became apparent.

Slowly, noisily, a thin, long proboscis slid out of a gap between the hairy plates of the bug's underbelly. On the end of the fleshy stalk there was mounted something so obscenely human that I knew it immediately for what it was.

It was red, and engorged, and headed straight for me.

'Oh fuck, NO!' I yelled, pushing against the thing with all my strength, realising with horror that its hairy legs with those hairy fucking mutant hands were scrambling around on my chest, and down my legs, and across my arms, as if trying to figure out what part of me went where, and which bit of my anatomy was for what purpose, and all I could do was thrash around and flail like fish and try to fight it off.

Exasperated, the spider bit down on my neck, not to wound, but to hold me in place.

I screamed as acid fire raged through my body, and then something...amazing...happened.

My field of vision narrowed, grew dark, and

then multiplied.

I realised I was staring at my own face through eight sets of eyes. The bug's brain, its...*essence*, if you like, was lurking in the back of my own mind, crouching, waiting to pounce as it waited in the physical world. I knew, somehow, that it could feel me in the back of its own mind, and then seconds later, I processed the implications of the weird mind-meld that was going on.

GET. OFF! I roared, in my head.

The Scuttlebug flinched, squealed, reared up on its hind legs.

An axe, *my* axe, whizzed past my nose and crunched into the spider's belly with a satisfying force. Agatha panted, yelled her own war cry, yanked the axe free, and swung again, just like she was chopping wooden pallets in a neighbour's barn.

Such a good girl, I thought, teetering around on the brink of madness.

Agatha kept chopping, grunting, and ululating like a banshee, great gobbets of spider gloop flying around her as she brought the axe down time and time again. I thought I'd never seen a woman look so beautiful before, and probably never would again.

The bug eventually rolled onto its back, legs jerking about erratically, and finally, finally had the good grace to die.

Silence rolled slowly back across the fields and the highway beside us, soothing, peaceful.

I cautiously assessed the damage as I lay on the ground, too overwhelmed to move. My head ached from the unexpected, psychic invasion. My neck throbbed and was wet with my own blood from two large puncture wounds. There were multiple other cuts, scrapes and bruises, but, in essence, I was still in one piece.

Despite everything, I was still alive.

Something cold and wet landed on my closed eyelids. I opened my eyes, and saw tiny snowflakes drifting down, gently, from above.

Agatha giggled, suddenly, and then the giggles turned into great guffaws of laughter.

'What?' I said, sitting up cautiously, and staring at her open mouthed. 'What is so fucking funny?'

'Were you just nearly ass-raped...by a spider?' she managed, between bouts of uncontrollable mirth.

I had two choices, really. I could be pissed at her, or join in.

I started laughing too. I figured that as we were both still alive, so why not make the most of it?

* * *

AFTER THAT DAY, we didn't see any more Scuttlebugs for a while. I guessed, correctly as it turned out, that they were headed for more densely populated areas. We decided to do the opposite.

Cruel Works of Nature

We hot-wired an abandoned jeep, loaded it with any supplies we could scavenge, bundled Peter the dog in the back, and drove pretty much due west, headed for Nantahala Lake.

When I was young, my family rented a cabin on the shore of that lake almost every summer. I remembered one distinct thing about it: the cabin was actually situated on a tiny island connected to the shore by a small spit of sand. Which meant there was only one entry point into the island, unless you came from the lake itself.

And I was fairly sure spiders couldn't swim. Not that well, at least.

Could they?

At any rate, I had plans for that cabin. I could dig a channel, cut the island off completely from the mainland. Build defences. Make it safe.

So that's what I did, and that's how I've lived, for a while now.

Until your little drone turned up with its message on board.

* * *

SO, we're all caught up, now aren't we? And so it's time to get to the crux of the matter- the reason you sought me out.

Imagine my surprise when your little flying messenger-machine landed on my jetty this morning, its little blades whirring in that self-important manner they have. You're lucky I didn't blast the thing out of the fucking sky with my shotgun, I mean, for fuck's sake, the world is overrun with an infestation of giant, mutated spiders, and you send me something that looks like an overgrown mosquito? Come on, guys. At least *try* to make it look a little less threatening. Tie some fucking flowers onto it, or paint it pink or something. Jesus.

I suppose it says something about the state of the world now that you sent a drone, instead of a real person, to recruit me. I don't know why I'm surprised. I hear that these days, the CDC and a bunch of other scientists, government officials and army folk are holed up under the mountains, safe beneath the layers of rock. How you found me, I'll never know. I guess our satellites are still going strong. Maybe you followed a rumour or two, or maybe you found me by accident.

None of that matters. What matters is what you want from me.

Because, you need me, don't you?

You need me because I was bitten, and I survived.

So far, as far as I know, and I'm only basing this on other survivors I've met, rumours I've heard, whispers over walkie-talkies I've salvaged...so far, by some miracle, good ol' 'just-trying-not-to-fuck-this-up-Frank' survived the spider-bite, and more interestingly for you, I'm the only one so far who has.

You want my blood to study. You want my brain on a petri-dish.

And what happens if I don't want to come over there and help you out?

I like my life at the moment. I'm safe out here on my island, or I have been so far. I can fish, and there is fresh water. I sleep okay. The Scuttlebugs can't get to me yet.

Agatha is here too, although her mental state is not so great at the moment. She needs more time to process the end of the world and the loss of her parents. Peter the dog is a good source of comfort. He's a cool guy, Peter. He's surprisingly good at fishing trout, too.

So yeah, life in the apocalypse is actually kinda good.

And I've learned, after years of experience that if it ain't broke, well. Don't fix it.

So I think I'll stay put, if that's okay with you.

Thanks for the invitation though.

THE PATH THROUGH LOWER FELL

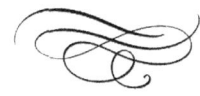

I T WAS THE KIND OF DAY THAT MADE YOU FEEL GLAD TO be alive.

The sky overhead was a deep, satisfying shade of blue. Butterflies drifted lazily around us as we walked through the countryside, flitting past our faces, landing gently on the spring flowers that had finally, finally blossomed after weeks of freezing, shitty weather. The world felt like it was shaking off the oppressive mantle of winter, stretching out in the sunshine like a cat does after a long sleep. I felt like that too. The skin on my arms tingled, enjoying the fresh air, having been swaddled in thick layers for far too long. My feet struck the ground with energy, and enthusiasm.

Yes. It was a good day to be alive.

We walked, Jim and I, one in front of the other. Dew coated our walking boots, and a warm, pleasant sun shone down on the backs of our necks. Sweat was already trickling down from underneath my armpits.

We'd been going for about an hour, an hour spent in comfortable silence, the sort that develops when two people have grown accustomed to each other. We liked to walk on the weekends, to leave the city behind us, as they say. Today we'd chosen a new route, a twelve-mile hike that would take us over hills, across ridges and down through lush, green valleys and meadows. My heart rate was up, and I could feel that my cheeks were flushed from the exercise. God, it felt good to be outdoors.

We reached a bend in the footpath we were following, and Jim stopped, checking the map. He seemed strangely preoccupied with something.

'Okay?' I said, coming to a rest behind him and wrapping my arms around his waist. He felt a little stiff in my embrace, but I didn't make too much of it - I knew that he hated to be distracted when he was concentrating on something.

'Mmmmm,' he said, not looking up from the map.

'So which way?' I said, letting him go and swigging from a water bottle I had stashed in my backpack. The back of my neck was beginning to feel too warm. I rustled around in my bag some more, and brought out a thin scarf, wrapping it around me to protect my pale skin from the sun.

'God, it's a beautiful day,' I continued, rather pointedly, when he didn't answer. The words hung in the air.

'Mmmmm,' he said, again, and I sighed. Jim really could do only one thing at a time. I smiled to myself then, and waited.

Eventually, he seemed to decide on a route. He pointed further down the path we were already on, towards a large stand of oak trees in the distance.

'That way. If we keep going that way for another mile or two, we should come to a large meadow, behind those trees. It's called... Lower Fell.' He gestured to a point on the map that I couldn't really see. 'If we take the path across it, it should bring us out the other side of this farmland, and then we follow the stream until we hit the main road again.'

I smiled and shrugged, taking his word for it. 'Let's go then,' I said brightly, but Jim didn't seem to share my enthusiasm. He looked lost in thought, and the corners of his mouth curled down in a serious expression that I hadn't seen for a while.

I reached out, touched him lightly on the shoulder with one hand. Was it my imagination, or did he flinch at my touch? A little tendril of uncertainty curled around my happy mood.

'Are you sure you're alright, Jim?' I asked, concern in my voice.

He avoided my gaze, and set off walking.

'Yeah, I'm sure,' he said.

But his voice seemed heavy, weighed down with something.

I felt a sudden flash of annoyance at this moodiness. What more did he want? The sun was shining, the birds were singing, and all was right with the world. I took a deep breath, filling my lungs with fresh country air, and shrugged it off. He'd tell me what was bothering him sooner or later.

We continued trudging along the trail.

As promised, after a mile or so, we came to the oak tree ridge. Set amongst the trees was a rickety wooden fence, and set into that was a rickety wooden gate. It hung lopsidedly on one hinge, a hinge that squealed with rust and age as we pushed it open.

On the other side of the gate lay a small, shady footpath through vast, green trees which were so tall I had to crane my neck as we passed beneath the canopy to be able to see the top of them. We walked through what felt like enchanted forest, eerie, and cool, and green, and then, suddenly, without warning, we were out the other side, back into the blinding light of day. Squinting, we came to another fence, with another dilapidated gate providing access beyond.

Behind that lay the meadow of Lower Fell.

We latched the gate shut, turned, and froze. As our eyes adjusted to our new setting, we just stood there, gawping.

Before us stretched a huge, green, verdant swathe of knee-length grass. It was so green, so rich, and so thick, that it made my eyes ache, trying to process it all. The grass looked alive, almost, rich and dense like glossy animal fur. It shimmered in the sunlight. The brilliant blue sky overhead added a layer of primary colour that was so intense, the whole scene looked... unreal. Great, tall oak trees like the ones we'd just left behind lined the meadow the whole way around, and a picture-perfect, winding, babbling stream cut through the heart of the meadow, from left to right.

My heart sang as I took in the view, astounded by the beauty of Lower Fell. The air was thick with swooping and buzzing insects that made themselves busy upon wildflowers. A gentle breeze rolled through the meadow, ruffling the tall stalks of grass and creating a quiet rushing noise like that of the sea, if it were very far away. A fragrance crept into my nostrils: the thick, heady perfume of nature.

'Well, would you look at that,' I breathed, and turned excitedly towards Jim to see what his reaction was.

He was frowning, and looking at something in the distance.

'What?' I said, irritation once again bubbling to the surface, despite the day, the surroundings, the sunshine.

'Well... it's just a bit odd, that's all.' He shaded his eyes with one hand, still looking at something some distance away.

'What is?' I tried to see what was taking his attention away from me so effectively.

He pointed.

'There, at the bottom of the meadow. That herd of cows, can you see them?'

I shaded my own eyes from the bright sun, and looked.

Eventually, right at the far end of the meadow, lurking in the tree line, I saw them. A large herd of cows, big ones by the looks of it. I tried to see if any of them were bulls, but they were too far away for me to focus properly on. I could make out the colour- they were black. They seemed fairly stationary, and placid. They just stood there, huddled together, watching us as we watched them.

I shrugged, and turned back to my boyfriend. 'They're just cows, Jim. They won't bother us.' He shook his head.

'No, it's not that. It's the grass. Why is it so...

long?

Don't cows eat grass?'

I shrugged again, not really caring.

'Maybe they don't like this type of grass. Does it matter? Look at this place, Jim! It's magical!' I threw my arms out, gesturing to the gorgeous vista that lay beyond, spinning around, a poor man's Julie Andrews in *The Sound of Music*.

Jim watched me, and I saw that his eyes had grown soft, moist even.

I smiled hesitantly back at him, but the smile died on my lips, and worry took over as I began to wonder what exactly was going on. Because something was definitely wrong.

My mind went over multiple possibilities. Was he sick?

Was he sad? Was he just feeling romantic?

Was he... Oh, God. Was he about to propose?

Holy shit! I thought, and, as if to confirm my suspicions, I saw him put his right hand in his right jean pocket.

That's it.
He's going to do it.
He's finally going to do it!
We're going to get married!

In the distance, I heard a faint lowing sound: one of the cows, calling out. The noise was deep, and mournful. I barely registered it, and instead, excitement surged through me as I stared at my lover, my heart beating with increasing ferocity in my chest.

Jim gulped, and put his spare hand up to caress my face.

'Amelie,' he said, softly, and I felt my heart flip right over inside of me. It was perfect. This place was perfect. He must have planned it, must have always intended to bring me here, so that he could ask me to be his wife. Tears threatened in the corners of my eyes, but I held them back, struggling to keep my composure.

'What?' My voice was shaky, and weak.

'I've got something... I need to say.'

He looked down at his feet, shifting his weight from one to the other. I heard another cow lowing, and then another, softly.

'Yes, Jim?' I could barely breathe, I was so nervous.

Once more, a cow lowed in the distance.

Shut up, cow! I thought, furiously. *Don't you dare fucking ruin my moment! I've waited years for this!*

Jim seemed to be struggling to get the words out.

'What is it? You can tell me.'

My eyes were wide, and my mouth curved into a small, gentle smile of affection, of love.

He took a deep breath, and brought something out of his pocket. I began to tremble in anticipation.

He handed it to me, and said the four words I'd been longing to hear.

'I'm leaving you, Amelie.'

Wait.

What?

I looked down at my hand, and saw that he had pressed something into it that definitely wasn't a diamond ring.

It was his copy of my front door key.

He was giving me back his front door key.

What?

I stood, stunned, on the edge of the meadow. Flies still buzzed around us, only now I realised they weren't interested in the wildflowers, but rather, they seemed more interested in the cow shit that I spotted suddenly, hiding underneath the grass. In a moment of pure disconnect and surrealism, I thought how strange it was that the shit, which I now saw was lying thick on the ground almost everywhere, all across the meadow, all around our feet, well, it was peculiar, but it seemed to be a light, fleshy pink. Cow dung was usually brown, wasn't it? Brown and grassy? This stuff... it looked spongy. Meaty, somehow.

Gross, I thought, absent-mindedly, and then: *Oh, and Jim's leaving me.*

'Amelie?' Jim said it with what sounded like real concern in his voice. 'Did you hear me?'

'Okay,' I said, in a voice that didn't sound like mine.

He sighed, and looked as if he were about to cry. He tried to put an arm around my shoulders, but I reared back, and kept him at arm's length.

'Let me explain, Amelie. I just... for some time

now, I haven't been happy. I can't believe you haven't noticed. I think I need to take some time for myself... be selfish for a while... maybe travel... take a sabbatical at work... does that make sense?'

'Is there someone else?' I asked, a headache beginning to play around the edges of my temples.

'What?' The question startled him.

My voice grew angry, and dark. 'You heard me. Have you met someone else?'

He avoided my gaze, and I knew, with a sinking sense

of inevitability, that he had. I snorted with bitterness.

'What's her name?'

There was a pause, as Jim struggled with himself.

Then, reluctantly, he told me.

'Louise. Her name is Louise.'

We stood there facing each other in silence. It felt as if time had somehow eloped. Water sang and chuckled in the nearby stream. I heard the sound of cows lowing again from the bottom of the meadow, and swallows screaming as they swooped through the sky above.

It was at that moment that I noticed something about the cows. It was one of those absurd things that you fixate upon when something bad happens. A distraction, so that I could avoid thinking about what was actually happening to me at that exact moment in time.

The cows were somehow closer than they had been before. They had moved from the tree-line, and still stood in a huddled, eerily silent group, squashed up against each other to form a single mass of cattle. Only they were about ten feet further into the meadow than they had been when I'd last looked. Not a single one of them had lowered its head to graze on the long, thick grass, and I registered at last that this was odd, wrong, in fact. They just stood there, staring in our direction. In silence.

At the front of the herd stood a large bull, huge, wickedly curving horns pointing forward on its massive head. Even from this distance I could see that it was a huge creature, its coat glossy and black as tar, with great solid slabs of muscle rippling underneath.

It opened its mouth and lowed, deep and long. The herd echoed the cry, and the weird, otherworldly sound of twenty or so massive animals calling out in unison swooped across the meadow.

My headache doubled in intensity as if in response to the herd.

'Amelie?'

Jim had not noticed the cows. His gaze was still firmly fixed on me. It was clear that he was trying to assess the damage that he'd done with his sudden announcement.

I looked at him, feeling my world, my little happy world, begin to crumble down around my ears.

'I... I don't understand.'

My vision swam. My ears began ringing with a peculiar buzzing sound.

The herd shuffled closer. I saw them out of the corner of my eye. A few of the biggest began stamping their feet, pawing at the ground.

My gaze returned to the cow shit at my feet. Why was it so pink?

And why was the grass so long in this meadow?

Ignoring Jim, I studied the grass and the flowers around my knees intently, a sensation of unease slowly spreading through my body, pushing aside the shock of Jim's betrayal.

After a few moments of scanning the ground, I spotted something partially hidden in the grass, something that looked out of place. I moved forward and crouched down to get a better look. My hand reached out, pushed aside the grass, the red poppies, the blue cornflowers, the yellow buttercups. Pushed it all aside, and saw what lay there, hidden, covered in a thick, indelicate layer of curiously pink faeces.

It was a skull.

A human skull.

Half-shattered, and scarred with great, dented holes and deep gouges that looked like...

...That looked like teeth marks.

Behind the skull, thrusting out of the earth like strange, white weeds, were the stripped, gnawed bones of a ribcage.

A human ribcage.

Further out, scattered around like confetti, were smaller, tiny fragments of bone that could have once been an arm, or a hand, or a foot.

The skull stared at me with its dark, empty sockets. The grass moved gently, singing in the breeze.

The cattle lowed again, in unison. I covered my mouth with my hand, my brain slowly making the connection.

The cows in this field don't eat grass.

I rose, slowly, cautiously, looking for the herd.

Jim- stupid, unobservant, cheating, shit bag Jim carried on as if nothing were happening.

'I know it's hard Amelie. I know. And it's so...sudden. But I just can't... I just can't keep lying to myself, Amelie.

It'll be better for both of us, in the long run. I know it will.'

His voice faded into insignificance as I met the gaze of the herd once more.

They had moved closer still. They stood watching me as I watched them, huge, dark eyes rimmed with long fluttering eyelashes. Their tails whipped around them, swatting flies, and their mouths chewed endlessly on the cud. Or was it?

The cows in this field don't eat grass.

Oh God, what were they chewing on?

Aside from the incessant side-to-side movement of their lower jaws, they might have been carved from stone, or marble: great, solid, bovine statues that terrified me beyond anything I'd ever been scared of before.

The bull who must have stood easily six feet high from the ground up, put one hoof out in front of him, cautiously, as if testing for something. His horns glinted wickedly in the sunlight.

He opened his mouth, and bellowed again, and this time it sounded defiant, and hungry.

'Run,' I said, softly, and the bull, and the rest of the herd, moved forward as one.

I turned tail and sprinted back the way we'd come. I heard Jim swearing behind me, but didn't look to see if he was following.

Fuck him.

This was about survival.

The ground shook and thundered with the unmistakable sound of multiple sets of hooves stampeding towards me. I pumped my arms and legs as fast as I knew how, thanking my lucky stars that I was in shape, fixing my gaze on the gate that had led us into the meadow, the rickety gate that was no more than ten feet away at most. Those ten feet suddenly seemed like ten miles, and no matter how hard I ran, the distance between myself and the gate never seemed to close.

Behind me, I heard the cattle lowing, making a frenzied chorus in the air all around me, and my headache intensified once more, again as if in response to the creatures. I felt something crack under foot and knew what it was: bone. It made me run faster still. How many had died in this field? How many ruined bodies lay hidden beneath the grass?

My fear lent me wings, and I sped up still more. I could hear Jim behind me, panting 'Oh, fuck! Oh, fuck! Oh, fuck!' over and over again as he ran. I could tell from the intensity of the vibrations running up my shins when my feet hit the earth that the herd were almost upon us now. My vision swam with sudden tears as I began to despair. I was going to die in this field. I was going to be trampled. I was going to be eaten.

The gate loomed close, finally, blessedly close enough to reach out and touch.

I hurled myself at it, throwing myself through the air to cross the final distance more quickly. I hit the gate hard, and scrambled over it, hoping the old, rotting wood would be enough to keep the cattle at bay, because I was winded, and as I landed with a crash on the other side of the gate, my legs caved beneath me, turning to jelly. I sobbed in relief as I slumped into the dirt.

'Amelie!'

I heard Jim scream my name. He had not reached the gate yet.

I heaved myself unsteadily to my feet, my head now throbbing with pain as if it were being held and squeezed in a vice. I looked for Jim, and what I saw made my blood freeze solid in my veins.

He was still running, face screwed up in panic, mouth hanging open, arms and legs working to propel him forward, hands outstretched towards me in a pleading gesture. He was only slightly ahead of the bull who thundered after him like a huge, black bullet speeding towards a target across the green meadow. Its head was down, lowered with the exertion of movement, and I could see frothy white saliva flying from its mouth. Its eyes were black, and flat, and intense, gaze fixed hungrily on Jim as it closed the gap between them. I saw streaks of something red on its hide.

The herd closed in behind the bull, a great, surging wall of hooves and eyes and frothy, wide-open mouths with pink tongues and horrible, huge, yellowing teeth. They mooed and lowed and jostled each other as they stampeded, and the closer they got, the more excruciating my headache became, a pressure building inside my skull so great I thought my head would split open.

Jim was now only a hair's breadth away from the fence, and the gate. I extended an arm out, shakily, feeling as if I were about to faint. He crashed into the gate with the full force of his body and scrambled to get a foothold. His gaze met mine as he struggled to climb over the gate. The black, terrifying shape of the bull loomed enormous behind him.

Suddenly, I could suddenly make out every

tiny detail on his terrified face, every pore, every hair, every line and imperfection.

I stared at him, and thought about the years we'd spent together. The love I had lavished upon him, day after day, naively, as it turned out. The blind faith and trust I'd had in him, trust which had been grossly misplaced, because all along he'd been fucking this Louise woman over his office desk. I thought about all those evenings where he'd told me he had to 'work late', how I'd just thought nothing of it, praised him, in fact, for his worth ethic, his dedication.

I had a flashback, suddenly, to our conversation a few moments earlier. To Jim's face as he pleaded with me, delivering his insincere non-apology.

'I just can't keep lying to myself,' he'd said, and the words replayed themselves over and over in my throbbing, tortured head.

'Her name is Louise,' he'd said.

I felt something snap inside of me.

Our eyes locked, and my vision cleared.

My headache lifted.

I saw things as if for the first time. As if the world had been suddenly encased in a clear and solid layer of crystal.

Jim, arms stretched out towards me, looking to save him. Eyes wide with terror, mouth agape with exertion.

The bull, rising up behind him, improbably tall, breath steaming out in foul, fetid clouds, spurting through its nostrils like geysers erupting from a hot spring. It opened its mouth, and inside I saw hell.

And something else.

An opportunity.

An answer to my pain.

Revenge.

'Fuck you, Jim,' I snarled, and pushed him, hard.

He flew through the air.

His hands clutched for me as he wind-milled his arms around, trying to balance, failing... falling.

He crashed backwards into the herd.

The cows fell upon him, roaring in victory. His cries were muffled by the noises of countless hooves trampling him underfoot, countless mouths tearing into his flesh. He screamed, and I stood there, watching as the bull ripped out his intestines with two swift, sure shakes of its head. It wore them on its horns like a spring garland.

Then, it tossed its head, pawing at the ground, and stared at me, its posture dominant, a magnificent display of predation and superiority.

I reached out my hand, tentatively, and patted it on its neck, feeling the muscles under the satin-smooth sheen of its coat. Blood and entrails dripped down its horns and hung in thick, glutinous strands from its hairy lips.

I stroked the creature, gently, gazing at it in

awe.

Jim's cries had stopped. The herd closed over the top of his ruined, flattened corpse, and set to work feeding off his body.

The cows in Lower Fell don't eat grass.

I stayed with the herd, and watched until they stripped the body clean of meat, until his bones shone clean and wet through the tall, whispering grass.

Then, I watched as the bull deliberately, and with great precision, stood on what was left of Jim's skull. It groaned, and squeaked, and then finally cracked under the pressure. Pink, wet brain matter squirted out onto the soil.

I watched as a butterfly, redolent in crimson and black and orange, landed on a shard of jawbone, probing the remains of Jim's teeth with a long, curled proboscis. Its wings shuddered gently in pleasure as it supped on the red nectar of my former lover.

I turned and walked away.

Behind me, the cows of Lower Fell lowed, softly.

Gemma Amor

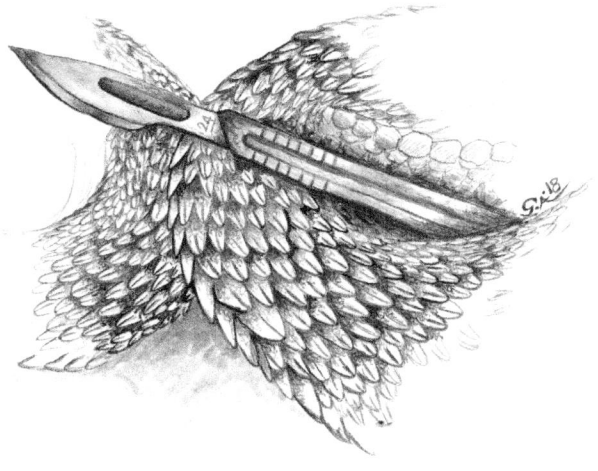

HIS LIFE'S WORK

A MAN ONCE TOLD ME THAT 'THE MOST BEAUTIFUL THING we can experience is the mysterious.'

He was apparently quoting Albert Einstein, although I did not know (or care about) this at the time. He told me this moments before trying to murder me. The sentiment, in context, was rather lost on me.

I don't think he saw it as murder, per se. I think that he saw my death as a necessity. Part of a grander scheme, a wider picture.

His name was Mr. Halo, and he told me he was a scientist. I was nothing more than part of his grand experiment, and my demise was the final piece of a jigsaw puzzle that represented his life's work.

It is a tragedy, in some respects, that he never lived to see his experiment through to its unforgettable and grisly conclusion.

It is also a tragedy, in many other respects, that I did.

❋ ❋ ❋

MR HALO'S house was the sort of house that hid in plain sight. It's hard to describe exactly what I mean, but I'll try. The house somehow avoided attention. Like a shy person at a party, it clung to the peripheral, lurked in the shadows. By which I mean you could walk by the damn thing a thousand times in a month, and not notice it at all. As indeed was the case with me. I had passed by the house many times during my working week, out on call, visiting patients around the town, but had no particular memory of it, despite this being my neighbourhood. I am not an unobservant human being, and I like to think I know my town as well as the next person, but still, as I made my way along the street and towards the place, I thought it was curious that I had never paid any real attention to this particular house before.

The property hunched down behind a low fence that was thickly entwined with ivy, honeysuckle and jasmine. Tall, spindly shrubs peered out above the fence and robbed the ground floor windows of both light, and a view of the street. The proliferation of greenery was such that I had an impression, as I walked along the road and double checked the address written on one of the many scraps of paper stuffed into my pocket, that the house was indeed camouflaging itself, reinforcing the feeling that it didn't want to be noticed at all. The property was deliberately innocuous somehow, unremarkable, a standard redbrick terraced house from the mid-thirties, not discernibly different from the house to the left of it or the house to the right. The front garden was a little unkempt but not wild, the window panes were grubby and peeling but the glass within them clean, and the outside bins were full to the brim, but lined up in an organised fashion out front.

As I approached, checking one last time that I had indeed gotten the correct address, my cheeks and eyes stinging from the bitter cold of early winter, I tried to remember my new patient's first name. My brain churned groggily through the details I'd been given: he was an elderly gentleman with a live-in carer, the latter being the person who'd made the appointment. I thought back to the notes we keep recorded on our system. The old gent had, if I remembered correctly, not long been diagnosed with suspected early onset vascular dementia. But that was not the purpose of my visit. I was there to assess two large, open sores on his lower legs, and issue a general health check following a nasty tumble he'd taken over a footstool a few days ago.

If you haven't already guessed, then I'll make it easy for you: I am a Doctor, working privately with a home healthcare organisation. I visit the elderly and the infirm, and treat them when they are unable to visit the surgery. Providing, that is, that they have enough in the way of money to pay for the privilege. I can't say I am ethically comfortable with my move to the private sector, but the pay is far superior to my previous salary, and the workload, usually, much more manageable than working for the public health sector.

The house I was currently about to visit belonged, as I said, to one Mr. Halo. My patient. First name...Rod? Derek? Jacob? The names all blurred together into a jumbled mess and I sighed. I was at the end of a week full of double-shifts. We were understaffed due to a savage outbreak of norovirus and the flu, the latter not uncommon at this time of year. When this happened, patients could not go unseen, so I picked up as many of the other visits as I could.

Mr. Halo was the last stop on that day's round. It was late afternoon, and I had been on my feet for roughly eleven hours straight. My back ached, and my neck felt stiff, as if my head had become too heavy to carry around comfortably.

I walked up the short path leading to the front door and noted all the familiar hallmarks of an elderly person's home: thick metal hand railings lining the path on either side of me, large mobility handles screwed into the wall next to the front door, a key-safe box tucked discreetly away inside the porch. I had the code for this key-safe, along with instructions to let myself in. I rooted around in my pocket for the details, pulled out another scrap of paper, and found the code. I could also see I'd written the name 'Ronald' next to the key-safe code. I breathed a sigh of relief. It always helped to relax a patient if you could use their first name. Ronald Halo. Ron to his friends? Who knew? I doubted many of his friends were still alive. My records told me that Ronald was edging towards ninety-seven years of age. The fact that he was still living in his own home was both remarkable, and worrying. Worrying because it was only a matter of time before he tripped over something else, and did more damage to himself than a gashed leg.

I punched in the code, found the spare key inside the key-safe, shouldered my bag and made my way inside, glad to get away from the biting cold December wind that had swelled up as I'd marched briskly across town.

On entering, I found that the house smelled curiously clean, and not like an elderly person's home at all. Usually, I am assaulted with a pungent aroma when first arriving at a patient's house: stale urine, more often than not, mingled with the scent of cat or dog and that all-pervasive, miserable stench of illness and infirmity that lingers so stubbornly in the air. Sometimes this is hidden clumsily under a layer of scented air-freshener, which in my opinion only serves to make the house smell worse, like putting perfume on a corpse. I hated thinking like that, but there it was. An unpleasant reality of being a Doctor who deals largely with geriatric patients.

But there was none of that smell here. In fact the house smelled like nothing in particular at all, as if someone had come along with a great vacuum cleaner and sucked all the scent from the air. I marvelled at how clean and tidy everything seemed, and put it down to the fact that Mr. Halo lived with his carer. She must do the housework too, or at least have employed a cleaner. It made a refreshing change.

I heard a growling, mewling sort of noise, and looked down. A cat perched on a threadbare hallway rug in front of me. It was fat, and old, one long front tooth dangling out from beneath its top lip. It stared at me suspiciously as I called out.

'Mr. Halo?'

No reply, but that was not unusual with a lot of my patients. They were often asleep or in the bathroom when I arrived, so I shrugged at the

Cruel Works of Nature

cat, waited a moment and called out again.

'Mr. Halo? Ronald?'

I listened hard, but still heard nothing. The house had a weird, muted quality to it that was a little unnerving.

I decided to investigate, hoping this would not be one of those dreaded days where I found my patient had quietly crossed over to the land of the dead in their sleep.

Looking around, I could see several doors leading off from the hallway, all of which were closed. I assumed the furthest door, situated at the end of the hallway in which I stood, must be the kitchen, and the other two a living room or lounge and a dining room, maybe. I hedged my bets, conscious that I didn't want to startle the old man, particularly if he was asleep. Those struggling with the early stages of dementia are often most disoriented when waking up, and I didn't want to add to his anxiety by appearing like some ghoul from the shadows.

But also, I had work to do, and I was tired myself. I didn't want to be in that one house all day, so I deliberated for a moment, and then stepped towards the door immediately to the right of me. The ancient cat continued to stare at me, his eyes giving nothing away.

I was just about to reach out and turn the door handle when I heard noise and movement behind me. It was the sound of someone approaching from the front garden, followed by the jingle of keys being drawn out of a pocket and slotted into the front door lock. I waited patiently as the door opened and revealed a small, young woman, dressed in a nurse's outfit. She must be the resident carer, the live-in nurse who enabled Mr. Halo to stay in his own home at such an advanced age. I had wondered where she was. I breathed a sigh of relief. This would make my visit a lot easier.

'Sorry, you must be the Doctor,' she panted, her eyes bright from the cold, as she bustled in. 'I meant to be back in time for your visit, but I got held up in town- bloody Christmas shoppers!'

She was slender, and pretty, and I felt myself straighten up instinctively as these facts registered. Lucky old coot, ending up with this one as his day and night nurse. She couldn't have been a minute over twenty-five, and had sparkling eyes, rosy cheeks and a smile that could stop a train dead on its tracks. I blushed a little, embarrassed at myself, and shook my head to cover my thoughts.

'No problem, 'I said, more gruffly than I'd intended. 'I was just about to look around the place and find Mr. Halo'.

'Oh, he'll be in the back, tinkering in his 'laboratory'' She smiled indulgently, as one would with a child who had a new hobby.

Laboratory? I assumed she meant a workshop, or shed, not unlike my own: a place to store tools, fiddle with electronics, fix clocks or just pretend that I was any good at DIY, which I wasn't.

The cat got up, stretched and yawned luxuriously, his old bones cracking and creaking as he moved about. He then started washing himself, bored with our chit-chat.

'Who's this?' I asked, more by way of making conversation than from any real desire to know the cat's name. I despise cats.

The nurse snorted, and I could tell she shared my disdain. 'Oh that smelly thing. That's Oppenheimer.'

'Oppenheimer?'

The nurse smiled again. 'I see you've not met Mr. Halo before.'

I shook my head, my curiosity piqued. 'I don't follow.'

'Mr. Halo is... was... a Scientist, you see. Oppenheimer was...'

'I know who Oppenheimer was.' I smiled so that I did not appear patronising. I found myself becoming more intrigued by the minute. I was also, however, becoming acutely aware of the time, which was slipping away. I glanced at my watch and the Nurse understood.

'Sorry,' she apologised again. 'We mustn't keep you. I'll show you through.'

I gestured silently and she walked ahead of me. I tried hard to keep my eyes fixed at shoulder-level, feeling once again a little embarrassed at how I was behaving around the Nurse. She was nothing but friendly and professional, what on earth was I doing, leering surreptitiously like some horrible old pervert?

'Here we are,' she said, abruptly interrupting my train of thought, and I jumped, guiltily.

She opened what I had earlier assumed to be the kitchen door, only now, as it swung noiselessly on well-oiled hinges, I could see I was very wrong. I had also been wrong to assume that the 'laboratory' the nurse had mentioned earlier was some sort of shed, or cubby hole.

My mouth dropped open. I stared.

What lay before me, illuminated with countless bright lights, was a large, sterile, organised and incredibly well equipped laboratory.

I don't mean it was decked out with test-tubes, a Bunsen burner and a few petri-dishes. I mean a fullblown, scientific laboratory, that looked state-of-the-art in terms of its dimensions and the equipment installed within. For a moment I couldn't process what I was seeing fully. I'd been so sure that I was about to walk into a kitchen. I acclimated to my unexpectedly futuristic surroundings.

It was obvious, the more I looked, that this had indeed once been a kitchen, although long ago. The tell-tale signs were still there. Gas pipes now sealed off, old food cupboards that had been re-purposed as storage cabinets, an old oven hood that had doubled as an extractor fan. You had to look hard for these clues, however. The sense

Cruel Works of Nature

of purpose and industry was so intense in the lab, that it was hard to imagine it had ever been anything else than what it was- a vast, organised space filled with tubes, pipes, computers, screens and machinery that I simply had no knowledge of, things I'd never seen in my life before, and I'd been to my fair share of labs in my time.

A pristine, white polished counter ran around the circumference of the laboratory, broken only by the indents made by the door we were standing in, and a large door set into the wall at the other end, which I assumed led into the rear garden. The door at the far end had an odd feel to it, something that I couldn't quite put my finger on, and it jarred the vision somehow, jogging something in my mind, although I couldn't determine what. It was lined with a thick layer of what looked like silver-backed insulating foam, and in the centre of the door, there was a huge mechanical lock, or at least, what I assumed was a lock. It had masses of wires coming out of it like tendrils of coiled, yellow hair. The wires led to various machines, and those led to various other machines. An alarm system maybe? Some sort of battery for the door to make it open automatically? Who knew? It seemed a very complicated way of getting into one's own back garden.

In the centre of the room, in between myself and the far door, was a chair, an examining chair not unlike those you find at the dentist's. Leaning over this chair, humming to himself loudly enough to be heard over the cacophony of beeps, whistles, pings, squeaks and rumbles that the assorted machines and tubes emitted around him, was an old man. Mr. Halo, I presumed. He was tinkering with one arm of the chair, a flat-headed screwdriver clamped between his teeth, a pair of tweezers in one hand and a soldering iron in the other.

I watched him for a moment as he worked, reluctant to surprise him and also intimidated by the sparkling clean lab that was his kingdom. I glanced down at my shoes and checked for mud. There didn't seem to be any, which was something. The thought of tracking dirt across the flawlessly white floor made my skin crawl.

Mr. Halo soldered some loose wires together in a small recess in the chair's headrest. As the soldering iron hissed and the molten metal sizzled, he called out over his shoulder.

'You can come in, I don't mind dirty feet!' he said, sounding jovial.

I jumped. So much for not surprising him.

The nurse, who I'd forgotten about, and who was clearly enjoying my reaction to all this, patted me on the arm sympathetically, that humorous twinkle still there in her eyes. 'I have some jobs to do,' she said, kindly. 'I'll leave you gentlemen to it. Call if you need a hand with anything.' I couldn't figure out if she was talking to me, or to Mr. Halo, but before I could think about it any further, she exited the door through which she'd come, and closed it softly behind her.

For a second, I thought I heard a noise like that of a bolt being drawn into place, but the door was insulated like its partner across the lab, and the noise was so muffled it was impossible to tell for sure. I shook my head, feeling annoyed at myself. As if she would lock me in here with him.

I stared at Mr. Halo, but didn't say anything for a few moments. Truth be told, I was discombobulated by the whole scenario: the house, this lab, my patient's apparent state of tremendous energy and health. As visits go, I was well out of my comfort zone, and found myself wishing instead for some poor old lady with a bad cough who did nothing more adventurous than sit in front of her television all day. Something I could treat simply and quickly, with no real drama. This was already turning out to be one of the most peculiar visits I'd ever made. I wasn't sure I had the energy for any more surprises.

'Come in, and know me better, man!' chuckled Mr. Halo.

I moved across the lab hesitantly. Mr. Halo straightened, stretched, and turned to greet me properly, setting down the tools on a metal trolley standing nearby, and pushing a thick pair of glasses up to the top of his head.

'Welcome,' he said, extending a hand to shake my own. I accepted the handshake and returned it lamely, feeling as if I had wandered somehow into the twilight zone. Mr. Halo was old, but looked nothing like the ninety-odd years he was meant to have under his belt. At a glance, I would have said seventy, at the most.

As I said previously, I specialise in treating the elderly, which means I've met a good number of aged men and women in my time, many of them in their nineties. But I can safely say I have never met anyone who looked as good as Mr. Halo looked at his age. I tried hard to mask my shock as I continued to study his face.

His eyes, a deep shade of blue, were bright and clear, with no fogginess, no thick, milky cataracts. The glasses on top of his head appeared to be more for his protection against the soldering iron than for poor vision, and his gaze locked onto mine with a fierce intensity that took me aback. He had the stare of a hunter, and reminded me somewhat of an eagle. His profile reinforced this impression. He had a strong, hooked nose and a prominent brow with great, white, sweeping eyebrows perched high up on his forehead. His hair was a smoothly coiffed mass of thick, white thatch, that showed no signs of thinning, or falling out.

All in all, he was a picture of health. He was tall, taller than me, and I'm a tall man, and he barely stooped, although when I shook his hand I sensed a nagging pain perhaps in one shoulder, because he withdrew his hand quickly, one eye twitching in that tell-tale sign, although not before gripping my fingers so tightly I winced. The old coot was trying to impress upon me how strong he was, and suddenly, I felt back in familiar territory. My patients always struggled to admit that there was anything wrong with their health, or that they needed help from me. They bore their stoicism like a badge of honour, pride being everything when you are so old you have little else left to call your own. Mr. Halo was no different, it seemed. Despite everything, I began to relax a little.

He was watching me still, and then he smiled, and I was reminded again of a predator. The smile was sharp, and his eyes gleamed. *You old wolf,* I thought to myself, swallowing. *What's your game?* A machine pinged softly behind him, and then began to spit out a long, thin stream of paper, a readout of some sort. He rubbed his hands in glee, and ignored me completely as he tore off the readout and began mumbling to himself as he scanned through the contents.

Was this how the dementia was manifesting itself? In obsessive collecting, tinkering, messing about with machines? Was any of this stuff even safe to be around? Some of those test tubes were smoking, giving off coloured gasses occasionally. Other machines sparked, and crackled with what I assumed must be electricity. Was this grand experiment, whatever it was, even stable, or was I about to be blown into the stratosphere by a mad old scientist?

I glanced around at the laboratory, wondering again what all the equipment was for. Scientist, the nurse had said. Was he? Or was it something more sinister than that? Was he merely going through the motions, trying to keep in touch with his past before he lost his mind completely? He wouldn't be the first old man in denial to try to recapture his youth before his memories dissolved.

Or was he indeed still working? Given his apparent fitness and health, it was a real possibility. Perhaps he was volunteering for a scientific institute. Maybe he was one of those types of folks that needed to keep working, or give up: it was not uncommon for men, in particular, to fall into ill health shortly after they retired, as there was simply nothing useful for them to do any more. Maybe he'd decided to keep going, rather than sit about growing fat and soft and useless. I had to admire him for it, if that was the case.

He interrupted my train of thought. 'You're wondering what all this is about, I suppose,' he said.

Mad or not, I couldn't get drawn into this anymore. I had a job to do. I took a deep breath. 'Well actually, Ronald, I'm here to take a look at those legs of yours.'

I gestured to his lower legs, hidden behind perfectly pressed and creased trousers. I could see what looked like a damp patch spreading just below his left knee, a wound that was leaking

Cruel Works of Nature

through a dressing, no doubt. Mr. Halo seemed to pay it no heed.

'Ron,' he said, jovially, and I nodded in acknowledgement.

'I'm Doctor Richardson,' I offered, looking for somewhere to put my medical bag. 'Or Robert, if you prefer first names. Now let's take a look at those legs.'

Mr. Halo smiled, and cleared a space for me on the polished counter. I put my bag down carefully, and motioned for the other man to sit down. Seeing as there was a large examining chair already available in the middle of the room, I waved speculatively at it, eyebrows raised in query.

My patient chuckled to himself, and moved obligingly over to the chair.

'I'll need those trouser legs rolled up, please,' I said, in the no-nonsense tone that I found worked best with my patients. He bent over with no problem, no mean feat for a man of his years, and nimbly rolled up both trouser legs. Then he perched gingerly on the chair, which was, on closer inspection, a real piece of work. It looked antique. I had seen an Italian vintage barber's chair much like this in a trendy salon in town. It was at odds with the rest of the room and the modern, minimalist technology and equipment that surrounded us. It had a deeply upholstered seat lined with thick, smooth, black leather. The arms and footrest were worked from what looked like highly polished chrome, with pads set into each arm for comfort. Ornate scrolls of moulded metal formed a footplate that was raised up on gleaming, cast chrome arms. It was set into a large, round base with a pedal attached to the chair's stem to enable someone to raise, or lower the seat to whatever height was convenient. The more I looked, the more I saw true workmanship oozing out of every curve, every surface. It dominated the room in the same way that Mr. Halo dominated the room, in an unexpected, commandeering manner.

The most noticeable thing about the chair, aside from its unexpected beauty, was that it seemed to be fully plumbed in, so to speak. Wires and tubes came out of each arm, the headrest, and the underside of the chair, and travelled to each corner of the laboratory where they were assimilated by machinery or fed into a computer, of which there seemed to be dozens. I wondered idly how he could afford all of this gear in his retirement. Clearly his pension was a lot healthier than mine would ever be.

I shook myself, aware that I was being distracted, again. I longed for this visit to be over so that I could go home and sleep. My eyes felt scratchy, and dry, and my head was beginning to throb. These long shifts were killing me.

I knelt down to look at my patient's legs. They were indeed weeping, the two sores hidden behind stained dressings that looked freshly applied. The nurse had obviously been keeping the wounds as clean and sterile as possible. I nodded in approval, and carefully cut the bandages away.

We kept a polite silence for a few moments as I worked to remove the bandages, and then peered at the wounds on both legs. I hissed slightly in sympathy when I saw the deep, long gashes in both shins. 'Took a real tumble, did you Ronald?' I said, stating the obvious but hoping to imbue a sense of normality into the situation. 'This must have bled a lot.'

Mr. Halo snorted agreeably. 'It did that. There was blood all over the floor, it was most inconvenient. Still, you don't get to my age without tumbling over now and then, Dr. Richardson.' I nodded my head in assent, and put my face closer to the wounds, prodding the skin around the gashes gently, looking for any signs of swelling, or discolouration, indicating infection. The elderly man did not move a muscle as I did this, although it must have hurt. He sat there motionless, statuesque, reminding me of that damned eagle again, watching, waiting, and staring down at the top of my head. I grew uncomfortable under his gaze, and busied myself with more conversation.

'Well, it looks like the nurse has got things nicely under control, although it's always best to double check. There's not much more I can do at this point, I don't think it needs stitches. They are seeping a little, but there doesn't seem to be any sign of infection, or sepsis. Keep the lacerations clean and dry for at least another week, and call me again if it looks like it's not beginning to heal, or starts smelling bad, or leaking anything yellow or pussy instead of clear liquid.' I began unravelling a clean dressing from my medical bag.

The man grunted dismissively, as so many men of his age do when asked to do something.

'Catherine will keep an eye on it for me. I'm afraid I'm not much good at looking after myself.' I chuckled, dryly.

'Who is, these days? I'd be lost without my wife telling me where I am supposed to be all the time. Besides, I can see you're somewhat... preoccupied.' I thought it was time to face up to the elephant in the room, and gestured to the lab, one eyebrow raised quizzically.

'I mean, with all this equipment...Are you inventing a time machine?' I said, jokingly, wrapping his legs in fresh bandages.

'No, no, not a time machine.' Mr. Halo managed to somehow look dignified and predatory even with his trousers rolled up to his knees, knees which were curiously hairless. I felt more as if I were polishing his boots than providing a medical service, and did not like the sensation at all.

'Whatever it is looks highly involved,' I said

neutrally, trying to keep my growing dislike of the man out of my voice.

'This?' he said, sighing and gesturing with his hands theatrically thrown wide for emphasis.

'This is not just involved, Dr. Richardson. Robert. No, sir. This is my life's work.'

He said it as if making a grand announcement, with a sense of rhythm and ritual attached to the words. He leaned forward, and I had to stop myself from flinching away. The more I was around him, the more my instincts told me that something was very off with this man's brain.

'You're a man of science, Doctor, as much as human biology can be called a science, I suppose.'

I blinked, but didn't have the energy to be offended by his snobbery.

He continued, his voice echoing sonorously around the otherwise muted laboratory.

'Tell me, do you believe in God? Heaven? Hell? An afterlife?'

I shook my head, slowly. 'Sadly, not. I am an atheist.' I continued hesitantly, not sure what answer the old man expected. 'There doesn't seem to be anything in science that proves those things exist, at least not to my meagre knowledge'. I wondered at how I was suddenly being drawn on matters of theosophy. That confident, arrogant way of questioning. The self-aggrandising behaviour. It wasn't normal in a man. How I longed suddenly for my bed.

'You are not alone, Dr. Richardson. I myself, a firm follower of science, an acolyte of Newton and Einstein and Galileo, of Hawkins and Schrodinger, I remain, as you would expect, firmly sceptical. But, as Einstein said, 'the most beautiful thing we can experience is the mysterious', and I am inclined to agree.

'You say there is not much in the way of scientific proof of life after death, or other existences. But I put it to you also that no-one, thus far, has been able to provide definitive, scientific proof that these things do *not* exist.'

I sat back on my heels, drawn further into the conversation despite myself. 'And so, what, you're trying to disprove the theory of... God?' I said, frowning and trying to keep the incredulity out of my voice.

He leaned down and hissed at me ferociously. 'Not quite, Dr. Richardson. Not quite. What I am trying to do is to explore the bounds of what we know of as reality. To see if there is, in fact, something beyond all of this.' He gestured again, by which I assumed he meant the world, not just this bizarre terraced house with its bizarre, secret laboratory hidden within.

'I am in the business of debunking the mysterious, Dr. Richardson,' the old man continued, and I noticed a faint line of sweat collecting on his top lip. He was growing excited, and as his excitement grew, I became more and more nervous. I felt as if he were building up to something, and regretted not taking the diagnosis of his mental deterioration more seriously. This kind of nonsensical, delusional ranting fitted very well into the dementia profile.

'Right, well. That does sound fascinating, Mr. Halo. Ronald.' I fumbled to find the right words, trying to remember that patients with delusions this strong do not like to be reminded of reality, or argued with, or made to see reason. It upsets them. 'Debunking the mysterious. Trying to find...another dimension, or world, beyond this one?' I surreptitiously packed away my equipment and rose, hoping he wouldn't notice that I was about to edge towards the door through which I'd come.

Mr. Halo didn't reply, just watched me instead. He then rose, and moved towards me, suddenly, as I stepped hurriedly back. I started, and he spoke in a lowered, almost hushed voice.

'It's been my life's work, *Robert*,' he said, and I could tell he was mocking me for having used his first name so informally earlier on. He moved closer and closer. My hands began to sweat, and my heart began pounding in my chest, so loudly that I thought he could surely hear it.

'My life's work,' he repeated, 'Just to get this far. To calibrate the machines, make the calculations, do the maths, procure the equipment, make the hypotheses. I've been laughed at and spurned by scientific institutions all over the world. They think I'm a hack, but what they don't know is that everything I have done has led me towards this day, this momentous day, when I put the final piece of my experiment in place.'

I had heard enough. I turned hastily to find the door handle, needing to get some distance between myself and this creepy old fanatic and his creepy laboratory. I was tired. I needed my bed.

But there was someone in my way. I stopped in my tracks. The door was blocked by a figure, dressed in a white nurse's outfit. Catherine. She was smiling at me in a brisk, blank, no-nonsense manner, and clutching a huge syringe filled with a clear liquid.

Before I knew what was happening, she thrust the needle of the syringe into my neck, held me by the throat with surprising force, and depressed the plunger.

I felt something cold slide into my veins, and then I began to feel woozy.

'What the fuck...' I mumbled, as I collapsed slowly, slumping against the nurse who held me firmly against her small frame. I heard Mr. Halo let out a deep, satisfied breath and finish his speech.

'My whole life, building up to this one sweet moment, Doctor. Imagine how that feels, can you? Something you poured your heart, your whole being into, every day of your adult existence, ever since you were a young, gangly man with not a penny in his pocket.'

Cruel Works of Nature

My eyes rolled in my head, and I could not keep them open. 'What...' I muttered hopelessly again, and I felt the nurse hook her hands under my armpits to hold my increasing deadweight.

Mr. Halo continued to eulogise.

'Words cannot tell you what I am feeling right now, Doctor. You see, today, I will know the answers to my questions, either way. And what I've been lacking, Dr. Richardson, is that knowledge, that certainty. Well, that isn't the only thing I've been lacking. I've also been without a worthy test subject. There was just no need for one before this point in the experiment. But now... well, I must say, it's so kind of you to volunteer like this. To donate your body to science...that takes real courage.'

I fell into a deep, black hole of unconsciousness, a distant part of me hoping that this was nothing more than a bad dream, a nightmare from which I would wake.

It was not.

❊ ❊ ❊

I OPENED my eyes and found myself dazzled by several glaring beams of light, from standing lamps trained on my face. It took seconds for me to realise where I was. I felt cold leather against my skin, and cool chrome. My feet were elevated, and supported by a large, solid footplate.

I was in the chair.

I jerked, and began to struggle. I found quickly that I was strapped in. I lay there panting, panic coursing through my body in thick, hot waves.

I gradually grew accustomed to the stark lighting, and began to slowly make out the shape of Mr. Halo, standing above me. He materialised gradually, his body morphing from a thin, fuzzy shadow into the shape of a tall, insane man.

'Hello Dr. Richardson,' he said, reaching out a hand to adjust something above my head. Whatever it was tugged against my scalp, as if it were attached to me. I hissed in pain.

He straightened up, turned to an electrical panel beside him, and hit a switch, mumbling to himself ceaselessly a sort of mantra that sounded not unlike a mathematical equation. My eyes widened, and bulged as I felt the chair move beneath me, and I realised it was rigged up to some sort of power source. Then I realised that it was rotating, steadily at first, and then with greater speed, until it came to a hard halt, having spun me a hundred and eighty degrees.

I moaned, feeling sick. A gag tied tightly across my mouth muffled and distorted my voice horribly. I now faced the far door, the one that was festooned with wires and cables, the door that held that bizarre, huge metal lock into which all the wiring ran.

The door was as unsettling now as it had been before, and I suddenly realised why that was.

I had found the rest of the house and laboratory strangely devoid of odour, but now, as I faced the back door, my nostrils began twitching. A foul smell leaked into the air from the direction of that far wall, and within moments, it had become overwhelming. I gagged against my bonds, finding it suddenly hard to breathe. It was a smell like no other, a smell of disease, of sickness, of decaying organic matter; of rot, stale sweat, and bodily secretions. I knew it to be the smell of the dead, or dying. The smell of the hopeless, the ill at ease, the smell of people whose lives had run their painful, fraught course, and were now drawing to a close.

With all my training, and all my years of exposure to that smell, I was still unprepared for the sheer force of it. I fought to retain the contents of my stomach. The bile rose, and I swallowed it urgently, but it rose again. I began to buck and strain against my bonds once more, knowing I wouldn't be able to hold the vomit in any longer, and not wanting to drown myself in it. I tried to lean forward as I heaved involuntarily. My skin broke out in a cold sweat, and my arms and legs began to tingle.

A pair of thin, strong hands whipped the gag from my mouth, and then Mr Halo was there. He swung a plastic bowl underneath my chin just in time to catch the torrid fountain of hot, steaming puke that erupted from me. I heaved, and heaved, the smell, that awful, awful smell getting inside my mouth, up my nostrils, into my ears and throat and everywhere, all over me, like a horrible, slimy, second skin, suffocating me with its putrescence. I vomited until there was nothing left in my stomach, and then I dry-heaved for a good ten minutes, unable to do anything else but succumb to the sickness.

Eventually, exhausted, I slumped back into the chair, and that's when I felt it, that's when I realised what had felt odd about my body. I hadn't been able to process it upon waking, but now I could see, and feel, something that made me cry out in panic once more.

Wires. There were wires coming out of me. And tubes. Sprouting from my legs, my arms, the backs of my hands, even my temples. I was plugged into the chair like a battery, and as my eyes, watering in pain, followed the lines of the tubing, I saw that they in turn connected with the wires that fed into the door, or more specifically, into that great door lock in the centre of the door. I was wired into the lock.

I felt a twinge in my left leg, a tugging sort of twinge that corresponded with the nurse making a movement to one side of me. She watched me as she worked, a small, amused grin on her face. I stared, and realised she was typing on one of the laptops connected to the chair. My left leg twanged again, and I yelled out as I saw my blood draining out of me, slowly, through the tube jammed into my skin just above my left ankle.

'Why are you doing this?' I moaned, finding my voice at last. 'What do you want from me?!' Dull pain began to creep up my leg, and my arms. I saw red liquid whizz past my peripheral, my blood, sucked from my skull like water from a tap, inching along the tubing, making its way inexorably towards the door lock with a terrible speed and finality.

'Why are you doing this?' I repeated, sobbing. 'Why don't you just get on with it and kill me?!'

'Don't be ridiculous,' said Mr. Halo, scoffing at my lack of imagination. 'I'm not interested in your body.' Catherine handed him a thin metal case, from which he drew a sharp, gleaming surgical scalpel. I began to whine in fear again, struggling against my bonds, acutely aware of my own sordid stench: vomit, fear, and piss. A warm patch soaked into my trousers. The nurse raised an eyebrow as she saw the damp spot on my groin spread. She shook her head, tutted.

Mr. Halo continued. 'No, no. Our bodies are immaterial, just a fleshy housing for what really counts, inside.' He tapped my trussed-up head with a long finger. *Oh God. Oh God,* I thought. *He's going to cut open my head. He's going to remove my brain.* I heaved again, but there was nothing left inside of me to bring up.

He continued, examining the blade under the powerful lamps overhead. 'I've never been able to understand the human obsession with our physical forms. They are such a mundane part of our overall existence, something to feed and hydrate occasionally, to exercise now and then. Even our brains, these swollen organs that set us so high above our natural peers, these lumps of grey matter that elevate us from bird, dog, cow and ape- well, it's all just water, and fat, sitting there, waiting to decay, like the rest of us eventually will.'

I tried to speak, the words coming out as a strained, raw croak.

'You're... fucking... insane!' I managed, before breaking into a coughing fit. My throat felt like it was on fire. I kept staring at the door, my eyes drawn to it unbidden, the smell still there, although not as overpowering now as it had been moments before.

'I'm not insane, Doctor. I simply have a mission, to complete my life's work before I die. And for that to happen, I need something from you, something that will complete my experiment. Now. Enough talking. Are you ready?'

'Noooooo!' I screamed, and he swung the scalpel down hard.

I felt the blade enter my right eye socket, felt the eye within resist momentarily, and then the contents of my eyeball began slowly sliding down my cheek. I screamed, and screamed, and yet somehow, above the sounds of my own terror and agony, I was still able to hear Mr. Halo say, with an astonishing brand of clinical detachment, the following:

'I don't need your body, Dr. Richardson. I need your soul.'

And with that, he thrust the scalpel into my other eye socket, and then everything went blissfully, mercifully black.

* * *

I AWOKE for the second time in the chair, and found I was spinning, whirling around in circles so fast that I could feel my hair standing on end.

And despite everything, despite the ruined mess of my eyeballs flooding down across my cheeks, despite the searing pain in my head from the double stab wounds, despite the taste of my own blood pouring into my mouth and the sound of droplets splattering around the room as I spun, faster, and faster, I could, somehow, unbelievably... *see*.

I could see the door, which stayed strangely and firmly locked into view, despite the fact that I was hurtling around in a three hundred and sixty degree arc every twenty seconds or so. Was it possible? Was it... growing *larger*, the more I spun? It grew, and grew, until it almost filled my vision. I could see the tubes feeding my blood into the lock, the wiring carefully arranged so that it did not tangle or interfere with the spinning motion.

The frantic sounds of machines working overtime echoed all around me. Things beeped, and chortled, and groaned in a deafening crescendo of hellish noise, and I thought to myself: *This isn't real. I've gone mad. I'm hallucinating.*

My eyes. He took my eyes.

I spun faster still, until it felt that my body would surely fly apart into little pieces, and then I realised dully that the word I had thought of earlier, 'battery', was an apt one. I knew enough about basic physics to understand what a centrifuge was. As I rotated, faster and faster around the fixed point that the chair was anchored to, I knew that I was being drained of my life's energy, that I was hooked up to this chair for a purpose, and that purpose could only be to open the door into which I was plugged.

As I spun faster, I began to black out again. The chair slowed ever so slightly, and my consciousness recovered. Then the chair sped up, and this pattern carried on for what felt like hours, with me drifting in and out of the blackness like a jet pilot in free-fall.

Then, when I felt sure that I could take no more, when my very skin felt ready to burst with momentum, the chair slowed, one last time.

I could hear Mr. Halo and his assistant nurse panting in anticipation behind me.

The lock on the door began to glow an unearthly, toxic shade of yellow, and it was...humming, no- *pulsing*.

Cruel Works of Nature

The glow grew brighter, and as it did, I felt a curious lifting sensation inside my body, as if something were freeing itself from me. The hollow emptiness it left behind was all-consuming. My mouth opened in a wordless cry of immense pain, and loss, and grief.

The glow reached a critical point of brightness that threatened to wash everything in the room away, and then suddenly, the lock melted, the thick iron running down the door and pooling into a molten puddle on the laboratory floor.

'*Yes!*' screamed Mr. Halo, jumping up and down on the spot. The nurse wiped tears away from her eyes, her chest heaving.

The door opened.

Mr. Halo collapsed to his knees clumsily, his own tears running down his cheeks. 'My life's work,' he whispered, looking suddenly old, ancient, and decrepit.

At this point, I was beyond caring about what happened to me. I watched through my bloody, pulpy eyeballs, detached, spent, my purpose served.

And that's when the things began to slither in through the open doorway.

Mr. Halo cried out, overwhelmed, in a state of rapture, as the beasts hissed and slid into the laboratory, looking about themselves with an avid, hungry curiosity.

Catherine shrieked, began running for the door that led back into the hallway. She never made even halfway across the lab. A creature, its body long, scaled, and lithe, like that of a giant snake, pounced upon her, the great muscled coils of its tail acting as a lasso. Its rough skin bulged, and rippled, and I thought for a second that I could make out the shape of faces underneath, mouths agape, hands pushing against the skin from the inside, trying to claw their way out.

The beast turned to look at me as it took hold of the nurse. Its head was completely, perfectly humanoid in appearance. Staring at me with a grinning, insane and vulpine malice was the face of a man, a thick-set man with dark hair and long, yellowing teeth like those of the cat who had greeted me as I entered into this damned house all those hours ago.

It smiled, and I began to cackle madly as it wrapped the nurse up in its loving embrace. My brain was stretched as tight as an elastic band about to snap, and yet still, somehow, I clung to a small semblance of sanity, enough to remain present, enough to watch the spectacle unfolding before me.

The petite nurse struggled, and choked, her cries becoming more and more strangled and futile as the coils tightened. I could hear her bones cracking, her skin tearing, see her eyes bulging in that once pretty face. She grew first red, then purple, and then blue. Blood seeped out of her. Her body split open like overripe fruit underfoot.

The man-snake squeezed the life clean out of her, until she looked like a limp, discarded, bloody glove.

Then, impossibly, it unhinged its human jaw and opened its mouth wide, wider than I could now comprehend. It fed the nurse into its massive maw slowly, methodically. I watched, empty, as she disappeared, inch by inch, until only the soles of her feet were left. The faces underneath the skin writhed and shrieked in a wordless frenzy.

The feet disappeared, and the human face relaxed, contented.

'Beautiful,' said Mr. Halo, softly, as the second beast made its way resolutely across the room towards him, mouth opening in readiness, and at that point, my brain finally, blissfully gave up, and I fainted for the last time.

* * *

IN THE BLACKNESS THAT FOLLOWED, I dreamed. I heard

muted, distant screams and animal noises in my sleep, felt heat against my skin, tasted blood and ash in my mouth.

Then, as a high-pitched whine climbed higher and higher in tone until it threatened to scrape out the insides of my skull, everything was suddenly obliterated by the noise of a colossal explosion.

There was a sense of everything falling in on itself, of gravity disappearing and of my body, floating, despite still being strapped to the infernal chair.

Then, I dreamed no more.

※ ※ ※

YOU MAY BE SURPRISED to learn that I did not die.

I have no idea what terrible land was on the other side of the door that my blood and soul unlocked. I am never likely to know. When they found me, I lay in the middle of a blackened pile of smoking, charred rubble. Electrical fire and gas explosion, someone told me, much later. No surprise with all the dodgy equipment Mr. Halo had crammed into his house. A wonder the whole street didn't go up. I was lucky, they told me. It was a miracle that I'd survived at all.

I didn't feel lucky. It didn't feel like a miracle.

It felt as if someone had violated my body, and stolen my soul.

At any rate, they found no trace of Mr. Halo, and no trace of the nurse, Catherine, either.

Most importantly, the door had disappeared completely. Obliterated by the explosion, the only thing that remained was a hardened lump of molten metal and a few charred, yellow electrical cables.

I've since retired. I spend my days at home, in bed, living modestly, and quietly with my wife. My injuries and burns were severe, but not life-threatening, although my survival remains the stuff of legend back in the town hospital.

My eyes are ruined, punctured and to all intents and purposes, now redundant. I wear patches over them, or thick, dark glasses wherever possible to avoid frightening anyone with my ravaged appearance. My specialist tells me I have adapted remarkably well to having no sight. I don't have the heart to tell her that I can still see, somehow. Perfectly well, in fact.

Just not with my eyes.

And there are times when I wish so hard that I couldn't see anything, anymore. My whole concept of what is reality and what is not has been entirely rearranged. Is there a God? Very possibly. Hell? Another dimension, an alternative reality? Yes.

Albert Einstein's words come back to haunt me on a daily basis as I struggle to process what happened. They are bitter words to me now. Beauty may be found in the mysterious, but I want no part of that. I'm not a scientist, after all, and have no desire to be. I crave no legacy, and will leave none behind, for the portal has vanished, mercifully.

Except sometimes, I wonder. I wonder if something remained, something that slipped through the door. Occasionally, as I drift off into sleep, or if I'm lost in a daydream, I hear things, sibilant noises in the distance.

The sound of slithering, of sliding, of scaled skin travelling over rough ground at speed. The sound mingles with another.

The sound of laughter, of high-pitched, terrible laughter.

Beauty to be found in the mysterious?

You can keep it.

Cruel Works of Nature

SPECIAL DELIVERY

THE DOORBELL ALWAYS RINGS WHEN YOU ARE DOING ONE OF the following things: sitting in the tub, sitting on the john, or taking a shower. When my doorbell rang, I was doing the latter. It was a bright and sunny morning. Light poured in through my frosted bathroom window like syrup. I sang along to my favourite song on the shower radio. Yes, I have a shower radio. I like music. I *adore* music. A hot shower, and a hearty singalong is a marriage made in heaven.

Cruel Works of Nature

So I was kind of pissed when the shrill ringing of my front doorbell sounded out halfway through my rendition of *Unchained Melody*. I put down the shampoo bottle I'd been using as a microphone, and stuck my head out of the shower curtain.

'I'm not here!' I yelled in exasperation above the noise of running water and music. There was a moment's silence, and the doorbell rang again.

'I said, *I'm not here!*' I shouted, hoping whoever it was would get the message and piss off.

Another shrill ring carried up the stairs.

'Fuck it,' I muttered to myself, and put my head back under the stream of hot water. They'd go away if I kept ignoring them.

The doorbell rang another three times. On the third ring, whoever was at my door held their finger down on the bell button hard and long, so the ringing kept coming in a hideous, continuous assault.

'Okay, okay!' I yelled, switching off the shower and the music in a fit of pique, struggling to grab a towel, slipping on the wet tiled floor and stubbing my toe against the doorframe as I scrambled out of the bathroom.

'Owww, fuck!' I swore, hopping up and down on one foot while the fucking front doorbell continued to ring out like a fire alarm. My blood began to boil.

'*I'm coming!*' I screamed, wrapping the towel around my waist and limping down the stairs.

Whoever was out there was going to get a mouthful of righteous abuse. I *hated* having my morning shower interrupted. It put my whole day off-centre. And my toe hurt. I was half-naked, dripping wet, and hopping mad.

'This had better be fucking good!' I roared as I reached the front door, and ripped it open.

'This had better be *really* fucking...oh.'

'Hi,' said the woman outside, taking her elegant index finger off the bell, and smiling at me.

I gulped. Standing on my front porch, holding a large, brown cardboard parcel and dressed smartly in a brown UPS uniform, was the most gorgeous woman I'd ever seen in my life.

Her hair was a deep, rich red. It was pulled into a loose ponytail underneath her brown cap, thick, and long enough to tickle the top of her ass. Her skin was pale, and she had freckles. Her eyes were green. Her lips were pink and full.

Holy fuckballs, I thought to myself.

She smiled, displaying a perfect set of white, even teeth.

'Hi,' she said again in a husky, thick voice. 'I gotta delivery for a Mr. Ben Andrews?'

I became acutely aware of myself, and surreptitiously checked to see that my towel was still in place. I stared at her dumbly, and shook my head, unable to get my mouth to work.

'Hello?' said the UPS woman, smiling again. 'Anyone home, sir?'

I blushed, and snapped out of it. 'Um, yeah,

sorry. That's me.'

'Well, phew for that! Sorry to pull you out of your shower, but you gotta sign for this one, and I'm not allowed to take it back to the depot. Special instructions.' She had a jaunty, almost cocky way of speaking that I found adorable. She oozed confidence and warmth. Strands of red hair fell around her face from underneath the cap, and glinted in the sunlight. She was a stone-cold knockout.

I looked at the parcel. It was big, about the size of a box of old vinyl.

'What is it?' I said, trying to see if there was a delivery label or other clue. 'Who's it from? I'm not expecting a delivery...'

'Afraid I can't help you with that sir. I'm just the postman, or post lady, if you prefer. Now, can I give you this? It's kind of heavy.'

'Oh, shit, sure. Sorry.' I hastily reached out to take the parcel from her, and my towel slipped. I caught it in time to save my decency, but almost dropped the package in the process.

'Shit,' I swore under my breath, crimson with embarrassment.

The UPS lady sighed, and then laughed. 'Okay, how about this. You run upstairs, put some pants on, and I'll carry this into the kitchen for you. Then you can come back and sign for it. Going to have to be quick, though. I've got a schedule to keep to.'

I smiled back, sheepishly. 'Kitchen's right in

front of you. Thank you,' I said, and bolted upstairs.

I scrambled around in my drawers for underwear and a pair of pants, dragged a shirt over my head, ran my fingers through my wet hair, checked my teeth for any leftover breakfast, and took a deep, shuddering breath to compose myself.

I made my way downstairs with more grace than I had the first time. UPS lady was waiting in my kitchen, staring at the photos pinned to the front of my refrigerator.

'You like to drink at The Blue Lagoon too, huh? Over on Cheshire Bridge?' She pointed to a Polaroid picture someone had taken of me and my buddies at the aforementioned bar. We had that drunk, happy, bleached-out look young people get in pictures when they've been boozing.

'Funny I've never seen you there.' She put the parcel down on the kitchen table, and took out her electronic scanning device, holding out the attached pen for me. 'Sign here please,' she continued, moving closer so that I could reach the signature screen easily. I flushed again, aware of her proximity. I stammered a reply.

'Sure, ah, yes. Yeah, I mean, we go there a bit. Or I used to. I don't get out much these days, I have to admit. I'm taking a break from the booze for a while.'

UPS lady gestured to one of the men in the photo with me. 'That's Steve, right? I know him.'

'Really?' My eyebrows shot up. 'No way! We were at college together. Haven't seen him for a while. He's...kind of...pissed with me at the moment.' I rubbed the back of my head and looked around the kitchen, avoiding her eyes.

'Oh really?' UPS woman slotted the pen back in its holder on the device, and hooked it back on her belt. She didn't seem in a hurry to leave, despite her earlier protestations. 'Why, what did you do?'

'What did I do?'

'Yeah. What did you do to piss off Steve?'

I flushed red with embarrassment. 'I sort of...ahh...I can't tell you that, actually.'

'Oh come on,' she wheedled, her thick, velvet voice coaxing at my secrets like a snake charmer piping a cobra out of a basket. 'You can tell me. I'm just your friendly local UPS lady.'

'Yeah, but if you know Steve, then...'

'I said I know him, but I didn't say how well. We went on a date once. He got smashed and fell asleep in the toilets. It was a *great* night.' Her voice was droll, and flat.

I blinked, then laughed. 'That sounds like Steve, alright. Wouldn't know a good thing if it came up and hit in in the face with a baseball bat.'

She laughed, and it was an amazing sound: decadent, and passionate, a raw, natural noise that made me think of one thing and one thing alone: taking her clothes off.

I shook my head. *Jesus! Get a grip, Ben!*

'So come on,' she said, not letting it drop. 'What did you do?'

'I kind of...ah...I...sort of...ahhh...slept with his little sister. You know.'

She let out a breath. 'Oh, man. You broke the guy code.'

I shrugged, and smiled lopsidedly.

'Yeah, I did. I know. Bad Ben.'

She looked at me, square in the eyes. 'Bad Ben indeed,' she said, her gaze suddenly very fixed. I blushed, and squirmed on the spot. *Jesus H*, I thought, again. She needed to leave, before my threatening boner became a real-life boner. I didn't have a cushion to hand to save my dignity.

As if hearing my thoughts, she brought herself up, sharply.

'Well, I've got to make a move.' She nodded at the parcel on my table. 'I hope it's not from Steve,' she continued, winking at me. 'You know, a horse's head or something.'

I put on my best Brad Pitt voice. '*What's in the box?*' I said, playing for laughs. I got them.

'Awesome movie,' said UPS lady, shaking her head and chuckling again. 'Awesome ending.'

'Couldn't agree more. I mean, imagine if Gwyneth Paltrow's head *wasn't* in the box. What a let-down that would have been.'

She smiled up at me. 'Listen. I have a few minutes before I need to get on the road,' she said, her eyes flicking to the cardboard package.

'Why don't you open it? I'm intrigued.'

I looked at her thoughtfully, and then slowly went over to a drawer to take out a silver letter opener.

'Sure,' I said, shrugging again. 'Why not?'

'I'm excited,' she said, leaning in and rubbing her hands.

'Wait a minute,' I said, a sudden thought occurring to me. 'Before I expose myself to more potential embarrassment in front of you, can you at least tell me your name?'

'Sure,' said UPS lady. 'I'm Melissa. Lissy for short.'

I held out my hand. 'Nice to meet you, Lissy.' She took my hand and shook it, heartily. 'Nice to meet you, Bad Ben.'

I laughed, and turned to the parcel.

It was nondescript in terms of packaging. Just a simple brown cardboard box, with a UPS delivery sticker on the side. There were no other markings or postal stamps of any kind. Just a plain box, sealed with packing tape. There was no forwarding or return address.

I chewed my lip. An anonymous parcel I hadn't been expecting. My hand hovered mid-air, the letter opener clenched tightly between my fingers.

Perhaps this wasn't such a good idea after all.

I hesitated, and then had a hard word with myself. *Stop being so ridiculous,* I thought. *It's just a parcel, Ben. Get on with it!*

I took a deep breath and plunged the letter opener into the tape.

It gave, reluctantly. The parcel was well sealed. I struggled to hack through the tape and pull the flaps of the box apart. Lissy held her breath throughout.

When I eventually got the box open, I found a small wooden crate inside. Through the gaps in the crate I could see packing straw sticking out. Whatever was inside was evidently fragile. I gently removed the crate, and set it on the table. I looked inside the cardboard box. No letter, no receipt forms, no nothing. I frowned, and put the box on the floor.

'The mystery deepens,' said Lissy, leaning in. 'I reckon you could lever the lid off that crate, easily.'

I did as I was told, poking the letter opener into the crate's lid at one end, and using considerable force to lever it up. It was nailed down with brass staples, which eventually bent, and gave away. The crate lid popped open with a snapping, creaking sound, and I was left with an open crate full of packing straw, and something pale just visible beneath the top layer.

'Ooooh,' Lissy said, and, unable to help herself, she delved in with both hands, clearing the straw away while I looked on.

'Careful!' I said, as she dug around like a kid on Christmas morning. I had a sudden feeling of unease, of trepidation.

Cruel Works of Nature

'Oh my God,' she said, softly, and brought something out of the straw gently, with both hands cupped around it protectively, as if she were hoisting a small child up out of a crib.

I gaped. I don't know what I had been expecting, but this was not it.

It was an egg.

A *huge* egg, an egg bigger than my head, about a foot and a half in length, and easily a foot wide. It was smooth, and pure white in colour, with light blue speckles across the domed surface that reminded me of the freckles on Lissy's face.

Lissy cradled it in her arms, and looked at me excitedly. 'It's an egg!' she exclaimed, her eyes alight with curiosity.

'I can see that,' I said, scratching my head. 'Question is, who the fuck sent it to me? And why?'

She opened her mouth to reply, but before she had time to respond, a tiny, chirruping, cracking noise came from the egg.

Lissy and I looked at each other, shocked.

'Oh, you have *got* to be fucking kidding me!' I said, shaking my head and putting my arms out to ward off the unexpected new development occurring in my kitchen.

'Is it...is it *hatching?!*' Lissy cried, staring at the egg in her arms.

It jerked about suddenly, rocking back and forth, and the chirruping noise sounded again.

'Put it down!' I instructed, sharply. 'Put it back

down in the crate. Before it breaks open!'

She did as she was told, shaking with excitement. 'I can't believe this. I mean, this is fucking *unreal*.'

I stopped her from leaning in as the egg began to wobble once more, and then jerk and roll around in the straw, the chirruping noises intensifying.

'Don't get too close to it,' I warned. 'We don't know what it is.'

'It's gotta be a bird of some sort, an ostrich, or something.'

I shook my head again, helplessly. 'I'm no expert, but I'm pretty fucking sure there aren't any birds alive on this earth that lay eggs of that size. The thing is like a fucking dinosaur egg!'

A small crack appeared in the polished white surface of the egg. The chirruping turned into muted, tiny squeals, little angry noises of exertion. The crack fractured into a spider's web of other hairline fractures, and then the gap began to bulge, and pulsate, as whatever was inside fought to find its way out.

Lissy reached out and grabbed my arm with one of her hands. 'Is this really happening?' She whispered, her beautiful eyes as round as saucers.

'I think it is,' I breathed, as the egg jerked again, and the squeals rose in intensity.

We waited with bated breath, clutching each other's arms. The egg bulged once more, and then again, the cracks growing larger, the movements inside more frantic. Then, there was a moment's pause, as if the inhabitant of the egg were taking a break. After a moment or two it was back, heaving itself outwards with one, final, huge effort.

At last, the egg broke with a sharp crack, and then burst outwards in a shower of white shell and goop.

There was the wet sound of mucus-covered fur scraping against eggshell, and a weak, tired, mewling sound, and then we saw it, the thing from the egg, lying prone, panting, inside a large shell fragment, coated in bloodied straw.

'Oh my God,' Lissy whispered, gripping my arm tighter than ever. 'What *is* it?'

'I don't know,' I said, shaking my head. 'I have no fucking idea.'

The thing croaked, and moaned, softly. It had a tiny, gravelly, harsh voice.

'It's so...so...*ugly*,' Lissy said, her voice dripping with tenderness.

I looked at it in repulsion as it heaved itself unsteadily to its feet. Ugly it certainly was, there was no denying it.

The thing from the egg was a roundish ball of black, scraggly fur. It had two small, pink, skinny bald arms with hooked claws at the end. It had thin, long, rosy-pink legs that ended in two huge birdlike feet. It had tiny black gimlet eyes. Its head and body merged into a single lump. Most of this area was taken up by the thing's mouth, which was huge, wide, and curved like a Cheshire cat's smile. I saw twin rows of small, needle-like teeth, like the teeth of a shark, serrated, and curved inwards slightly, so that they looked like barbs. I knew instantly that this was a predator of some sort, and that one bite from that thing could be enough to sever a limb.

'Don't touch it!' I cautioned again, as Lissy moved forward. I could see she intended to pet the creature, and I snatched and held her hand back before she could. 'Look at its teeth. Don't put your hands anywhere near it.'

'But it's so cute!' she said, although a little more unsure of herself now she'd noticed the wicked fangs lining the creature's maw.

The thing moaned, and growled. Then it stood upright, wobbling around on its bandy pink legs.

We gazed at it, and it just stood there on my kitchen table, staring back, opening its disgusting mouth every now and then to let out a horrible, scraping, growling, mewling noise. It panted, still weak from its exertions. Mucus and slime dripped from its fur, pattering gently onto my table top. My lip curled in disgust. It smelled bad, too. Like ammonia.

'I need to call the animal control service,' I said, backing towards the telephone on my kitchen wall, and with that, the creature snarled at me, almost as if...

'Can it understand you?' Lissy said, horrified.

It looked at Lissy. A long, black, sticky tongue slid out of its mouth and licked its lips. Those little black eyes glittered.

'Lissy,' I said, quietly now. 'I need you to back away from it, slowly. In the drawer behind you there is a kitchen knife. Get it.'

She did as she was told, moving slowly and steadily backwards until her ass hit the kitchen counter. She fumbled behind herself, pulled open the drawer, and felt around inside.

'Ahhh!' she hissed, suddenly, and winced.

'Are you okay?' I asked, concerned but reluctant to take my eyes from the thing on my table.

'Yeah, I just…I cut myself on the knife, is all. It's not deep.'

She slowly brought the knife around in front of her, and held it out defensively. Bright, fresh blood dripped from her thumb, splattering onto the floor and forming a little puddle at her feet. I reached out and grabbed a tea towel hanging to the right of me.

'Here,' I said, handing it over to her, still without removing my eyes from the strange creature. 'Wrap this around it.'

She took the towel. She managed to clumsily stem the flow of blood while still holding the knife out in front of her.

The creature cocked its head to one side, and studied the blood on the floor. It shifted its weight from foot to foot, and then opened its mouth. Slowly, ponderously, its tongue slid out once more, only this time it glided across the room, a good three or four feet, like a snake gliding through the grass, and then it arched into the air, before dipping down into the red, glossy puddle and lapping at Lissy's blood like a cat at a milk bowl.

The tongue then recoiled, wetly, slipping back into the mouth as if retracted by a motor. The thing crooned with pleasure.

'*MMMmmmmmmmmmmmmmm,*' it said in a horrible, crackling, vile little voice.

'Ahhh...I think we should get out of here,' I said, in turn, my voice now wavering with fear.

'I think you're right,' Lissy said, and then, 'Oh my God... *look!*'

I was looking. I couldn't help but look. The creature was... growing.

Its skin rippled, then puffed out. The legs grew suddenly longer, by at least an inch. More teeth sprouted, and poked out of its gums, making a horrible noise as they did so. The tongue quested for the blood once more, and once more the monster groaned in pleasure at the taste.

'*MMMMMMMmmmmmmmmmmmmmmmmmmm,*' it said, lasciviously, and seconds later, it grew bigger still, its body swelling, puffing out like that of a toad.

'Back away,' I said, my voice now hoarse. 'Back the fuck away from it!'

But Lissy had nowhere to go. The kitchen counter was behind her. To her left was a dividing wall, and to her right, the creature. She was cornered.

I need to distract it, I thought, looking around me frantically for a diversion, or a weapon, and realising that everything useful was on the opposite side of the kitchen to where I was standing. I had a baseball bat somewhere in a box in the garage, but beyond that, all I had was my letter opener, and that was only made of...

'Arghhhhhh!' Screamed Lissy, as the thing's tongue whipped out and wrapped itself around her right wrist. It pulled, *retracted,* as before, and dragged Lissy slowly across the tiled floor toward it as surely and steadily as a fisherman reeling in a large catch. Lissy's skin hissed and burned where the sticky black tongue made contact, as if it were coated in acid. Lissy screamed again, and fought desperately against the pull, but it was futile. The creature was strong, and the creature was hungry.

'Do something!' she sobbed, hysterically, and then: '*DO SOMETHING GOD DAMMIT!*'

I sprung into action, leaping forward towards the thing. I lifted the letter opener high up into the air above my head, and then I plunged it down, with all the force I could muster. The dull blade sank into one of the creature's black, lump-of-coal eyes, which erupted. A drop of the creature's blood splashed onto my cheek and began to burn, instantly. I howled, and clawed at my face. God, it *burned,* so bad!

'*Ben!*' shrieked Lissy, '*Ben!*'

The thing was still reeling her in, despite the damage to its eye, which now sported the letter opener like a piece of fancy jewellery. The creature opened its mouth wider, that tongue still pulling like a steel cable, and Lissy was now mere inches from its face. With a sudden jerk, it yanked at her, opened its huge mouth further, and brought its terrible teeth together around Lissy's forearm. It bit down. The sound of breaking bone filled my ears. Lissy screamed and screamed and screamed, and then slumped to the ground, clutching at the remains of her right arm which now, instead of ending in a slim, white, delicate hand, ended in a mangled mess of bone, and gore. She turned a nasty shade of white, and then almost grey, and I knew she was about to faint. I looked at the monster. It was temporarily preoccupied with chewing, with tasting, with savouring the human flesh in its mouth. I knew what was going to happen next. The thing had eaten, and so it would grow, as all new-borns do. They just eat, and grow, and eat, and grow. Our only chance to escape was now, while it was chowing down.

I lurched over to Lissy, who was beginning to drift out of consciousness. I slapped her hard across the face once, twice, three times.

'Get up!' I said, as calmly as I knew how. 'Get up. You can't faint here. If you do, we will both die. Get up, now.'

She looked at me, not understanding, her brain beginning to shut down.

'I SAID GET UP!' I roared, and she stumbled slowly to her feet.

I knelt down, and grabbed her good arm. I hoisted her over my back in a fireman's lift, turned, and ran from the kitchen as fast as I could, which wasn't very fast at all, given my burden. Behind me I could hear the monster. I could hear its skin contracting, the legs and the arms growing longer, more teeth thrusting out through its gums. I whimpered, and moved my legs faster, reaching the front door, fumbling to get it open, and then racing out onto the street.

I emerged into sunlight, and green, and birdsong, and gentility. The contrast was like having a bucket of cold water thrown over me. The street was so quiet, so peaceful, as it usually was this time of the day on a Sunday morning. It was so far removed from the horrors behind me in my kitchen that I stood there, completely flummoxed, Lissy's head dangling down over my shoulder and chest, her ponytail touching the ground. Somewhere along the way she'd lost her cap.

Chest heaving, and ears ringing from what was probably shock, I shuffled forward. From the house behind me, I could hear movement, and knew that the creature was in pursuit. I looked around desperately for someone who could help. My eyes scanned the street and saw noone, no-one at all, until I spotted old Mrs. Kent from next door. She was in her front yard, about to start mowing her lawn. She bent down, and pulled the choke cord on her mower. It was an old- fashioned petrol lawnmower, the kind you needed to kickstart first by yanking on a handle. She tried a few times, her movements laboured, and unsteady, and then looked up as the engine roared to life.

She saw me, and froze, her mouth dropping open in shock. The mower idled in front of her, forgotten.

I started to move, my legs shaking from the effort of carrying Lissy, her blood leaking down my front, her skin growing increasingly cold to the touch.

'Help me,' I pleaded, staggering under the weight of the girl who had looked so beautiful that morning on my doorstep.

Mrs. Kent remained frozen to the spot, her mouth open. I realised she was not looking at me, but at something *behind* me. She raised an arm and pointed a trembling finger at what I knew was there.

A sound carried across the street, licking at my ears.

'MMMMMMmmmmmmmmmmmmmmmmm,' it said, huskily, seductively, *hungrily*.

The lawnmower purred on the yard ahead of me.

I heaved Lissy off of my shoulder, and thrust

her into Mrs. Kent's arms. She reacted automatically, having no choice- it was either carry her, or drop her. She was an old woman, but large, sturdy enough to just about bear the weight of the younger woman.

'Move,' I said, and grabbed the lawnmower. Mrs. Kent shook herself, the panic consolidating into stern resolve. She heaved Lissy over her shoulder in the same hold that I had used only moments ago. She was far stronger than she looked, despite her age. We looked at each other, her old, rheumy grey eyes searching mine for answers, and then hurried towards the safety of her house, Lissy's red hair trailing behind her.

I whipped the mower around to face what hunted me.

And I gasped, unable to help myself.

The thing from the egg was now *huge*.

It towered a good six feet above me, seemingly all arms and legs. The talons on its hands were as large and wickedly curved as scythes, and its bird feet also ended in vicious talons that were designed to rend and shred at flesh.

But it was its mouth that I couldn't bear to look at. It spread from one side of the thing's black, matted, furry face to the other, and, as it opened wide to slide that long, black tongue out into the air, as if testing for my scent, I could see row upon row of teeth, all curved inwards, all savagely sharp, receding right back to the darkness within, as if they protruded halfway down its throat. I'd seen the inside of an eel's mouth once, and it was the same as this. Endless teeth. Death for anything trapped within.

The tongue lashed out towards me, snapping out like a frog's, and I ducked, narrowly missing its slimy, corrosive embrace. It growled, and took another step toward me, a jerky, lurching step. Its arms twitched and spasmed by its side. The tongue lashed again.

This time, I caught it. My hand began to sizzle and the skin on the palm of my hand to blister, and burn, but I held fast, groaning. I dug my heels into the pristine green of Mrs. Kent's lawn, and pulled.

Now it was my turn to go fishing.

Now it was my turn to reel in a catch.

It struggled, and was stronger than I. The tongue, coated in whatever acid the thing's mouth secreted, sank into the flesh of my hand like cheese wire. I groaned, and pulled again, straining so hard I could feel all the veins in my neck bulging. Fear and adrenaline gave me strength I didn't know I had. The lawnmower still chuntered next to me.

I gave one last, final, huge tug on the creature's tongue, and it stumbled, its stork-like legs folding underneath it. It tumbled to the ground, its head mere inches from my foot.

I let go of the tongue, and grabbed the mower. And then I ran forward with it as fast as I knew how.

I was going to turn this motherfucker into grass clippings.

It was fast, but I was faster. Its arms were the first to disappear under the blades of the lawnmower. I held on tight as the mower jerked and protested in my grasp.

A high-pitched, alien scream keened out from beneath the blades, as the creature lost its arms. Panicking, I realised the thing's head was too large to fit under the machine. I yanked it back, and aimed at the long, bandy legs. Those went the same way as the arms, and the noise I heard as those thin, pink limbs chugged and churned under the whirling blades will stay with me for the rest of my life.

Mangled, dismembered, yellow blood seeping out across the yard, the grass turning brown and singed beneath, the thing looked at me, and opened its mouth. I wasn't quick enough. The black tongue whipped across the distance between us and made a burning tourniquet around my leg. I fell to the ground, shrieking. Dying, but still stubbornly, fixedly malevolent to its last breath, the creature dragged me towards its open, panting mouth, and then...

And then, there was a gunshot, inches above my head.

And then another.

The tourniquet around my leg loosened, slowly. I was no longer being dragged across the floor.

Sobbing, I rolled onto my back, and stared up.

Mrs. Kent stood over me, a shotgun held fast and steady in her blunt old hands. She took two more shotgun shells from her pocket, and slowly, carefully loaded the cartridges into the gun, took aim once more, and filled the dead monster with two more rounds. I watched as she did this. In the distance, I heard sirens winding their way inexorably up the street towards us.

'I think it's dead now,' Mrs. Kent said, and I would have kissed her had I not, in that moment, spent and injured, shocked and scarred, fainted onto the cool, green, well-kept lawn.

❉ ❉ ❉

WHY ME? I used to think, in those early days following release from hospital. *Why send the parcel to me?*

After a while, the question ceased to have any meaning. I didn't want those answers. I didn't want to know who would do such a thing. I just wanted to move on. To forget.

The remains of the egg, and the creature, and even the lawnmower, were removed by men in HAZMAT suits, who arrived while I was being loaded into an ambulance, and who I have never seen or heard of again. There was nothing in the news about it, which made me glad. Noone came to interview me, or Lissy, while we lay in our hospitable beds. Mrs. Kent stopped by to see me when I was released, and told the same story. Everything had gone right back to normal, as if the parcel, and the egg, and the creature had never existed.

The first thing I did when I felt well anough was to put my house on the market. Lissy and I grew closer as we struggled to come to terms things. My foot was fucked, and my hand was now useless, the nerves and tendons severed clean through. Lissy's wrist stump healed in time, but it was a long, and painful journey. Through shared rehab, we drew comfort from each other. As friends, all interest in anything else evaporated. We survived, in each other's company, and joked that between us, we had enough good limbs to make things work.

We moved, eventually, to the countryside. We gave noone our forwarding address. Our mailbox is situated a mile up the road away from our house, and is going to stay that way.

And on the rare occasion the doorbell does ring, on the *very* rare occasion that a delivery man, or woman, asks us to sign for a parcel, well.

We just slam the door in their face.

Once bitten, twice shy, as they say.

Gemma Amor

IT SEES YOU WHEN YOU'RE SLEEPING

Y<small>OU CAN LOSE A LOT OF HOURS OF YOUR LIFE, STARING INTO</small> an open fire. Trust me. I know.

The longer you look, the more you see. Movement, and light. Faces, where before there were none. Flames shift and writhe about, like people dancing. It's hypnotic. And the range of noises that a fire makes is complex, and rich: there's the crackle of flames, the shifting of embers, the snap and pop as wet wood dries out and launches small spark bombs into the air above.

On this particular night, those popping sounds reminded me of gunshots, ringing out, sharp and distinct. I flinched. Gunshots, short, deadly punctuations. I heard them, and then I saw the face of my sister. I wasn't there when it happened, but I imagined her face all the same. Beautiful, and scared. I wondered if she screamed, at all, if she had time. I stared at the fire, and waited for it to release me from its spell, but it wouldn't let me go. We gazed at each other, and the white-hot shadows danced for me, pulling me in, always pulling me in.

I should have been in bed. It was late on Christmas Eve, and I should have been asleep. Instead I was in my TV room, ensnared by the roaring fire and the dull ticktock of the clock on the mantelpiece, and the quiet, wellworn melodies of Christmas carols coming out of the ignored TV set across the room from me.

Go to sleep, I kept telling myself. *Go to sleep.* But then the fire would sing and new faces would appear and I just kept sitting there, feet propped up on a stool, and covered by Mona's thick woollen winter socks. She'd given me a pair of these socks every year at Christmas for as long as I could remember, right up to the point where I found out that she was fucking her boss, and we broke up.

Never mind her, the fire said. *Look over here. Look closely. Can you see them? There are things to see over here. Keep looking.*

Yeah, you can lose a lotta hours.

❉ ❉ ❉

SO, it was late when my niece came downstairs, wrapped in her duvet, looking cold and miserable. She found me, catatonic and fuzzy and bitter-hearted, swallowing down a whole meal of melancholy, listening to the fire concerto. Alice appeared in the doorway like a sleepy ghost, and although it took me a few moments to notice her, when I did, I didn't mind, not one bit.

'Uncle P?' she said, timidly, wiping at her bleary eyes.

The 'P' stands for Peter, in case you're curious, Pete to my friends. I frowned and then checked the clock on the wall.

'Hey, kiddo, you should be asleep! Santa won't come if you stay awake all night.'

'Yeah, I know. I was just wondering something.' Alice had a strange look on her face, a serious and scared expression that I'd not seen for a while, not since that cold, bitter night three years ago. I wondered, my heart suddenly heavy, if she was about to ask me about her Mom and Dad. I wasn't sure I was ready for that conversation, not on Christmas Eve. Not ever, really, although I knew the time would come soon. It had to. Alice was eleven, and a bright, curious kid. She would want answers, soon, answers that I wasn't sure I knew how to give.

I shuffled over on the couch and patted the warm space left behind.

'Come on,' I said. 'Take off a load.'

She came over gratefully and snuggled into my side. I popped an arm around her shoulders.

'What's bugging you, pigeon?'

Alice hesitated for a moment. 'Uncle P,' she said then, chewing her lip and twisting her hands together.

'Spit it out, kiddo.'

'Is Santa a bad guy?'

I snorted into my beer glass.

'Why would you think that? Kids at school been yapping in your ear again?'

She took a deep breath. 'It's just...well, I've been thinking about it. And, well, I think it's kind of... creepy that Santa is, like, watching you all the time, you know, all year round, to see if you are a good person or not.

And...I...'

I nudged her gently as she trailed off. 'And what?'

'I don't want him coming down the chimney and into my room while I am asleep! My friend Lucy says that grown men who come into little girls' bedrooms in the middle of the night are not good people.'

I stared at the fire once again, stunned, trying to think of some way to revive the poor kid's sense of Christmas innocence.

Cruel Works of Nature

Alice continued. 'And it's that song, you know, the one that goes "He sees you when you're sleeping, he knows when you're awake"...' She sang the last bit in a reedy, uncertain voice. 'Yeah, I don't like that song,' she finished, mumbling into her duvet, embarrassed and unsettled. 'I don't like it at all.'

I couldn't argue with the kid. That song *was* pretty creepy. And come to think of it, so was the idea of a big fat man with a bright red nose breaking into your house in the dead of the night and snooping around.

'Well?' Alice said, turning her sweet little face to mine and searching it for answers. The firelight flickered and cast soft shadows beneath her eyes, making her look older than her eleven years.

'It's at times like this, pigeon, that I wish Mona were here,' I said, sighing and pulling a strand of Alice's golden hair away from her face.

'I miss Mona too,' she said, and squeezed me with a big hug. 'Are you sure she won't come back?'

'Ah, pigeon,' I said, shaking my head sadly. 'I think we blew the lid well off of that one. I can't even get her to answer her damn phone. But...yeah. She would have known what to say right now.'

Alice sighed. 'It's okay. I just... I can't sleep in my room with the fireplace all... open like it is. It's like... it's like it's watching me, or something.

Can you come and block it up? Please, Uncle P?'

I looked at the clock again. Ten to midnight. I blew out my cheeks and shrugged.

'Block it up?'

'Yeah, or cover it with something... I don't know. I just don't like it.' She shuddered.

I thought for a moment. Then, I sat forward.

'What the hell. Sure,' I said, 'If it'll make you feel safe.'

That, there in a nutshell, is all I ever wanted for Alice after her parents died. I wanted her to feel safe. It had become my mission in life. Protect Alice. Make Alice happy again. Keep Alice safe.

'No, problem, pigeon,' I said, and ruffled her hair.

She smiled at me then, letting out a big sigh of relief, and the night felt a little less heavy. 'Thanks, Uncle P.'

❋ ❋ ❋

I GOT a large piece of stiff hardboard from the shed, a cordless drill and a box of multi-purpose screws. Alice watched me closely while I fixed the board over the mouth of the ornate, cast-iron fireplace in her bedroom. I'd actually been thinking of blocking it off for a while: it was an old house, and the drafts that came down into her room through the fireplace were getting worse as the years progressed, not to mention the soot and shit that blew in all over the carpet. Blocking it off should make her room a lot warmer and cleaner.

As I worked, I thought once or twice that I could hear muted scratching noises coming down the chimney. I heard the sounds several times, and worried about rats. I'd have to set some traps up another day when Alice was elsewhere. The board should keep them at bay for a little while, but rats could chew through pretty much anything if they had a mind to, and I didn't think it would take them long to do so.

When I had finished, Alice tapped the board firmly in several places, checking to see how robust it was. Then she nodded to herself, satisfied.

'Better?' I asked, folding my arms.

'Better,' she confirmed. Now it was my turn to sigh in relief.

The things you do for love, I thought to myself as I packed away the drill.

Alice handed me a note as I tucked her back into her bed. I opened it. It said, in large capital letters:

DEAR SANTA
PLEASE LEAVE ALL PRESENTS UNDER
THE TREE DOWNSTAIRS, NOT AT
THE END OF MY BED.
THANK YOU FOR UNDERSTANDING.

It was the politest eleven-year-old 'fuck off' I'd even seen. I chuckled. 'Sounds good to me,' I said, and pinned the note to the outside of her bedroom door. I flicked off the lights, and Alice's room descended into the low, blue glow of her nightlight.

'Now, get some sleep,' I said, in my sternest voice, which was never very stern at all. Since the kid's parents had passed, I hadn't been able to raise my voice to Alice ever, not even once. Not that I'd ever needed to. Alice was a good kid. She took after her Mother, my sister, for that. So far, she showed no signs of taking after her Father. I tried not to think about that when I looked at her, but I couldn't help it. I couldn't help... watching and wondering. Would the bad come out, in the end? Was I doing a good enough job?

Again, Mona would know what to think. Mona was a good judge of character.

'Night, Uncle P,' Alice said, drowsily. I waited outside her room for ten minutes, until I heard her breathing slow down, become more rhythmic. Hopefully she would stay asleep, this time. I didn't like it when she was upset. A kid that age, she should be dreaming of nice things like ponies and adventures and books and her favourite band, not creepy fat assholes with beards coming into her room late at night.

I descended the stairs, heavily, and made

straight for the fridge, pulling out another beer and cracking it open. It was past one-thirty in the morning, now, but I still couldn't sleep. Emotions always hit me harder during the holiday season. I remember the days, back when Alice was really little, when she would come over with her Mom and Dad on Christmas morning. Mona would greet them at the door with Christmas music and a tray of warm mince pies. We would eat, and open presents, and drink, and eat some more. Mona and I would try to ignore the strained smile on my sister's face, and all of us would ignore her husband, who would get quietly more and more blitzed in the corner of the room until it was time to roll him out of his chair and into the front seat of my sister's Chevy. I always hated that part: waving them off, knowing that there was a loaded gun in human form sat between two of the girls I loved the most in the whole world.

In the end, my instincts about him turned out to be right, but I took no comfort in that. No comfort at all.

But, that was then, and this is now, and the past belongs in the past, I thought, and what better time to let bygones be bygones than at Christmas?

I knew it was a bad idea, but I was feeling drunk, and forlorn. This was my first Christmas without Mona for ten years. Maybe...just maybe she would be feeling blue too.

I dialled her number, and waited, swigging my beer, staring at the fire. She hadn't answered my calls for months, now, although that never stopped me trying. But it was Christmas, and I had hope.

And to my surprise, this time, she actually answered, her voice thick with fatigue. My heart leapt. For months she had been screening my calls. Months.

'Hello, Peter,' she said, softly, and my pulse quickened.

'Hi, Mona. I'm early, but…Merry Christmas.' There was a long pause. Then:

'You're not early, Pete. It's nearly two in the morning. Merry Christmas, I guess.'

'I didn't think you'd answer your phone. I'm… glad you did.'

She ignored me.

'Pete. I have…I have a present for Alice. Can I come over later on and give it to her? I won't stay long.'

I thought about it for a moment or two. 'You can come,' I said. Then, hopefully:

'Stay as long as you like.'

There was a pause which I blundered on into. 'I brought this huge turkey…I don't…I don't know how we're going to eat it all, to tell the truth.'

Mona sounded relieved. 'I felt sure you'd say no.'

I shrugged, hoping she could hear it in my voice. 'Nahh,' I said, and decided that honesty was the best policy, for once. 'It's Christmas. I'm wearing the socks you bought me last year. I...ah, fuck, Mona. I miss you.'

I heard her clearing her throat, fighting back tears.

'I miss you too, Peter.'

'Then why didn't you answer any of my calls? I've been trying for months to...'

'Isn't is obvious? The things you said...you hurt me, Peter. You hurt me real bad.'

I sighed, wiping a hand across my face. 'I know. I shouldn't... I shouldn't have said any of those things. In my defence, you did, ah, well, you know. Sleep with your boss. So the hurt was mutual.'

She was openly crying now, and it tore at me. Even though this whole thing was her goddamn fault, it still tore at me. My sister always said I was a soft touch.

'I'll never forgive myself, Peter. I don't know why I did it. I don't expect you to forgive me, but I just...I don't know how many times I can say sorry before you'll believe me. And those things you said...the names you called me...I felt sure that was it between us. And it hurt, so I stopped taking your calls. It was easier that way.'

I cleared my own throat. This was the longest conversation we'd had in months. The trick now was not to screw it up.

'I believe you. I...I forgive you. And I'm sorry for what I said.' I was surprised to realise I meant it. I waited, to see what her response would be, my heart thumping raggedly behind my ribs.

'Can I...are you...are you alone right now?' Mona asked, something like hope carrying across the phone.

'Well, Alice is upstairs. Other than that, it's just me and this fridge full of beer.' Another long, loaded pause.

Then:

'I'll be over in ten minutes.'

I smiled, and my heart almost climbed up and out of my mouth.

'I'll wait up for you,' I said, joy bubbling up inside of me. I hung up and sagged with relief back into my chair. Mona was coming over. Mona was coming back.

This Christmas might not be so bad, after all, I thought.

The fire crackled on.

❊ ❊ ❊

CHRISTMAS MORNING DAWNED in the best way possible: Mona and I, naked and hung-over, tangled in a sweaty pile of arms and legs and her long, thick hair in my bed.

We woke together as light came streaming in through the bedroom curtains. Mona sighed in comfort, and buried her face in my chest. I felt like I had come home after a long journey away.

Cruel Works of Nature

We lay in silence, breathing in a syncopated rhythm.

Eventually, I heard movement from Alice's bedroom.

'Wake up,' I murmured to Mona. 'We have to put clothes on. Alice is waking up.'

Mona raised her head, her tangled hair making a dark halo around her face. She smiled.

'Happy Christmas,' she said. I groaned as her smile took on a wicked accent and her hands started to wander.

'You'll be the death of me,' I muttered.

'I know you're in there Mona!' came a small, happy voice from the landing. Alice.

'I can hear you talking! I knew you would come back, I said that, didn't I Uncle P?!'

We froze, and then burst out laughing.

'We'll be down in a minute, pigeon!' I called, and her footsteps skipped away happily down the stairs.

'Five minutes,' I whispered to Mona, flipping her onto her back. 'It is Christmas, after all.'

'Merry fucking Christmas,' she gasped, and then, for a little while, there was nothing else but she and me.

❋ ❋ ❋

WE WERE unwrapping presents when I first heard it.

As usual, I had bought too many. I was never able to stop spoiling Alice. I figured, her Mom and Dad were dead, the kid should get spoiled a bit. I mean, the presents wouldn't replace her parents, but they might help...distract her a little from the great tragedy that hung over her life. And I wanted her to know she was loved. Because she was, so much.

Mona and Alice and I were sat in a circle on the floor of the lounge, still in our pyjamas, surrounded by crisp, hastily discarded mounds of wrapping paper. Alice was excitedly ripping into Mona's gift when the sound came, high and shrill and insistent. I didn't pay much attention to it at first, assuming it was the over-excited kids down the street goofing around.

But then the sound came again, long and loud and...Wrong, somehow. The kind of sound that makes the hairs on the back of your neck stir. The kind of sound that is a harbinger to grief, and lives altered beyond recompense. The sound I imagined my sister made when she was shot and killed by her own husband on a Christmas Day not that dissimilar to this one.

My head snapped up. I held up a hand to the girls, to get them to quieten down. Alice stopped ripping paper, and put the box down carefully, looking at me with wide eyes, solemn and serious.

'What is it?' said Mona, but then the screams came again, and this time, we all heard them. I lumbered to my feet.

'What is that, Uncle P?' Alice asked, nervously.

'I don't know. Maybe just some kids messing around.' I listened again, and found I could still hear it, shrieking that just went on and on, like a siren wailing.

My skin broke out in gooseflesh. I decided I needed to be neighbourly, and go check it out.

'Stay here while I take a look,' I said, bounding up the stairs to go and get my gun. Yeah, I'm one of those guys that keeps a gun in the house. I'm a security guard for a large bank, and I privateer sometimes for other gigs where men with steady hands and bit of experience are in demand. The gun comes with the job, although I'm what I like to think of as a careful gun-owner. I keep it locked in a safe at all times, and I don't even think Alice knew I had it in the house until that point.

I loaded it quickly, and then tucked it into the back of my pants, intending to keep it hidden until I was out the front door so as not to worry the girls.

'Stay here,' I said as I came back downstairs, trying to project an aura of calm, and hoping they would fall for it.

'Be careful, Peter!' Mona rose, and followed me to the front door. She hadn't fallen for it. Her face was stricken with worry.

'Stay in the house,' I replied firmly, cupping her face in one of my hands. 'I'll be back in a moment,' I said, turning and shutting the door behind me in haste.

I loped across my front lawn, towards the source of the screaming, which from out here was easy enough to identify. It was coming from the house two doors away, the Morris house. Ed and Lana Morris were a nice, welloff, middle-aged couple with a teenage daughter named Megan, who was only a few years older than Alice. She'd gone to the same school as her until she left for high school. Recently, she'd even babysat for me for a few times, when I'd been really desperate and had a work commitment I couldn't get out of. A nice kid, as teenagers go.

My skin crawled as the screams came again, and just kept going, and going, and going. It sounded like one person, and that person sounded young, and female... and like Megan.

I took out my gun, and approached the house, cautiously. Out of the corner of my eye, I saw other people falling onto the street, men mostly, slippers and dressing gowns slung over their pyjamas hastily as they came to check out the noise. I turned, and waved at Mona, who had opened the front door, and was standing watching me, holding Alice close.

'Get inside and call 911!' I yelled, and, grim-faced and pale, she fumbled in her pocket for her cell phone.

I slapped my palm against the Morris front door, loudly, wondering how I could get inside.

Cruel Works of Nature

The screaming shredded at my nerves, and I was now convinced that it was Megan making all the noise. My instincts told me that there was something seriously wrong going on inside the house. I rattled the front door handle, banging on the door again.

'Megan?!' I called, increasingly frantic. 'Megan, what's going on in there? Are you okay? It's Peter from up the road! Megan! Answer me!'

She carried on without pause, and I rattled the front door again. It was locked, from the inside, meaning noone had left the house yet that day. Why would they? It was Christmas, after all.

I put my shoulder into the door, shouting again. 'It's okay, Megan. I'm coming in, I'm breaking down the door, it's okay!'

It didn't sound okay.

A man's voice, urgent and out of breath, sounded out behind me. 'Move over, and I'll help,' he said, gruffly, and I did so, recognising Travis, another neighbour from farther up the street.

'On three,' I said, and he nodded. I took a deep breath.

'One...'

More screaming, insistent and nerve-shredding.

'Two...'

My heart thundered in my chest, and my gun felt cold in my clammy hands.

'Three!'

We both slammed into the front door, and something popped, then cracked. The door swung open. We got no further than a foot through it before Megan Morris came flying down the stairs, covered in thick, red blood from head to toe, screaming like an animal caught in a trap.

She flung herself at me, and I put my arms out instinctively to catch her before she sank to the floor. Something warm, wet, and fresh soaked immediately through my clothes and stuck to my skin. It was blood. A lot of blood.

'Megan!' I said, terror now flooding through me like a raging river. 'Megan, what happened?!'

'It's upstairs!!' she wailed, over and over, her eyes blank and uncomprehending, looking at me and seeing nothing.

'It's upstairs, oh God it's upstairs, it's upstairs, it'supstairsitsupstairs!!'

'Jesus fuck,' said Travis, his eyes wide as he registered the state of the poor girl clinging to me. She shook violently as I held onto her. A rich, thick blood scent filled the air between us.

'Call an ambulance, Travis, call one now,' I whispered, my throat tight. The room spun a little, and I felt faint, but I tried to focus, tried not to give into it.

Travis backed away from us, looked around frantically, and then ran over to the hall stand, where a phone stood. As he dialled with trembling hands, I realised how quiet the rest of the house was, apart from the girl babbling nonsense in my arms.

Too quiet.

Where were Mr. and Mrs. Morris?

I returned my attention to the girl at my feet, who had stopped screaming, but was now shaking, and whimpering, like a beaten dog, and muttering random strings of words to herself with a hoarse voice ruined from screaming.

'Where are your Mom and Dad, Megan?' I asked again, slowly and carefully, trying to get her to make eye contact with me, to break her out of her state of terror if only for long enough to find out what the fuck was going on.

Shaking harder now, as if she had a palsy, she stared blankly into the distance and pointed a single hand up the flight of stairs that led from the hallway to the upper floor. Then, she curled up into a foetal position on the ground, and refused to say anything else.

Travis hung up the phone, returned to us.

'Cops and ambulance are on their way,' he said, and I saw how white he was.

'Look after her,' I said, feeling as if I were suddenly very distant from things. 'Find her a blanket. Keep...keep talking to her. She's in shock.'

She's not the only one, I thought.

Travis nodded, and crouched down next to Megan.

'It's okay, sweetie,' he said, and I could hear something choking up his voice. 'It's okay. The ambulance is coming, and the police. We'll look after you, sweetie.'

Megan didn't reply, but then I didn't expect her to.

I gripped my gun hard in my right hand, which was now slick with sweat, and headed up the stairs.

As I climbed, I noticed bloody footprints coming down the stairs in the opposite direction towards me, as if someone had walked through a large puddle of blood, and then kept on walking. I moved over, trying not to destroy any evidence, and swallowing my fear as best as I could. I knew that what I was about to see would be terrible.

I just didn't appreciate how....oh, Jesus.

* * *

I SMELLED it before I saw it, if that makes sense.

It's hard to explain that smell, but I'll try. It smelled...rich, thick, and damp. It was heavy, and sweet, but sour, too. It filled the air like a solid red mist, that smell. You could almost see it swirling through the air, climbing into your mouth and up through your nostrils. I covered the lower half of my face with my free hand, bringing my gun hand up in front of me.

I knew death when I smelled it.

I hesitated on the landing, wondering which

room to start with. Then I looked down, and saw a trail of Megan's bloody footprints running from one door to another, starting with what looked like the master bedroom. Her parent's room. I blanched: there was a lot of blood, thick and rich and dense.

I closed my eyes, steadied my breathing, thought about turning back, then thought that maybe, somehow, despite the blood everywhere, someone in that room was still alive, and still needed my help. Shaking, I pulled my free hand inside my sleeve and, careful not to contaminate the door with my own fingerprints, I pushed it open, and went inside the master bedroom.

❊ ❊ ❊

WHAT REMAINED of Ed and Lana Morris was painted all across the walls of their immaculately decorated bedroom in a violent explosion of gore that looked like scarlet graffiti to my struggling brain. For a split second I thought I was looking at a prank, or a violent act of vandalism. I'd seen a car covered in red paint once, a whole tin of the stuff.

This room looked like that car.

But it wasn't paint.

I stood rigidly in the doorway, mind spinning as I tried to process exactly what I was seeing.

Red.

It was all red.

How can there be so much blood in the human body?

How?

It was everywhere, over every single surface, like a bomb had gone off while they were lying in bed together.

'Ahhhh,' I said, unable to form any coherent thought or sentence. 'Ahhhhhhhh...God. Oh, God.'

The silence that answered me was profound. Somewhere, something dripped onto a carpeted floor. Drip, drip, drip. Life, drained away.

I closed my eyes, and a cold surge of dizziness swept over me. I opened them again, and tried desperately to make out any remnants of human shape left on the bed, someone I could help, maybe, some vestige of a human being that I could return to the girl on the floor downstairs, or something we could bury, at the very least. I could find only wet, misshapen lumps, and unidentifiable, splintered bones.

I backed out slowly, my head spinning. I made a sort of animal noise in the bottom of my throat as I struggled to deal with what has happening.

I found myself standing on the landing, chest heaving, staring at my feet, trying to regain my balance. I saw more footsteps, leading further up the landing, away from me. I followed as if I were a drifting ghost, feet moving unbidden, my brain shutting down bit by bit.

The bloody prints led, of course, to Megan's room. I pushed my way in.

I had thought the parent's bedroom bad enough. This was worse.

This was much, much worse.

❊ ❊ ❊

HER ROOM WAS DECORATED for Christmas, with a small tree in the bay window and a red and green knitted stocking draped over the bedstead at the foot of the large, pink wooden bed.

Like a moth to the flame, I drifted closer, and this time, it took me even longer to process what was in front of me. Eventually, after several minutes of staring, I began to make out what I was actually looking at.

In the stocking at the end of the bed, something long and rigid stuck out, dripping blood onto the floor. I gagged when I saw what it was: a foot, attached to a leg, stuffed into the stocking like a goddamned candy cane.

A breeze blew across the room from somewhere as I stared at the foot, at the toenails, so carefully manicured. The baubles and ornaments on the Christmas tree rustled faintly in response.

Except, as I peered at the tree, confused, I realised that not all the things dangling and swaying in the breeze were baubles. I blinked, trying to make sense of it. Then it hit me.

They were eyes.

Glistening, shreds of optic nerve still attached. And there were ears, too. And... oh, God. Two severed tongues hung from a clear, viscous, stringy substance like fishing nylon, but... organic, somehow. Silver tinsel sparkled and mingled with shiny pink intestines, fairy lights twinkled delicately, and instead of an angel or a star on top of the tree there was...

There was a head.

I took an involuntary step forward, drawn despite myself. I caught a glimpse of matted blonde hair, moving in the same breeze that riffled through the branches. Empty, ruined eye-sockets. Something dripping, something else bone-white gleaming in the fairy lights.

And, attached to the topmost branches of the tree by more of that sticky string were a cluster of long, ricegrain shaped parcels, about six inches long from tip to tip. Each one was white, and had a gummy, tacky surface. They looked like poorly wrapped presents, left in the tree by a demented Santa Claus.

I made an incoherent noise and ran from the room.

Christmas would never be the same again.

❋ ❋ ❋

Cruel Works of Nature

I SAT with my head between my knees at the breakfast bar in the Morris' blue and green-tiled, Mediterranean style kitchen, as men and women in uniform moved through the rest of the house, going through the motions of isolating the crime scene. Blue and red lights flickered across the walls, thrown there by the emergency vehicles parked up outside. Blue, red, blue red. I closed my eyes, exhausted, head pounding, but when I did it was *all* red, so I opened them, and wondered if I'd ever be able to sleep again.

Megan was given powerful sedatives and taken away in an ambulance for medical examination. Her aunt and uncle were contacted, and I didn't have to go far to imagine how they would be feeling right now as they made their way to the hospital. My confused thoughts turned to my own niece, only two doors away, and I worried, thinking: *Is she safe?*

What kind of person could do something like that?

Is she safe?

I tried several times to leave the Morris house and check on my girls, but a young cop with blonde hair and a nervous smile had been instructed to keep me there, alongside Travis, until the police were ready for me. He took my gun away and kept bringing me cups of piping hot coffee in polystyrene cups from God knows where: certainly not the Morris kitchen. I shook as I accepted them, and both Travis and I asked several times if something a little stronger could be added to each cup, but the cop just shook his head ruefully at us and went back to his position on guard outside the kitchen door.

'How much longer you think they'll keep us here?' Travis said, gruffly, after our third cup of coffee.

I shook my head. Speech was still difficult for me. Every time I opened my mouth I saw red, heard the sound of a faint breeze tinkling Christmas ornaments, saw that... tree. I was amazed at myself for not puking. Amazed, but also I realised I'd sort of lost touch with my body, and almost... forgotten how to do things with it.

Travis sighed. 'I should have gone up there with you, Peter,' he said, patting my sore shoulder with a large hand. 'You shouldn't have had to see that all by yourself, man. I'm sorry.'

I stared at the floor, still not able to put the words together properly. Travis sighed again, and kept patting my shoulder, as if petting a nervous dog.

Red. So much red. A tinkle, and a movement of the branches. A cool breeze, blonde hair shifting, catching the light...

Something swam to me as I sat there, the walls of shock closing in. I took a while to let the thought rise up, not wanting to scare it away.

Red.

A breeze.

Wait...where...

...Where was the breeze coming from?

I lifted my head.

'Hey,' I croaked to the young cop on guard duty. 'Hey, do you know if the window in Megan's room was open?'

The cop turned to look at me, but before he could say anything, a tall woman in a suit moved past him and into the kitchen to join us. With a serious face she showed us her I.D. I took from her age, which was around fifty, and the way she held herself and approached us, that she was someone in authority. I could also tell that she was distressed, but doing a fine job of disguising it. Her skin was just a little too pale for it to be a completely convincing performance, and the muscles around her jaw worked a little too fast, as if she were clenching her teeth over and over, or chewing gum, really hard. This meant she had been upstairs, and seen what I had seen. Only she was in way better shape than I was.

I repeated my question, and this time I aimed it at her.

'Do you know? The window, in Megan's room...was it open? I can't... I can't remember...'

She looked at me for a long moment, measuring me with a pair of cool, grey eyes. I could see she was wrestling with herself, trying to establish how much she could entrust me with in terms of information.

'Please,' I continued, voice unsteady. 'I think it's important.'

She pursed her lips, then sighed. 'Okay, sure,' she said in a deep voice. 'The window was shut, actually. Why do you want to know?'

The window was shut.

So where had the breeze come from?

I had a flashback to the night before. To blocking up Alice's fireplace with hardboard. I'd been drilling holes, and I'd noticed a breeze, a cool breeze, coming down the chimney, and I'd wondered why I hadn't blocked the damn thing up years before, to save on heating bills.

'Have you...have you checked the fireplace?' I asked, and the woman cocked her head to one side.

'Why? What would we be looking for, exactly?'

'I don't know. But...when I went into the room...Megan's room...there was a breeze. It's what drew me to the tree in the corner, the sound of the breeze in the branches, kind of shaking the ornaments around...oh, God.' I passed a hand over my face, feeling nauseous again. I wished my stomach would hurry up and empty itself, and give me some temporary relief, but it never did. It just churned and gurgled as I sat there, gripped by horror.

'Sit down, Pete,' said Travis, guiding me back to a chair. I did as I was told, but carried on talking. I needed to make sense of it all before I went mad.

'And if there was no window open...the breeze

had to come from somewhere, right? I don't know how important it is, but...maybe...check the fireplace? The chimney...I don't know.'

'When you broke the door down, you said it was locked, from the inside?'

Travis answered for me. 'Yes, Ma'am. Locked tight. Took a big shove to get that door down.' She nodded.

'And as you entered the house, you didn't see any obvious signs of a break in? Smashed glass, a ladder on the outside of the house, anything like that?'

Travis shook his head. 'We were kind of distracted, Ma'am. The girl...she ran right to us, and we didn't get much of a chance to take anything in, if you understand what I'm saying. She was so upset. I just ran for the phone.' He cleared his throat, thinking out loud. 'Come to think of it though, if the windows were closed upstairs... well, these old houses, we got real big chimneys, you know. Pete might have a point.'

The woman continued to assess us, silently, for an uncomfortably long amount of time. It dawned on me, then, the reason we were being kept here all this time. As the first people on the scene, we were automatically suspects in a double homicide. The thought turned my blood into ice.

The woman eventually nodded, and spoke into a walkie she detached from a hook on her belt.

'Janice, come in.'

There was silence for a beat, and then another female voice, thick with Bronx and sounding harassed, rang out:

'Ah...yeah?'

'Can you pay special attention to the area around the fireplace and the chimney in the girl's bedroom? Our witness seems to think there is reason to look more closely around there.'

It stung to hear her use the word 'girl'. 'Megan', I said, in a defeated voice. 'Her name is Megan.'

The woman in the suit kept her voice neutral, ignoring me, and waited for a response. It came after a pause, crackling with static over the walkie.

'What, does he think the killer came down the fucking chimney like Santy Clause?!'

The woman shook her head, and shot me an apologetic look. Again, I had an impression that she was repressing a lot of strong feelings, and I reluctantly admired her strength of character.

'Just do it, would you? Check it carefully for signs of entry or otherwise. Shoe prints, scuff marks, soot, maybe even partial prints if we're lucky. Leave no corner of that room untouched, you hear?'

'Sure, fine. You know, I left a turkey roast behind for this. Merry fucking Christmas to me.'

The walkie snapped off, and I shuddered, folding my arms against a chill that would not subside.

'Thanks,' I said. Then:

'Are you a detective?'

The woman nodded, then reconsidered and shook her head. Then she stuck her hand out towards me.

I shook my head and refused the offer, gesturing at myself.

'I wouldn't,' I said, by way of explanation. 'I'm still covered in...well.' We both glanced at my brown, now crusty clothes, soaked in the blood that Megan had transferred to me when I first broke through the door that morning, blood that had dried, and felt... permanent, somehow. I was desperate to take everything off and shower until my skin burned, but I hadn't been allowed to leave, or wash, or do anything since the cops arrived.

The woman acknowledged the mess I was in with a dip of her head. 'I'm sorry we had to keep you here so long, like this. I know you're not exactly comfortable. With this being Christmas day and all, it's taken us a while to gather everyone up and get them over here. I'm sure you understand... we can't let you leave just yet, not until your statement has been properly recorded. For a case like this, we thought that would be best done by me.'

'And you are?' Travis sounded unimpressed.

'Sure, sorry, that was remiss of me. For the purposes of this chat, you can call me Helen.'

She pulled up a chair and sat down carefully,

bringing a digital tape recorder out and setting it gently down on a counter next to her. She then proceeded to reel off some legal jargon, and I knew we were about to be asked for our statements, and I knew we were about to be assessed as potential murderers. I knew she wanted me to relive that moment, that awful moment, when I pushed through that first bedroom door and saw what I saw. She would want me to recount my journey as I moved from there to Megan's room. She would want all the details, and I just... couldn't...

'I'm sorry,' I said, cutting in over her spiel. 'I can't. I just can't. Don't make me relive that. Not this second, not right now. I...can't...'

My shaking hands came up to my face, trying and failing to disguise my distress.

'You've seen it,' I said, through my fingers. 'You've seen what I've seen. How can you still be standing there, so...calm?'

'Peter,' she said, softly, and I raised my head to look at her because she just had one of those voices: when she spoke, you listened.

'I wish I could say it was the worst thing I've seen, Peter. But the sad truth is that I've actually seen worse, believe it or not, and years in this job have given me coping mechanisms. Plus my training. Extensive training in how to handle myself in the very worst of situations. I wish I could say it made me feel any better, but it doesn't.' She shook her head, wryly. 'I also drink a lot of wine come the evening.'

'What could you possibly have seen that was worse than... that?' I said, gesturing to the upstairs of the house, incredulous and on the verge of tears.

She just stared at me, and shook her head once more.

'Look, miss, you gonna let him go? I mean look at him, he can barely hold his head up straight.' Travis was getting angry at all the back and forth, which wasn't achieving much. 'At the very least have someone look at his shoulder. Way we broke that door down, I wouldn't be surprised if he fractured it or something.'

Helen nodded. 'Of course. But first-'

The beep of the walkie-talkie interrupted her.

'Boss?'

'Yes?'

The voice of Janice sounded less harassed now, and more subdued. 'We found something...in...ah...' The voice coughed, and restarted.

'In..?' Helen said, impatiently.

'Well, yeah. We found something in the chimney, boss. Jammed right up there... just like you said. You better get up here. And bring a flashlight.'

Helen looked at me then, and I knew it would be a while longer before she let us go.

'Stay here, please, gentlemen,' she said, holding her hand out in a holding gesture. It was almost a subconscious command: here was a woman who was used to being in charge, and used to having her every word turned to law.

And something about how fucking imperious she was set me off, suddenly. A small fire lit in my belly.

I stood up.

'I want to see,' I said, voice unsteady with feeling. We locked eyes. I saw irritation flare briefly, then get smothered.

'Wait a minute, Peter,' she said, suspicion in her eyes. 'A moment ago you were just about to refuse to give me a statement, and now all of sudden you want to go back up there? What happened to not wanting to relive it?'

I tried to make sense of it in my own mind, knowing how it looked.

'I... need to see. I don't *want* to see, but I need to. I need to understand what could... I have a kid, Helen. A niece. And my girlfriend... I need to see.'

And then, before anything else could be said, for the second time that Christmas day, I heard screaming.

It was high, and female, and it tore through the air like Megan's screams had only a few hours earlier, and I knew that whatever it was, it was happening again, and we were powerless to stop it.

I knew this, but I broke for the stairs anyway. Maybe there was a chance, a tiny, slim chance that this time, I could help someone.

There wasn't.

* * *

WE MADE FOR THE STAIRS, Helen, Travis, the young cop, and me. I managed to get out in front, taking the steps two at a time. I crashed into Megan's bedroom, shredding through yellow and black crime scene tape, and came to a dead halt when I saw what was happening in front of me.

Then I sank to my knees, whimpering.

I have a vague recollection of Helen running into the back of me, almost knocking me over, and all she could say as she steadied herself against me was 'What the fuck? What the fuck?!' over and over again, as if saying it would make it go away.

But it didn't make it go away. It didn't.

* * *

I TRIED to describe it to people, later. May as well have tried to describe what God looks like. Even now, I'm not sure what is real and what is my brain, gone rogue with despair.

It had a man's body, of sorts. The torso was too long to be completely humanoid, and it was covered with a bright red carapace. There were legs, but they were jointed in the wrong place, and backwards-facing. They ended in wickedly sharp hooks, which dug into the carpet for purchase. Weird, fused genitalia hung down obscenely, brushing against the floor as the thing moved. Its arms were oversized, and there were four of them, barbed with more hooks. It embraced the body of a woman, and, as we watched, it lowered its grossly oversized head which was covered in scraggly, white bristles, and tore into the soft flesh of her abdomen with a pair of small, sharp mandibles. The sound of rending, tearing skin filled the air between it and us, and the thing began dissecting what I can only assume was once Janice, with a delicate, surgeon-like precision. Rows of shiny, black eyes watched us as we watched it right back. It took its time, working up the body towards the neck like a tailor slicing through fabric, severing the woman's head and letting it drop to the floor with a weighty thump.

Then, eyes bright with awareness, it kicked the head towards us. Shiny, black hair caught the light as the head rolled, and came to rest mere inches from where I knelt.

We screamed, scrambled backwards. Vaguely, I heard someone click the safety off a gun, and then a shot roared out over our heads.

The thing flinched, and scuttled backwards with impossible speed, screeching in defiance at us and still hugging the headless body like a prize teddy won at the county fair. The young

Cruel Works of Nature

cop who'd fired the shot fumbled with his gun and dropped it, swearing and scrabbling around on the floor for it.

In the brief interlude, the thing in the room lifted up Janice's headless body and then, with incredible care and precision, neatly folded it in half at the waist, as if it were making a paper airplane. I heard the spine snap like a wet branch. I heard other things pop, and crackle. Pop, and crackle, just like the fire. The noises will live in my mind, always, until the day I die.

With the body compacted down into a manageable size, the thing moved backwards slowly, and steadily, using a foot to probe behind it for safe footing. Then, inch by inch, keeping eye contact with me the entire way, it disappeared into the gloom of the fireplace, and the body disappeared with it, inching its way backwards and upwards, until, at last, after what felt like a thousand years, all that was left of the scene was a scrabbling, scratching sound echoing down the chimney, and the disembodied head of a mid-thirties woman staring at us with a shocked expression.

I turned, and ran, pushing past Helen, who was still shrieking with a now hoarse voice, and the cop, one thought and one thought only in my mind:

Alice. Mona. My girls.

I fell down the last few stairs, rolled, swore, and crashed out of the front door, shouting to

Travis as I went. 'You need to go home and board up your fireplaces, Travis!' I roared, and I heard him hard on my heels, swearing under his breath.

Outside was chaos, as people gathered in the street, both uniform and locals, stared up at something on the roof of the Morris house.

'What the fuck is that?!' I heard someone say as I pushed through the crowd, and, despite myself, I turned and glanced back, and I saw it, sitting there in the early evening gloom which was falling like a dropped veil. The thing, crouched on the roof of the house, its prize, the body of a helpless, innocent woman, slung across its back like a sack of goddamn presents.

It hunkered down, watching us, and, behind it, a single star winked into existence in the night sky.

Then, seemingly on a whim, it let go of the body. The corpse rolled down the steep incline of the roof, and, with an air of finality, fell, landing with a crash onto the roof of a cop car parked next to the house. The car alarm blared out, and the thing raised its ugly head in response, opened its mandible-choked mouth, and let out a throaty roar.

Chaos erupted in the street. The nightmarish spell broken, people scattered and ran for their homes or their cars.

The thing on the roof scuttled across the ridge with incredible speed, lowered its torso, braced its legs, and then leapt into the air. It sailed through the sky and landed with a crash on the roof of the next house along.

The Atwood house. My next door neighbours.

One house away from my own.

I knew the Atwoods were away in Florida this Christmas, and I also knew it wouldn't take the creature long to figure that out. I could see Helen standing in the street and screaming into her radio, trying to put out a call for backup, but God knows how long it would be before they arrived, and I was pretty sure my house would be next on its itinerary.

I saw the thing make its way to the chimney top and then, somehow, fold itself into a thin, stretched out version of itself, cramming its body down the chimney until it was magically, impossibly gone.

Alice. Mona.

'Spread the word!' I yelled, once more, pumping my arms and legs and making for my front door. 'Block up your chimneys! It comes down the goddamn chimney!'

Faintly, I heard Travis, from further up the street. 'Be careful, Pete!' he cried, and then it was every man for himself, every man for his family, running to get to the people he loved most, before it was too late.

❖ ❖ ❖

I THUNDERED in through my front door.

'Alice? Mona?!'

Silence greeted me, and my panic almost consumed me.

I went from room to room, furiously searching for my girls, praying they were alive, praying they were in a room which didn't have a fireplace.

'Here!' I heard Mona say, and I stumbled in relief, then swerved to find them in the TV room, cosying up next to the blazing fire, which had been built up high again.

Alice was peacefully asleep on the couch, with her head on Mona's lap. She didn't wake as I came crashing in, and I almost collapsed to my knees when I saw her unharmed.

Covered in blood, eyes wild with terror, I must have looked a sight and a half, because the colour drained from Mona's face.

'Pete?' she said, shocked and scared. 'What's happening, Pete? We heard noises, but I didn't want to...I didn't want Alice to hear, so we came in here and put the TV on.'

I stood, chest heaving, gulping for air, an imposter in this peaceful scene. When I could, I said only one sentence:

'We need to block up the fireplaces.'

'What?' Mona said, incredulous, but I didn't elaborate. Instead, I picked Alice up gently, and led them both to the kitchen where there was no chimney breast, no fireplace, and a lot of sharp knives. 'Stay here,' I instructed, locking the back door, lowering all the blinds, and grabbing a carving knife. I shoved it through my belt.

Alice woke up, at last, rubbing her eyes and looking at me blearily.

'What's going on, Uncle P?' she said, and I knew she immediately understood the gravity of the situation from the look on my face: she'd been here before, on another night. She was a survivor, this kid, and it gave me hope, cemented my resolve. We would get through this. We would. I just had to keep the thing out of our house, and wait for someone in authority to come along and kill it.

'I'm keeping you safe, that's what's going on,' I said, and I hugged her once, hard, before kissing Mona fiercely, and then barricading the kitchen door behind me with a side-table.

It was time to go to work.

❈ ❈ ❈

IN HINDSIGHT, I don't know what I was thinking. I should have gotten them out of the house, into the car, and driven for the hills.

But some ancient instinct of 'defend thy castle' kicked in, and, instead, I ran around the house like a mad person.

There were six rooms in my house that were connected to two main chimney flues. I'd blocked up Alice's fireplace yesterday, so that left five open fireplaces remaining. I scrambled for the top floor, to the old, disused attic space, the closest point of entry. I pulled down the collapsible attic ladder, took a deep breath, swarmed up it with my carving knife held out in one hand, reached out with the other, shaking hand, and fumbled for the light-switch.

It pinged on, and the light of a naked bulb illuminated a largely empty, cobwebbed space filled with insulating foam and a few abandoned pieces of furniture I'd been meaning to sell.

A sense of desperate urgency dogged every second I stood there, scanning the attic for signs of the creature. *Keep them safe,* it said, over and over. *Keep them safe.*

I slid the knife back through my belt and rushed to an old wardrobe leaning against a wall. I put my damaged shoulder to it began to shove, bolts of pain shooting through me, the veins in my neck and on my forehead throbbing with exertion.

I'd managed to push it to within a foot of the fireplace when I heard something scuttle in the chimney. It sounded tentative, as if listening for me. I swore, and redoubled my efforts, a sick feeling rising in my throat.

Then, a little shower of old soot and cement rubble landed in the hearth, puffing out into a black dust cloud into the attic space.

It was coming.

Cruel Works of Nature

I was almost there. I heaved once more, and the wardrobe snagged on a screw sticking out of the floorboards, sticking fast and refusing to budge. I kept my eyes fixed on the fireplace at all times, seeing a dark shadow gathering there, hearing more movement, and odd, chittering, insectile noises.

Slowly, carefully, a single clawed, serrated arm extended out of the darkness of the fireplace and into the attic, testing the air, and then the ground beneath it, like a probe.

I yelled and pushed with every single muscle and fibre in my body. The wardrobe tore over the top of the protruding screw head and shot towards the fireplace in a sudden rush of release. I heard a snap as the creature's arm became jammed behind the wardrobe.

And then the thing shrieked in pain and in rage, and pushed the full weight of its body against the wardrobe, fighting back.

Crying now, sobbing like a baby, I planted my back and braced myself, feet anchored into the floorboards, pushing backwards as the wardrobe bucked against me and the thing scrabbled against the wooden frame, squealing with impotent fury.

Then, all of a sudden, the wardrobe crashed back into place and I fell backwards.

The thing fell silent.

I leaned, spent, against the wooden blockade, face wet with tears and sweat, gasping for breath.

Had it retreated? Had it given up?

I heard more muffled scrabbling inside the chimney flue, and realised, with dread, that it wasn't retreating.

It was simply climbing down, aiming for the next fireplace.

The next room down was Alice's room, which I'd boarded up.

The room beneath that was the TV room. The fire was lit in that room.

An idea blossomed. Could I trap it in the chimney flue, suffocate it somehow? Let the fire smother, or roast it to death?

My eyes fell upon an old, mouldy mattress not far from where I stood, panting. It was the kind of mattress you found on a futon, not a bed, which meant it was unsprung. Unsprung meant I could fold it in half, and stuff it up the chimney.

Scuttle scuttle, went the beast behind the chimney breast, inching its way down to the next level.

I don't know how I did it, but I did.

I dragged the wardrobe away from the fireplace once more, ran to the mattress, heaved it across the floor, rolled it into a tube shape, and stuffed it up the chimney. Then I dragged the wardrobe back, vaulted down the ladder, and raced down the hall to Alice's room.

I heard the thing tapping and slapping its legs against the boarded-up fireplace. I didn't stick around to see if it would break through or not. I tipped over Alice's desk with a crash and threw it against the hearth as an extra barricade. Then I ran downstairs again, this time to the TV room.

❋ ❋ ❋

I PUSHED THE DOOR OPEN. Everything inside was tranquillity.

The fire had died down, but was still glowing. The TV set in the corner of the room was showing the title sequence of a Christmas movie. As the text scrolled lazily up the screen, a tried and tested Christmas classic blared out cheerily.

'You'd better watch out,' the voices said. *'You'd better not cry...'*

Hysteria almost obliterated all thought and reason then, as I saw the Christmas lights strung over the fireplace cycle dreamily through different festive colours. It was like crossing from a nightmare into a dream where everything felt soft, and fuzzy, and surreal.

In the distance I heard Mona call out to me from the kitchen.

'Pete?' She called, her voice muffled through the door, and I could tell how scared she was. 'Pete? What's going on out there? What's happening?'

'You'd better not pout...'

'Keep them safe,' I muttered, and then the fire

began to sputter, and I saw legs emerge from the mouth of the chimney.

'Pete? Pete, we're scared, and Alice has to use the bathroom. Answer me, Pete! What's going on?' I heard the kitchen door rattle and then thump into the table I'd pushed against it as a barrier.

But I couldn't answer her. All I could do was stare at the fireplace and wait for the thing that was coming.

And, inch by inch, carefully, like a spider creeping across a web to a struggling fly, it emerged. One arm was mangled, but this didn't deter it. It slid down the chimney and out into the room like a living nightmare, black and red, with white whiskers all over its head, its disgusting eyes scanning the room and finding me, its legs and arms coming into an angular formation beneath it, the mandibles in its mouth rubbing together with an audible, juicy squeak.

Dimly, I heard the kitchen door shove open again, and the squeak of furniture being pushed back as Mona fought her way out.

'Pete?!' She cried, as the thing and I faced each other. 'Pete, why won't you answer me?!'

The knife was still in my belt. I could feel the tip of it pressing dangerously into my thigh.

But then, a sense of despair overtook me. What good would it do, really? One measly knife against this...abomination?

'Uncle Pete?' a little voice said from the doorway behind me.

I froze, almost doubling over, as if I'd been punched in the gut.

Alice. She must have slipped through the gap between the dresser and the kitchen door to come and find me. I could still hear Mona struggling in the background, the door banging against the dresser with more and more urgency.

'Uncle Pete?' she said again, and suddenly, time became nothing. We were dolls in a display, flies trapped in amber.

The thing slowly turned its hideous head, and fixed its malevolent gaze upon my niece, my Alice, my beautiful, brave girl, who stood, with her thumb in her mouth and a strand of hair threaded through the fingers on her other hand, locked in place, immobile with fear, incomprehension in her wide blue eyes.

I swam up from my shock and shouted at her.

'Get away from here! Run!'

She started, and then turned, stumbling against the doorframe, trying to make a run for it, trying so hard, but she hit the doorframe rigidly, and it sent her off balance, so that she stumbled.

The beast reared up onto its back legs, pulled its head back, and lashed out at her.

A single long leg shot through the air and latched itself onto Alice's foot. It yanked her off her feet, and then the thing began pulling her towards it, gibbering in demented triumph.

'NO!' I roared, and I heard Mona, who'd finally made it over the barricade, shouting the exact same word: 'NO!'

Alice screamed and struggled, but the beast was stronger than her, stronger than me, stronger than any of us. I lunged for her, and saw Mona do the same, but it all seemed too inevitable, too beyond my control. Her body flailed and fought, to no avail. The creature reeled her in like a trout on a line, tensing its entire frame as it did so, bracing some hidden, internal mechanism it used for just this purpose: capturing prey. A part of me wanted to liken it to a spider, but it wasn't like a spider at all, more like a preying mantis, a killing machine, an ungodly primal abomination, trying to survive, to feed, to exist, just like we all were, every day of our lives.

I grabbed hold of Alice's arms as she whipped past me, and she shouted in pain as she drew to a sudden halt. I realised then, with horror, that I was caught in a momentary tug of war with the thing, a fight I knew I would lose if I didn't want to rip the tiny, fragile girl in half.

'Mona!' I screamed, feeling her right behind me. 'The knife! The knife in my belt!'

Mona fumbled at my belt and yanked out the carving knife. Then, with a quick, downwards slashing movement, she sliced through the limb holding on to Alice's ankle.

The beast roared and launched itself at us in a renewed attack as we tumbled backwards in a ball of arms and legs. There was shadow, and a rotten, putrid stink, and then it was upon us, slashing with its arms, rending at our flesh with its hooks, spitting and working its mandibles until, suddenly, there was a sickening *crunch!* And the thing squealed with a pain so palpable that I felt my eyes roll back in my skull, and blood start to trickle out of my nose.

There was a glint, a flash of fairy lights on steel, and the crunching sound came again, followed by the splatter of liquid, and I realised it was Alice, who was born a survivor, Alice, who had only been a small girl when her Father shot her Mother and then hung himself in his prison cell six weeks later, my Alice, my brave girl, brandishing a carving knife and systematically stabbing each one of the beast's beady, black eyes until they were ruined and leaking, Alice, who then stuck the knife into the small, fleshy gap between the beast's bright red carapace and its whiskered, distorted head.

There was a sticky noise, and the creature's arms and legs began to jerk in an uncoordinated display, like a puppet with its strings all crossed, and the blade rose and fell, rose and fell, until suddenly, the thing wasn't moving anymore, and Alice burst into tears and sat back on the floor, the knife falling from her fingers.

Without hesitation, I picked it up, grabbed hold of the twitching creature's ruined head, and sawed the damned thing right off, just to be sure.

Then I threw it into the embers, which glowed with renewed vigour, sending showers of sparks into the smoky chimney while Christmas carols played out on the TV behind us.

* * *

'WE THOUGHT we were dealing with a serial killer, you have to understand,' Helen told me, days later.

We'd been evacuated from our house and settled into a temporary home. Men with masks and decontamination suits had arrived only minutes after the police and army had showed up. I'd pointed to the charred, gently smoking head in the fireplace, and they'd stared at me from behind safety visors, like I was an alien.

Helen continued.

'I'm a behavioural analyst, you see. There was... another case, that very same day, in Michigan. Not far from you. An easy enough distance to drive, within an hour or two. An older couple, the grandson found them. Same M.O. Well, we *thought* it was an M.O. A severed head, dismembered limbs, the savagery of attack, the fact that the victims were asleep while it happened. The... arrangement of the limbs and internal organs around the room. We thought it was a man, a psychotic man. We thought it was escalating behaviour.' She laughed, bitterly. 'I drew up a

Cruel Works of Nature

profile, made sure that we held anyone found on scene for questioning. I was trying to figure out if *you* matched my profile when...oh, God.' She sighed with a deep, heartfelt remorse. 'I don't know how I could have gotten it so wrong. I should have seen that there was no rationality behind any of it, no pattern, no discernible profile. It was just...well, it was just an animal. A "cruel work of nature," as Darwin once said, I believe.'

Helen gripped her coffee mug miserably, and avoided eye-contact.

I stared into my own steaming mug and asked: 'Did I?'

'What?' The analyst looked confused.

'Did I fit the profile?'

She shook her head. 'No, not really. I mean, age, sex, and ethnicity, sure. But I was convinced we were looking for someone with a record of assault, someone with abuse in his background, someone who lived a transitory lifestyle and had perhaps spent several years perfecting his technique...ugh.' She waved a hand, embarrassed. 'What does it matter? None of that matters, now.'

'Why do you think it did it?'

'What?' Helen frowned at me. 'You mean, killed?'

'No.' I shook my own head. 'I mean, why did it...you know, decorate?' I struggled with the word, but it was the most fitting term that sprang to mind. A vision flashed through my mind: a severed head, instead of a star, at the top of the tree. Blonde hair, illuminated by flashing lights, moving in a faint breeze.

She folded her arms and chose her words carefully. 'I can't... divulge too much of this, firstly because it's been taken off of my hands now, but secondly because, what I *do* know, I overheard when I shouldn't have been listening. But it made sense to me, I guess. Do you remember anything else about Megan Morris' bedroom, Pete?'

I thought about it, and something niggled, a loose end, but I couldn't bring it to mind clearly enough to voice.

'Something, but...my memory...well, I'm running blanks, if you know what I mean. Probably my brain's way of coping with the trauma. Or whatever. You're the shrink, you know what I mean.'

'I'm not a shrink, Peter, I'm an analyst. But that's beside the point. In the tree, Peter, aside from the human remains we found there. We also found...well, for want of a better word, we found eggs. In Michigan, too, in the Christmas tree, just the same.'

A memory shot out of the fog and into the clear. White, sticky parcels, shaped like grains of rice, about six inches long, and attached to the Christmas tree with a milky, white fibre.

'Oh,' I said, and my skin prickled with realisation. Eggs. Helen continued.

'It was building a nest, the experts believe. They've called in a slew of bug and infestation people on this one. The CDC, too. I heard them on a conference call when I was handing the case over. No-one's seen anything like this, but what they do know, or what I could glean at any rate, is that certain insects decorate their lairs and nests with the carcasses of their prey and other items. Wasps build nests out of multi-coloured paper. Other bugs like to keep food around...well, for their offspring to eat. When they hatch.'

It was just trying to survive, I thought, remembering the ferocity with which it had torn off Janice's head. We'd disturbed its nest. It was protecting its young, just like I'd been protecting Alice. Trying to build a home for its offspring, feed them, build a world where they could thrive.

I turned my head and looked out the window. Alice and Mona were in the backyard, mooching around in a thin blanket of snow that had fallen overnight. I looked at them, and Mona glanced up, caught my eye. Alice had her head down, and was subdued, quiet, gazing at the snow, her face pale, and drawn.

Damaged, the full extent of which we would never know. Her, and Mona, and me too. All damaged. Just like Megan, and Travis, and even the stoic Helen, who sat calmly in front of me with her straight back and carefully arranged hairstyle and neatly pressed trousers.

Damaged, but alive.

Mona mouthed the words 'I love you' at me through the window. I made up my mind then and there that I would marry her, when this died down further. Stop fucking around, stop wasting the precious days, and just get on with the living. Care for Alice, maybe give her a baby cousin to play with.

Survive.

'You have a lovely family,' Helen said, softly, watching me as I watched them. 'And that child... what a remarkable child.'

'I know,' I said, and then, ever so gently, it began to snow. I stared at the snowflakes the same way I used to stare at the fire in my TV room, watching patterns swirl and form in the sky, only there was no noise, no crackle or pop of gunfire, only peace.

And I thought to myself, remotely, as if someone else were thinking the thought and not me:

You could lose a lot of hours of your life staring at the snow.

You could.

But why waste them?

Cruel Works of Nature

351

SKETCHBOOK

I N MY NIGHTMARES, YOU ARE FIVE YEARS OLD AGAIN.

I hold you in my arms. You bury your face into my neck, shaking. Your skinny, strong legs are wrapped around my waist. Your breath is hot and ragged against my skin. You are heavy, but it's a weight I cannot feel. The only thing I can feel is this huge, crushing burden of terror, terror that threatens to snap me in two like a dry twig.

I am frozen to the spot. And all I can manage is to hold you tight, your fear coursing through my own veins.

'Make him go away, Mommy!' you shout, but I can't move, I can't do anything. I just stand there and hold you, watching our death approach on spindly, awkward limbs.

The twisted figure of an impossible man moves unsteadily towards us.

He trails a long-handled axe across the floor. It shrieks as it drags across the tiles of our kitchen, and whispers with intent as it hits the thick-pile rug by the door. The man laughs, an idiot, chuckling laugh. It fills up the air between us with ravenous, wicked intent.

His proportions are wrong. His legs are thin, and crooked. His arms look like the branches of a dead tree, his fingers like sticks. His left shoulder sits higher up on his body than his right. He has an awkward, limping gait as a result. His head is cocked stiffly to one side although his gaze never wavers. His eyes are two bright, white spots in a sea of murky, scribbled black.

Around his neck hangs a grisly wreath, made of blood, and bone, and hair. A small infant hand dangles from the centre of the wreath, and I cannot take my eyes off of it, no matter how hard I try. The tiny fingernails are stained red.

I scream, because I do not know what else to do, I do not know how to keep you safe.

'Mommyyyyy!' You cry, but the word dies in the air and hangs there, impotent.

The twisted figure lets out a bubbling, lunatic laugh once again, and takes another step forward.

It's the Bogeyman, and he has come for you.

* * *

WHEN I WAKE, you are a grown man, staring at me with concern on your face as I lie here in my hospital bed, things beeping and whirring all around me. Hospitals are desperately noisy places, and I hate being here, but the sight of you warms my heart and chases the nightmare away.

Nightmare, or memory?

I hardly know, these days.

You take my hand and smile at me with that devastating smile of yours, and an unruly blonde curl works its way free from the thatch on your head. For a moment I see the five-year-old version of you staring back at me again, instead of the man you've become since. Sparkling eyes and devil-may care, gap-toothed grin. Hair in desperate need of ruffling. Cheeks that just had to be pinched and kissed.

A white, long scar winds itself across one of those cheeks, now. I run a single finger along it, gently. I remember the night you got that scar, and shudder, a familiar sensation of sickening dread pushing up the gooseflesh on my arms as the nightmare rudely forces its way back into my mind.

All these years later, and I still dream about that night.

It's a small price to pay to have you here with me, now.

'Mom?' You say, softly, in a man's deep and assured voice. 'Mom, are you awake?'

I don't have the strength to answer you, not yet. Instead, I let myself drift off onto a melancholy train of thought, still drowsy from all the medication I've been given.

The Bogeyman is not done with me yet. He pulls me straight back into the nightmare.

❊ ❊ ❊

HE GRINS, and hefts his axe in his horrible, distorted hands.

'Henry,' he croons, and his little pinprick eyes glow fiercely. His voice is ghastly, and you whimper and clutch me even tighter, shaking violently now. I can't stop staring at the severed hand at his neck. So small.

'Don't be afraid, Henry,' the thing says around a mouthful of dirty, square teeth, all the while getting closer and closer, and slapping the butt of the axe head into the palm of one hand.

Slap, slap, slap.

'Go away!' I scream, finding my voice at last. 'Leave us alone!'

What am I going to do? I think, panicked, desperate, over and over again, a deer in the headlights.

How am I going to keep you safe?

'Go away!' I scream again.

Head already cocked to one side because of his lopsided shoulder, the Bogeyman widens his smile.

'NO!' He hisses, and raises the axe high above his head.

❋ ❋ ❋

I'M AWAKE! Oh, thank God.

Beep, beep, beep goes the infernal machine behind my head. I've been told it's keeping me alive, but I'd really rather it didn't, unless it can do it quietly. Dying has been a noisy affair, so far. Noisy, and slow.

'I love you, Mom,' you say, bringing me back into the moment, and I don't trust myself to reply, not yet. I just smile like an idiot, and enjoy the feeling of you being there, tall, and strong, and no less precious to me than you were when you were only five years old.

'So handsome,' I manage to say, at last, smiling at you.

'Such a handsome boy.'

You laugh, gently. 'Hi, Mom.'

I'm filled suddenly with pride, looking at you. I know that you are going to be okay, when I die, after I have gone, and that is all we can ever hope for our children.

'Have I ever told you about the day you were born, Henry?' I ask, my voice weak. But, before you can reply, the memories come rushing in, clouding my vision, and I sink back into them gratefully, as if falling asleep on a deep, thick pillow.

* * *

I REMEMBER the day you were born. Amazing how clear the memories are, when you're on your way out.

I remember the contract I made with myself on that day.

I had awaited a long time to meet you. Thirty years and nine months, to be exact. If that seems like a long time to wait for your life to begin, well, you're right. I mean, I was happy, before. I was young, and healthy, and I had your Father. We made a good team.

But I knew I needed you. I needed you to make my life complete.

And then, you arrived, with a rush of pain and frantic activity. They handed you to me, and I looked, speechless, at your tiny, wrinkled face, coated with blood and thick white mucus, your little, angry, blue fists clutching tightly at my finger. You cried, and it pierced my heart.

We locked eyes. They were steady, and clear, just like mine. A promise passed between us. The contract, signed in love. A promise to protect you, no matter what the cost, no matter what the risk.

I laughed, and you closed your eyes, and even that tiny movement was perfect.

You were here, finally here: my son was born. And so was I.

* * *

THE SOUND of you crying fades, and the hospital of the past fades into the hospital of today. *Beep, beep, beep,* reminding me of how ill I am. I know it is only a matter of time, now.

A nurse is in the room with us. She is talking to you in hushed, respectful tones.

'It won't be long now,' she says, echoing my own thoughts, and I hear you hitch in your breath.

'Will it... will it hurt?'

'No, she won't be in any pain,' the nurse says. 'She'll get more and more drowsy, and fade in and out of consciousness, and then eventually fall asleep, and that will be it. Just be there for her if she gets confused, or distressed. Call me if you need anything at all. I'll leave you in peace.'

'Thank you, nurse,' you say, sighing heavily, and I feel your hand cover mine once more.

* * *

TIME PASSED. You grew into a toddler, and that toddler became a small boy of five years old in the blink of an eye.

Five. My favourite age, if I'm honest. So grown

Cruel Works of Nature

up in so many ways, and just a baby in so many others. Old enough to display some independence. Young enough to still need me.

You were five the first time you displayed any interest in drawing.

You were five when we got you the sketchbook.

❖ ❖ ❖

WE HAD A ROUTINE, you and I. A way of passing the time together. And sometimes, on a Saturday, that routine meant that I took you to the toy shop, to buy you a treat. Indulgent, yes, but when I was a child, I was too poor for such things, so I had a tendency to spoil you whenever I could, because it felt good to be able to do so.

As we wandered around the store on one particular Saturday, looking at trucks and action figures and construction kits, you turned to me.

'Well, sweetie?' I said, prompting you. 'What would you like to choose? We can spend up to ten dollars. Can you remember what the number ten looks like?' You rolled your eyes as five-year-olds do.

'Of course I know what ten looks like, Mommy. But I don't want a toy for a treat.'

'Oh?' I said, surprised. 'Well, what do you want?'

'I want a sketchbook,' you said, firmly. 'And

some coloured pens. Like we have at school.'

'Oh,' I said, taken aback but secretly delighted. 'Right, then.' There was enough plastic crap in our house to keep ten small boys entertained. A sketchbook would make a nice change. I marched you out of the toy shop and into a neighbouring book store before you could change your mind.

If only we'd walked for five minutes more, chosen a different shop. But we didn't. I was so eager to make the most of your newfound enthusiasm for art that I panicked, dashing into the first place I could find. I've been back, since, tried to retrace our steps, find the shop. It isn't there anymore. Somehow, given the things that followed, this doesn't surprise me.

It was a curious, dusty, dishevelled place, books piled high from floor to ceiling in a haphazard manner. It wasn't really suitable for a five-year-old, but I knew they carried stationary and could see they had a good selection of notebooks, sketchbooks and art materials. These were kept at the back of the store, in a small alcove which was dark, and quiet. There was no store-owner to be seen, so we went straight to the back and started rummaging.

'I'm going to choose, Mommy,' you said, pre-empting me as I picked up an age-appropriate sketchbook covered in dinosaurs.

'Okay,' I said, backing off. 'Of course you can choose.'

You took your time, screwing up your face and humming, something you always did when you tried to concentrate on anything. You shifted through the piles of stationary, fingering the different covers, hardback, softback, patterned, plain, lined, unlined, thick, thin.

Eventually, you made an excited noise. I watched as you pulled at a book at the bottom of the pile, and before I could do anything, the entire pile then collapsed, landing on the floor and scattering everywhere.

'Oh, Henry!' I admonished, but you were in a world of your own, holding your brand new sketchbook out in front of you with a bright, excited smile.

'I want this one!' you said, thrusting an enormous, red book at me. It looked huge in your small hands, and was covered in a thick leather binding that gave it an antiquated feel. I took a moment to appreciate your good taste, and then waggled my finger at you.

' "I want this one... please" ', I corrected. 'And you aren't getting anything until we tidy this mess up.'

You rolled your eyes again, so sassy, even at that age.

'UGHHHHHHHHH,' you complained, but I held firm.

We picked up the other books and stacked them neatly back on the table. I looked around for the store owner, but could see no-one. On further investigation, I spotted an honesty box near the front door.

I shrugged, looking for a price sticker on the sketchbook. When I turned it over in my hands, I spotted a yellowing label with a handwritten message on it stuck to the rear cover.

It read:

Pay only what you think I'm worth.
No refunds or returns.

I shrugged, and put ten dollars in the honesty box, which I thought was adequate for the book and a pack of coloured pens. Then we left. You clutched the book tight to your chest in glee the whole way home.

I had no idea what I'd just done, what I was about to bring into my house.

How could I have known?

This doesn't stop me from blaming myself, every day, for what it did to you. But on that day, we were both oblivious, walking side by side in the sunshine, a happy little unit without a care in the world.

And then, well.

Then, it all went to hell.

❊ ❊ ❊

'HENRY?'

Cruel Works of Nature

My voice sounds alien to me. It sounds thick, and heavy, and cracked, and old. Because that is what I am, now.

You raise your head from your hands and look at me.

You look so tired. My poor boy.

'Mom? What is it?'

'Do you still have it?' I ask, and you know immediately what I'm talking about. You sigh, and rummage around in an overnight bag you have next to you. After a few moments, you pull something out of your bag, and hand it to me. A scent follows the book into the sterile hospital air: evocative, rich, exotic. The smell of cinnamon. I breathe it in.

I take it carefully, with trembling, clumsy fingers that are knotted and spotted with age.

'I thought you had destroyed it,' I say, turning the leather-bound book over in my hands.

'I tried,' you reply. 'I tried a hundred different times. I tried burning it, and throwing it into the river, and once I even tried to feed it through a shredder. The shredder blew up, and the book remained as it is, without a scratch on it.'

'This book was meant to belong to you,' I say, and then, before I lose my courage, I ask you what I've been wanting to ask you all along.

'Henry,' I say, holding you with a firm gaze. 'I want you to draw something for me.'

We stare at each other, and the notebook lies between us, listening, waiting for the inevitable.

Gemma Amor

* * *

WE GOT HOME, and you took your new book and your pens and settled down on the small table in your bedroom. I started preparing a sandwich for your dinner. Peanut butter and jelly, the only thing you would ever ask for. I was in an indulgent mood, so I made it for you as a treat, fully aware that I was going to Mom hell for preparing something so beige and lacking in nutrition.

I was just cutting the sticky, disgusting sandwich into triangles for you when I heard you shout.

'Mom!' You cried, and I could hear excitement in your voice. I wiped my hands on my shirt, and came to find you in your room.

You stood in the middle of your bedroom, covered in pen. You held the sketchbook open in both hands for me to look at, and pointed at the drawing within.

'Look, Mommy, I drew a dog!' You said, and, as I drew closer, my mouth dropped open.

You had, indeed, drawn a dog.

Standing there on the paper, bold as brass, was a large, enthusiastically realised, multi-coloured dog, with a long tail, floppy ears and a black, shiny nose.

I'd been expecting...well, scribbles. Maybe a stickman, at best. I gaped.

I mean, it wasn't perfect. The perspective was

warped, as you would have expected from a five-year-old, and there were too many legs, and the edges were all jagged, and hasty. But it was such a lively drawing, so full of character and warmth, and I was genuinely at a loss for words.

I tore my eyes away from the dog and searched your face intently.

'Did you draw this, sweetie?' I asked, wondering if the book had already been used by someone else before we bought it.

'I did,' you said, chest swelling out. 'I drew it all by my own! He's called Toby.'

I stared at you, still stunned, and gently prised the book out of your hands so that I could get a closer look. I walked over to the window where the light was better, and pressed my face right up against the paper.

I got a whiff of the stiff leather cover, and the starchy pages. They smelled strange, musty, but with a hint of...what was that? Cinnamon?

As I puzzled over the strange scent, trying to put a name to it, out of nowhere I heard a soft, sharp *Yip!*

And then again, once more, almost right inside my ear.

Yip!

Just like a dog, barking.

I jerked my head back, shocked, heart leaping in my chest. Toby the dog grinned at me from the sketchbook, as if laughing at a joke with a punch-line I didn't understand.

I laughed, shaking my head at my own stupidity, nerves still fluttering like moth wings.

Of course the goddamn drawing hadn't barked at me! Ridiculous.

I handed the book back to you, shaking my head sheepishly.

'Darling,' I said, stroking your hair. 'It's wonderful. Shall we put it up on the fridge for Daddy to see?'

'Yes!' you said, beaming that smile at me again, 'and then maybe he can take it to work with him!'

'Maybe,' I said, smiling back at you.

✽ ✽ ✽

I STUCK the drawing to the fridge, as promised. You ate your dinner, and slurped at a glass of milk I set down in front of you absentmindedly.

'What shall I draw next, Mommy?' you said, with your mouth full.

'Hmmmm...' I replied, thinking. Something in me still felt a little unsettled, and I glanced at Toby the laughing dog, who seemed even more lifelike now that he was pinned to our kitchen wall than ever.

'How about... a nice bird?'

'An eagle?' You said, enthusiastic. I shuddered, and shook my head, laughing nervously without knowing why.

'No, not an eagle, please. Something smaller. How about...a robin?'

'But it's not Christmas!'

'Doesn't matter. Robins are my favourite.'

You smiled at me. 'Alright, Mommy.'

Robins are not my favourite birds anymore.

❈ ❈ ❈

AT DINNER TIME, your Father came home, and I showed him the drawing of Toby the dog. He was impressed.

'Did Henry draw that? Really?' He said, echoing my own earlier sentiment of disbelief.

I nodded. 'Looks like that school is teaching him something, after all,' I said, and we both stared at Toby. We fell silent as the scribbled animal stared back at us.

'There's something so... so... lifelike about it,' said your Father, sounding a little creeped out, and I shivered in agreement.

'I know. I mean, it has like, eight legs, but... I know exactly what you mean.'

Your Father took off his glasses, and wiped them with the corner of his shirt, peering once again at the drawing.

'It's like... it almost looks like it's about to move, jump right off the damn paper,' he said, laughing. 'I feel like I should be throwing a stick for it to fetch. I can't believe Henry drew this.'

At that moment, we heard you scream.

'Mommy! Daddy! Come *now!*'

You were shouting, and your voice sounded urgent, panicky. Your father and I looked at each other for a few seconds, then rushed to your room.

We found you cowering in the corner, the sketchbook clutched to your chest. On the floor in front of you, a ripped out page from the book lay, discarded. It was blank.

You pointed wordlessly at the paper, and then at the window. We followed your finger, wondering for a brief moment what the problem was, and then I saw it, and my hands fluttered up to my mouth in disbelief.

A bird flapped and screeched at your window, flying into the glass windowpane again and again and again in a desperate bid to escape the confines of your room and get outside. Each time it hit the glass it made a meaty thudding noise that shook the windowpane in its frame, and each time it came away from the window it chittered and cried out with a strangled warbling sound of frustration and pain.

'Mommy!' You shouted, your face twisted in your own, private panic. 'Mommy, make it stop!'

The bird attacked the window one more time, screaming in a high, manic, wild bird voice, and this time, as it hit the stained and smeared glass, there was a thick POP! And then a fragile, crunching noise.

Cruel Works of Nature

The warbling sounds cut dead in an instant, and the bird fell to the carpet.

'Mommyyyy!' you wailed, and your Father rushed across the room to sweep you up in his arms.

Cautiously, I crept across the bedroom towards the dead bird. As I approached, I saw its feet twitch once, twice, then stop. Belly up, body twisted and frozen in death, it was clear that the poor thing's neck was well and truly broken.

On the windowpane itself a large, red smear was spattered across the glass like graffiti.

I looked down at the bird again, and noticed its red breast, a red that was not blood.

Was it a...

Was it a robin?

My skin prickled, and the hairs on my arms stood to attention.

Draw me a robin, I'd said, and now here was a robin, laying in a bloody cloud of feathers with its neck broken on the bedroom floor.

Your father soothed your tears.

'Shhh,' he said, rocking you. 'I'm sorry buddy, sometimes these things happen. Poor birdy. It must have come in down the chimney and panicked, looking for a way out.'

'Hmmmm,' I said, absentmindedly, staring at the blank sheet of sketchbook paper on the floor, and knowing full well that we'd blocked the chimney in your bedroom up years ago with newspaper, to stop the drafts, and anything else that was undesirable, from coming down it. I felt very far away, all of a sudden.

'I just wanted to draw something nice for Mommy,' you sobbed, and my blood ran like ice.

I said looked from the dead bird, to your face, to the paper once again.

'I drew you a robin like you asked, Mommy,' you continued, struggling through your tears. 'I drew it for you, and then it flew into the window, and, and..!'

You burst into fresh convulsions, and hugged your Father tight. He hugged you back.

I crouched down once more to examine the bird, a strange, tingling sensation running down my spine. I picked it up delicately by one twiggy leg, holding it with distaste between my thumb and index finger.

As I looked at it, *really* looked, I began to feel sick. The robin had a smooth, oddly featherless body. From a distance, it bore the right colours, but up close it was blank, and flattened, and almost plastic looking. It had a weird, two-dimensional feel to it, as if I were holding a cardboard cut-out of a bird. A single, black, beady eye gazed lifelessly at me. A broken beak, which looked like it was too long for the bird in the first place, hung pathetically from the oversized head. The feet, instead of ending in small, delicately formed bird claws, ended in strange, straight, thin appendages that looked like broken match-

Cruel Works of Nature

sticks. The wings were leaf-shaped, instead of wingshaped.

All in all, it looked exactly like a bird would look if a five-year-old had drawn it.

I looked at Henry once again, thinking back to the dog he'd drawn earlier, and the barking noise I thought I had heard. Blood rushed in my ears, and I thought to myself: *Am I going mad? What is happening here, exactly?*

'Poor birdy,' you said, and we all agreed, sadly, whilst inside, my stomach churned.

Poor birdy.

❋ ❋ ❋

YOUR FATHER TOOK you off to watch some cartoons and try to forget about the dead bird which I disposed of using a dustpan, a brush and a lot of newspaper. I swiftly carried it through the house, wrapped it up like a burrito, and threw it in the bin.

The newspaper unrolled as the bird hit the bottom, and the weird, mutant creature stared accusingly at me from the bottom of the trash can where it lay. I banged the lid down with an air of finality, brushing my hands together to rid myself of it mentally.

I went back into the kitchen, and glanced at the sketch of Toby the dog.

I froze mid-step, and gasped.

The piece of paper with the disturbingly lifelike dog drawn onto it was now blank.

Henry the dog had disappeared.

With shaking hands, I unpinned the now blank page from the wall. I did not know what to think. Were you playing a prank on me? Surely not. At five years old, your sense of humour was nowhere near this sophisticated. Had I pinned the wrong thing to the wall by mistake? But no, your Father had come in, and we had been looking at the dog when you called to us from your bedroom. Noone had come into the house, and swapped the paper over for a blank sheet- that was simply ludicrous.

My mind flashed back to the blank, discarded sheet of paper on your bedroom floor, the one you had pointed to before we saw the deranged robin at your window.

Pieces of a peculiar puzzle started to slot together in my mind, but I was reluctant to believe what instinct and common sense was trying to tell me: that the paper was blank because Toby the dog no longer lived in the sketch.

Toby the dog lived in the outside world, now, instead.

'Don't be stupid, Caroline,' I muttered fiercely to myself. I marched over to our drinks cabinet, and pulled out a dusty bottle of brandy, knocking back a shot of the stuff before I knew what I was doing. We weren't big drinkers in our family, and the brandy was usually reserved for emergencies, but somehow, this felt serious. And my nerves needed fortifying.

My eyes tracked back to the pinned sheet of paper on the kitchen wall, and stayed there, contemplating. I was still staring at the empty page when you came into the kitchen with your Father to kiss me goodnight.

I shook myself, and knelt down. I gathered you in my arms, holding you tight and running my fingers through your curly hair.

'Get some sleep, buddy,' I said, softly. 'You've had a tiring day.'

'Daddy's gonna tell me some extra stories tonight.'

'Fine,' I said, absentmindedly. Then I levelled your father with a serious, stern look.

'Just no scary stories, please. Not at bedtime. No Bogeyman, or the like. I don't want him waking up having nightmares. Especially after today.'

Your Father raised his hands up, a picture of innocence. I repeated myself, because suddenly, it felt very important that he understood.

'Okay? No Bogeyman. Please.'

'Alright, alright,' he grumbled. But I knew he wouldn't listen to me. He just couldn't help himself.

❋ ❋ ❋

THE NEXT DAY, we had an argument, you and I.

Most children are stubborn, but by God, you had a talent for it. You caught me when I was tired, and still preoccupied with the events of the day before. The argument blew up into a tantrum before I knew what was happening, as arguments with stormy children always do.

I stood in your bedroom, looking at a chaos of toys, clothes and Lego strewn across every available surface, and folded my arms, my mouth turned down disapprovingly.

'What's this?' I said, incredulous. You must have turned out every drawer and cupboard on purpose to make this amount of mess. It looked like a toy bomb had gone off dead in the centre of the room. I could barely walk across the floor.

You shrugged, sullen, and I could tell from the circles under your eyes that you were tired, that you hadn't slept either. You stuck your lip out, surly.

'I felt like making a mess,' you said, and I felt my temper rise.

'Well, this is not acceptable Henry, do you hear me? No more cartoons or treats of ANY sort until you tidy this mess.'

'But I don't WANT to, Mommy! I just want to play!'

'Not until your room is tidy.'

'NO! You do it!' You lowered your brows moodily, and stuck your bottom lip out even further.

I put on my most authoritative voice.

'If you don't tidy this mess up, I'll cancel the trip to the zoo on Saturday.'

The lip wobbled. I could see you struggling with something you were not old enough to articulate. I know now that it was stress, and an underlying feeling of things not being quite right in your usually sunny and simple universe.

'But that's not fair, Mommy!'

'Well it's not fair that I should have to clean up all your mess! Mommy works hard enough as it is. It won't hurt you to tidy away a few toys.'

'NO! I DON'T WANT TO!'

'Okay,' I said, in a matter-of-fact voice. 'No zoo trip, then. I'll tell your Father to cancel.'

'NO!! I HATE YOU, YOU'RE A MEAN MOMMY!'

I tried to grab you, but you were too fast. You snatched up the damned sketchbook which never seemed to be far from your reach, hugged it tight to your chest with a wounded, furious expression, and ran past me, stopping on the way to kick my left ankle, hard. It hurt, and you ran off, fully aware of how naughty you were being, but not willing to stick around and suffer the consequences.

I let you go, and sighed, and rubbing at my ankle, wondering if it was too soon to re-visit the brandy bottle. I knew you'd calm down, eventually.

I waited twenty minutes, and then went to find you, knowing exactly where you'd be.

I found you curled at the base of the walnut tree in our back yard, red-faced and sniffing, scribbling furiously in your sketchbook.

'Hey buddy,' I said, approaching cautiously and crouching down.

We held each other's gaze a moment. Then your eyes filled with tears, and your resolve crumbled. A stricken, worried expression took over where anger had been only moments before. I realised that you weren't scribbling in your sketchbook, but rather, trying frantically to erase something. Whatever it was, wouldn't rub away.

A strange feeling of premonition took hold of me, and

I felt cold.

'Henry?' I said, cautiously.

You stared at me with those huge, blue eyes.

'I drew something really bad, Mommy,' you whispered, and showed me the book which trembled in your hands. I gasped.

'Oh, no, Henry. Oh, Henry'. I didn't know what else to say. I felt sick to my stomach.

An angry, jagged sketch of a tall, angular man dominated the page.

He had pinprick eyes, shoulders that were mismatched and sloped, arms that dangled too far down his body, and a horrible, fixed leer on his face, a leer filled with a great many square, crookedly arranged teeth. You had drawn bright red splashes of blood on those teeth. My eyes dropped from the thing's face and down its body, where a grim necklace lay like a bloody garland around its neck. Hanging from this was a small, dismembered hand, chopped off cleanly at the wrist.

The man clutched a long-handled axe, which was also covered in blood. You'd coloured in splashes of red all over the page.

On the floor in front of the horrible, black figure lay a body, a stick-figure really, but one with long, brown hair just like mine, and a white shirt, just like mine, and blue jeans, just like mine. You'd drawn eyelashes around my blue eyes, eyes the same colour as yours, and my mouth was a wide open 'O' of surprise. I was quite clearly dead.

I shivered as I looked at the hateful sketch, and then back at you. You burst into tears.

'I'm sorry, Mommy!' You said, throwing yourself into my arms. 'I'm sorry, I didn't mean it! I tried to take it back but it...it...won't rub out!' Your tears took over and I soothed you, stroking your hair and rocking you gently.

'Don't worry, baby,' I whispered, staring at the drawing in the book. 'It's just a sketch, darling. It can't hurt me in real life.'

I cursed your Father inwardly. He'd told you a bedtime story about the Bogeyman, despite my warning, and you'd done exactly what I was afraid of: drawn him, in a fit of rage, and sent him after me.

In the distance, a dog barked, and I shuddered.

※ ※ ※

'WHAT DO you want me to draw, Mom?' You ask me, and I'm back in the present, and my body is feeble and frail once again. I can feel the dull ache of a cannula piercing the thin skin on the back of my right hand. I long to yank the thing out, but it's drip feeding me pain relief, and I lack the energy anyway.

You look at me, concerned. 'I don't...I don't use this thing much, anymore, Mom. It's dangerous, you know that.'

'I know, darling,' I say, my breath rattling in my throat. 'But I want you to use it...just one more time. For me.'

'So what do you want me to draw?' you ask again, but the waves of medication are swelling and rising, and I am swept out to sea once more.

※ ※ ※

THAT NIGHT, your Father rang to say he would have to stay out of town for a last-minute conference he'd been invited to. I rolled my eyes at him down the phone. Now wasn't a good time for him to be away, but he assured me he there was no choice, told me he loved us, and hung up.

I decided to break my usual rule and allow you

to sleep in the same bed as me, that night. For some reason, I wanted you close. As the evening crept on and the light faded from the sky, our usually warm and comfortable house took on a cold, almost sinister feel. I checked and locked every door and window while you got dressed into your pyjamas, all the while listening for any unusual noises, and hearing only the distant barking of that damned dog once again. I tried hard not to think about that, or the missing Toby dog from the paper in the kitchen.

After I was sure that the house was secure, I put the sketchbook into a cupboard high up where you couldn't reach it, tucked behind tins of fruit and beans and soup. Tomorrow, I would take it out into the yard and burn it. From now on you could draw all over the damned walls for all I cared, just as long as you didn't touch that cursed book any more.

I made us some cocoa, and we snuggled up in bed together. I told you a story about a little boy who found a magic sketchbook. The boy used the book to draw a door, and the door led to a happy, safe place where there was only love, and light, and laughter. It was a place without monsters. A sanctuary, I called it. The Safe Place. You smiled as you listened, and my love for you raged fierce in my blood.

We fell asleep within moments of each other, the dog still barking somewhere out there in the distant night.

※ ※ ※

I AWOKE WITH A START, knowing immediately that something was wrong. You slept soundly by my side. I slid my now dead arm out from underneath your head and flexed it to get the feeling back.

A noise rang out from downstairs, and I froze.

The noise came again, louder this time, and more distinct.

Something was in my house. Something large, and slow, and noisy. Moving around.

I slipped out of bed, left you, sleeping. My heart yammered in my chest, but I forced myself to walk towards the landing.

I stood there at the top of the stairs, straining to hear and shivering in my nightgown, goose-fleshed, cold, and terrified.

The noise stopped.

Silence regained its hold over the night. I leaned my whole body forward, desperately listening for any more alien sounds, wondering if I was going mad, or was maybe even still asleep.

The noise came again. This time, it was closer. It rustled and scraped. It growled, long, and low.

I held my breath, willing my very heart to stop beating in my chest for fear of being heard.

And then a voice rose out of the darkness.

'Hennnnnryyyy?' A horrible, nightmarish

Cruel Works of Nature

voice. It called to you, softly, from below.

'Henry, *dear* Henry, where are youuuu?'

I knew then, without a shadow of a doubt, that the Bogeyman was in my house, and he was coming for us. You had drawn him in the sketchbook, and he had come to life, just like the dog, just like the bird.

I snatched up the heaviest object I could find that was within arm's reach: an ornamental lamp-stand made of polished marble. I yanked the cable from the wall and wrapped it around my arm, then descended the stairs, softly.

All I could think was that I had to lead it away from you.

Time seemed to slow down.

No, no it didn't. Of course it didn't. That is a cliché, a lazy narrative to help me better process what was happening. Time moved at its usual pace, and I was swept along with it as I gingerly felt my way, step by step.

'Henrrrryyyyy?' The Bogeyman called, once more, louder this time, and I bit back a sob.

Eventually, my bare foot hit the cold wooden floor of the hallway. I stood there, panting softly, holding the lamp out in front of me with a quivering arm. I was drenched in sweat, from head to toe, but freezing at the same time.

My heart felt so big I thought it would smother me from the inside out.

There was a pause, an unbearable amount of time where I could not tell what was happening at all, and then your small, thin voice spoke up.

'Mommy?' you said, and I jumped almost clean out of my skin.

'Mommy, what's happening?'

Everything stopped. Then, out of the gloom of the hallway, a shadow detached itself from the wall and came towards us. Its outline was huge, murky, and confusing.

'There you are, Henry,' said the Bogeyman, and he began to laugh, a hyena laugh that pierced my ears.

'Get behind me, Henry!' I shouted, and the Bogeyman approached a strip of orange light which, cast from the streetlamp outside, sliced through the half-shuttered window blinds, bifurcating our hallway. It was dragging something across the floor, something heavy, something solid and metallic. It made a scraping, ringing noise as he moved.

He came steadily into the light, and I saw that he was holding an axe. I saw the grisly necklace about his neck. I saw his horrible smile.

I lost control of myself, and a loud, horrified cry fell from my open mouth.

Do you know how nightmarish every day, normal, mundane things look when five-year-olds draw them? Cats with legs like stilts, demented houses with ten windows and smoke pouring out of deformed chimneys and sloping, Picasso style walls and roofs? Humans with single strands of bright yellow hair and unbalanced eyes and expressionless mouths and mismatched limbs too long for their bodies?

Multi-coloured dogs with extra legs where there shouldn't be any?

Do you know how fucking *terrifying* five-year-old sketches can be?

Now imagine your child was actually trying to scare you, deliberately drawing something disgusting, and twisted, and malformed, and beastly.

My mind went back to the afternoon, to your beautiful blonde head bent angrily over your sketchbook, to the awful picture you drew. The look of panic on your face as you tried and failed to erase the Bogeyman.

You had drawn him, and he had come. For me.

You leapt into my arms, and I dropped the lamp, and just stood there whilst that... that thing... came towards us.

'Go away!' I screamed, and then...then, I heard something else.

A low, dark growling noise.

And then Toby, the brightly coloured dog you drew, the strange, energetic cinnamon scented mutt, emerged from the shadows on eight legs, long claws clacking against the floorboards, lips curled back to reveal sharp teeth that were too large for his snout.

He barked, crouched, and then leapt at the Bogeyman, furious, savage. Defending us.

I snapped out of my stupor.

The sketchbook. We needed to get to the sketchbook.

'Come on, Henry!'

I hoisted you higher up in my arms as the dog fought with the Bogeyman, who raised his axe high into the air, and brought it down hard. As I left the hallway, slamming the kitchen door shut behind me, I heard a crunch, and a yelp.

'Tobbyyyyyy!' You wailed, but I just kept moving.

The sketchbook was in the cupboard. We had only a moment or two before the Bogeyman would come for us. I put you down on the countertop and rummaged around desperately for the book, thrusting it into your hands, and grabbing a pen from the nearby noticeboard.

'Quick, Henry!' I shouted, as you stared at me in confusion, tears streaking your face.

'Mummy...'

'You need to draw! We can only beat the bad man with something from the book, do you understand?'

You nodded, sobbing, and my heart broke, for your face looked so old, suddenly.

'You can do this, baby,' I said, cupping your face in my hands. 'My big, brave boy. You can do this for Mommy. Draw me something. Draw me something I can use to beat the bad man!'

The kitchen door ruptured, and then exploded inwards, a shower of splinters raining onto the floor.

Cruel Works of Nature

The Bogeyman stood in the remains of the doorway, his long-handled axe clutched in his twisted, weird hands. He was covered in what I could only assume was the blood of Toby the dog, and even though the damn dog hadn't been real, I felt a sudden rage. You had drawn that dog. He had defended you. He was your friend. And this... this *thing* had brutally slaughtered it.

The Bogeyman took a slow, deliberate step across the threshold, towards us. I put my body between it and you. 'I'm drawing, Mommy!' you shouted from behind me.

'Hurry up, baby!'

The Bogeyman chuckled again, knowing we were cornered, and took another step forward.

I heard scribbling behind me, heard a page tearing, felt paper being thrust into my hand, and I had a moment to look at the sketch before it changed under my fingers, grew heavy, and solid, and metallic.

'Well done, baby!' I cried, as the sketch transformed in my hands. 'Now I just need you to draw one more thing, darling!'

Just one more thing.

'What, Mommy?' You were whispering, almost halfdead with fright, and I reached behind me to touch your knee.

'Draw a door to the Safe Place, baby,' I said, as the Bogeyman took another step forward. 'Remember the Safe Place from my story? Where the monsters can't go?'

'But Mommy, what about you?!'

'Yes, Mommy, what about you?!' The Bogeyman leered at me, and brought himself another step closer. I turned, away from him, and smiled at you.

'I'll be along in a minute,' I said, gently.

You lowered your shaking hand to the paper and began to draw a doorway. The paper shimmered as the pen moved across it.

'Go!' I shouted, and whipped my head back around to come face to face with the Bogeyman, who suddenly stood mere inches away, breathing a foul, fetid cloud of stench into my face, a stench that was tinged with the distinct, all too recognisable smell of cinnamon. Distantly, behind the blood pounding in my ears, I heard a door slam.

Relief poured into me. I threw back my head.

'Did you think I wouldn't defend my own child?' I snarled, and lifted my new sword up in front of my face.

The pinprick eyes bore into me, and the axe flew for my head.

I thrust the sword into the Bogeyman's neck while his arms were raised, and I yanked sideways. There was a strange tearing, screeching sound, and the axe clanged to the ground as the Bogeyman let out a roar that quickly died as I pulled the sword back on itself, and thrust again, this time yanking in the opposite direction. I felt something give, and snap, and then there was a sensation of release.

The Bogeyman crumpled to the floor in a sickening heap. His head tumbled along the kitchen floor and came to rest, eyes up, by the fridge.

I stared at the bloody sword in my hands.

Then, I spun around, and saw the door you had drawn, a hasty, oblong square of white in the dark of our kitchen, with a simple circle for a handle.

I pulled the door open, and saw you sitting in a green meadow, with sunshine all around.

I drew you into my arms. My boy, my darling boy.

I would do whatever it took to keep you safe.

❋ ❋ ❋

THE MEMORIES HAVE RELEASED me back into the care of this hospital, but not for long, not for long.

'Henry, are you there?' I ask, awake once more, and afraid.

'I'm here Mom. What do you need?'

'Remember when you were a boy, Henry? And I would tell you about the Safe Place?'

You swallow, overcome with emotion. 'A place where the monsters can't go,' you say, voice breaking.

'Make me a door, Henry,' I ask, tears rolling from the corner of my eyes and dropping to the pillow beneath me. 'Make me a door. It's time.'

There is the sound of a pencil scratching against paper. I close my eyes. I am tired, so tired.

'Thank you,' I whisper, taking your hand one last time. 'Thank you. I love you, Henry.'

An object is thrust into my hands, and I nod weakly, knowing what it is, and why you have given it to me.

A door squeaks open, and a golden light leaks in under my heavy, crusted eyelids.

And there will be no more nightmares, and no more pain, and no more anything. For I am going to the Safe Place. And I am going to take the sketchbook with me.

AUTHOR'S NOTE

Thankyou for reading *Cruel Works of Nature*. Please remember to **honestly rate and/or review this book** on Amazon or Goodreads, if you can.

It's the best way to support an author and help new readers discover their work.

ABOUT THE AUTHOR

Gemma Amor is a horror fiction author from Bristol, in the UK. Her debut collection of short stories, *Cruel Works of Nature*, was published in 2018. Gemma also writes for anthology audio dramas like the wildly popular NoSleep Podcast. She is co-creator, writer and voice actor for horror-comedy podcast Calling Darkness, and is writing a spooky cowboy show called *Whisper Ridge*. Her next book will be paranormal mystery novel *White Pines*, followed by another short story collection called *Till the Score is Paid*.

gemmammorauthor.com

Facebook.com/littlescarystories
Twitter.com/manylittlewords
Instagram.com/manylittlewords

OTHER BOOKS BY GEMMA AMOR

DEAR LAURA

COMING SOON

TILL THE SCORE IS PAID

WHITE PINES

Printed in Great Britain
by Amazon